AFTER THE FLAMES

ROBERT SILVERBERG
NORMAN SPINRAD
MICHAEL P. KUBE-McDOWELL

CREATED BY ELIZABETH MITCHELL

BAEN
SCIENCE FICTION
BOOKS

A Baen Books Original

Baen Enterprises
260 Fifth Avenue
New York, N.Y. 10001

First printing, December 1985

ISBN: 0-671-55998-2

Cover art by Richard Hescox

Printed in the United States of America

Distributed by
SIMON & SCHUSTER
MASS MERCHANDISE SALES COMPANY
1230 Avenue of the Americas
New York, N.Y. 10020

These stories have appeared previously, in slightly different form, as follows: "The Election," *Analog Science Fiction/Science Fact*, © 1983 by Davis Publications, Inc.; "World War Last," *Isaac Asimov's Science Fiction Magazine*, © 1985 by Davis Publications, Inc.; "When Winter Ends," *The Magazine of Fantasy & Science Fiction*, © 1985 by Mercury Press, Inc.

THE HELICOPTER WAS STILL A FEW YARDS ABOVE THE GROUND WHEN HE REALIZED THAT STOPPING WAS A MISTAKE

The town was intact, yes. Inhabited, yes. But reestablishing constitutional democracy was pretty much beside the point here, Jansen suspected. All the signs indicated that what he had chosen for the first stop of his tour was a town of crazies, thrown off balance by the heavy burden of the doom that had come over the world.

In the bright summer sunshine he saw images of death and the fear of death wherever he looked.

They had fallout rods mounted on every building—groups of three narrow metal dowels, one red, one green, one yellow, rising out of little steel domes painted with bright lightning-bolt patterns. About as effective for warding off fallout as a parasol would be, but try to tell a crazy that.

Outside the post office they had erected something that looked like a canoe with wings, a crudely carved object that was supposed to represent, he guessed, an intercontinental ballistic missile. It had an American flag painted across its nose, the Soviet hammer-and-sickle on one of its wings, a rough drawing of Christ on the cross on the other. Figure that one out, Jansen thought.

He realized he was being watched. Eyes, beady, suspicious, peered from every dismal dingy window. He let his hand rest lightly on his hip-holster.

CONTENTS

1985 marked forty years since the end of World War II. It is right and proper to recall the events which have shaped our lives, and the U.S. media took up this anniversary challenge with fervor. Television brought us everything from solemn remembrances in French churches to a song-and-dance reprise of the Big Band era.

One very special offering was PBS's airing of "Normandy to Berlin: A War Remembered." Compiled from many hours of film shot by a special unit of professional photographers under the "command" of Hollywood director George Stevens, it included the only battlefield footage taken with the brand-new color process.

The crew filmed D-Day at Normandy, the liberation of Paris, and the Russian-American linkup at the Elbe. Yet they were detoured from the final triumphant road to Berlin. South through the fields of Germany they rode, to a place none would ever forget. Dachau. Where American soldiers who came to liberate could not describe what they had found and demanded that the film crew record it for the world.

The Jewish people have sworn never to let the world forget that holocaust. If we are alert, if we are aware, perhaps we will never suffer another. Yet if we do, Robert Silverberg cautions in "The Election," we may lose more than lives and cities.

We must be alert. We must be aware.

THE ELECTION

Robert Silverberg

1.

"You better go right on upstairs," the Secretary of State said in that slow easy Kentucky drawl of his. He was leaning against the frame of his office door, with his thumbs behind his lapels like some old-time courthouse politician. "The President's waiting for you, Lloyd. You know Ben don't like to be kept waiting long."

"*Acting* President," Jansen said.

"You smartass Philadelphia lawyer," said the Secretary of State. "All right. The *Acting* President don't like to be kept waiting long."

Jansen nodded. He knew that. Everybody knew that.

"Not my intention to keep him waiting," he said. "I was helping to hook up the phones over at the Party building. I got down to the White House as fast as I could."

3

"Well, it wasn't fast enough, and the President's pissed off," said the Secretary of State. "This day and age, you don't keep the President waiting. The *Acting* President, pardon me. You can figure on getting your ass kicked a little. But I suppose it was about time for your turn again anyway."

"I suppose," replied Jansen, shrugging. He didn't particularly fear the President's temper. He was accustomed to Ben Thurston's volatile moods by this time. What he wasn't accustomed to yet was thinking of him as the President, or of this ramshackle old three-story building as the White House.

He moved along past the open door of the State Department and the closed one of the Department of the Treasury just beyond it, and up the creaking stairway. The second floor belonged to the Department of Defense. Defense's door was open; Jansen caught sight of General Ralston and Air Marshal Tolliver riffling through a huge pile of flimsy yellow sheets. Tolliver looked up and waved and called out, "Your chopper will be ready in two-three hours, Lloyd."

"I thought I wasn't going to go by chopper."

"Then think again, fellow." Air Marshal Tolliver pointed significantly toward the ceiling. "Orders from on high: Jansen takes the chopper. He's been trying to find you all day long, and he's plenty pissed off."

"So I hear," Jansen said. "I'm on my way up."

Tolliver gave him a thumb's-up sign. Jansen grinned and went onward, taking the last flight of stairs two at a time. But he paused on the third landing and glanced uneasily toward the door of the Oval Office. He could hear Ben Thurston's voice clear through it, shouting, "Speak up! Speak up! What about this man Broderick? What? You say *what*?"

Jansen drew a deep breath and knocked.

"Come," Thurston boomed. "Door's open!"

He nudged the knob and stepped inside. Thurston was hunched down behind his battered old fire-scarred desk, yelling into two telephones at once. "Speak up, will you?" he bellowed. "Talking through this thing is like using two tin cans and a piece of rope! You say that Tennessee is—what? What? Ah, to hell with it. I can't hear you worth a damn. Call me back in half an hour and maybe the line'll be better." He put down one phone, shouted for a moment into the other, slammed that one down too. Then he looked up, glowering, at Jansen. "About goddamned time," he muttered.

"I'm sorry, Ben. I was up at the Party headquarters. They wanted me to lend a hand wiring up the phones."

"Phones? Party? Christ, there are times I think we'd be a lot better off without either one." Thurston tugged at his jowls, pulled at his left ear, worried at the long curling strands of graying hair lapping over his collar. He was a big man, powerfully built, starting to get a little bald now; he looked like a former pro football player going beefy in his middle years. Jansen figured he was fifty, maybe fifty-five at most. Before the Blowup Thurston had been a congressman from one of the Louisville districts, elected when very young, thirty-two or so. The way Jansen had heard it, everyone had expected him to have a brilliant career, three or four terms in the House, then Senator or Governor, and a clear shot at the presidency by the time he was in his fifties. Well, here he was in his fifties, and he was going to be President, all right, but not exactly in the way anyone had imagined.

Jansen had been on his staff six years now, joining him at a time when the Anarchy was still raging in Kentucky and the surrounding states were in pure chaos. Maybe everything was still more or less in chaos elsewhere, but the days of the Anarchy in Kentucky were over, and it was Ben Thurston who had put an end to them. Jansen admired Thurston intensely: it surprised and even embarrassed him some, the degree of admiration he felt for this man. He stood silently, waiting while Thurston fidgeted with himself. At last the Acting President said, "Consider yourself reamed out for making yourself unavailable when I was trying to summon you. Next time let someone know where you're going, hear? Now: what the hell is this they tell me about your not wanting to go to Ohio by helicopter?"

"That's right, Ben."

"Why not? The copter's in good condition. You know how to fly the damned thing. We've got decent supplies of fuel."

"Not a whole lot of fuel."

"We have enough. The fuel issue is bullshit and you know it. What are you really objecting to, Lloyd?"

The big man's eyes drilled into him. Jansen tried to meet the Acting President's gaze levelly, but it was work.

He said after a moment, "I don't like the whole idea of flying to those towns. I'd like simply to drive one of the jeeps across the river. It seems more human, somehow, than dropping down out of the air like some sort of god. We aren't pretending to be gods, are we? And people aren't used to seeing airborne vehicles any more. If I come in that way, it'll intimidate them."

"It'll impress them," Thurston said. "That's not the same thing. We need to impress them. If people don't take the Provisional Government seriously the whole goddamned thing falls apart. You understand that."

"Take us seriously, yes. But *worship* us? Is that what we want?"

Thurston began to look impatient. "Those are still Americans over there, boy, not a bunch of fucking savages. They won't drop down on their knees and salivate if you come down into their towns in a helicopter. But they'll be impressed. They'll see that we have things functioning again in Kentucky, that we're putting it back together, that we're ready now to reach out and take them into the Republic and that it would be to their own benefit to come in with us. You show up in a car, that doesn't accomplish the same thing. Everybody's got cars. Even in the Anarchy states they have some cars. But a chopper? That's a different story. It'll make an *impression*. It'll make us look governmental. You've got to make that kind of impression when you go across the river. You can't just go into Ohio like a goddamned peddler of pots and pans riding some old jalopy, don't you see?"

"Ben—"

"Listen to me. You're not going there simply as an advance man sticking up a bunch of election posters. You'll be a representative of the Provisional Federal Government, which is the only government this country has had in too goddamned long, and you'll be the first of our people to set foot over there. You'll be practically an ambassador. As well as an espionage agent and half a dozen other things. You've got to arrive in style. You take the copter, hear?"

"I still don't like it. It's not *my* style."

"I hear that. You're overruled." Thurston grinned. "Is that too autocratic for you, boy? You want to put it to a vote? All right, let's vote. All in favor of your taking the copter, say aye. *Aye.* Motion carried." Thurston looked up and stared at him. The chilly green eyes, implacable, determined. There was no resisting that stare of Thurston's, Jansen thought. It was the stare of power, the stare of unanswerable command. Kings and pharaohs had stared at their prime ministers like that for thousands of years. Whatever force it was that made people obey, that was the force Ben Thurston had. Which probably was why he was going to be President, once there was something for him to be President of.

"You always get your way, don't you, Ben?"

Quietly Thurston said, "I have to. Right now I have to, Lloyd. Later on, when we have a Congress, when we have a Supreme Court, things will be different. You think I want to be a fucking dictator?"

"I never said—"

"Do you? Come on, boy. Do you think I want to be a dictator?"

"Ben, I know that isn't what—"

"Damned straight it isn't. I mean to be the constitutional President of a democratic nation, and don't you ever get any other idea. Congress will pass the laws and I'll carry them out, if I'm elected. Just as it was supposed to be in the old days. But right now I'm only Acting President. I've got no Congress and goddamned few laws, and if I want something done I've got to bull it through on my own. I don't have time for the finer procedures. Not now. Not yet. Next year, maybe. Not now." Thurston looked very tired, suddenly. The keen edge of his stare softened. "Listen, enough of this shit, Lloyd. Take the chopper and go do the Ohio mission. I think it's best if you take the chopper. In my judgment, that's the way to go. Take the chopper. You hear me?"

Jansen was silent a moment.

"Yeah," he said. "I hear you, Ben."

2.

He flew northeast over green rolling fields. Looking down on that land of low hills and broad farms you would never think that anything had happened. But then, nothing much *had* happened to this part of Kentucky, or to south-central Ohio on the far side of the river. You went up to the slagheaps that rimmed Lake Erie, the places that had been Cleveland, Toledo, Detroit, and you'd form a different notion. Or up to the real destruction zone that ran from Washington to someplace north of Boston, where there was nothing left but hot blackened pits. Or even just over here to Cincinnati, which hadn't been hit at all during the Blowup: Cincinnati, Jansen had heard, didn't look so good either. This was not an ideal time for being a city-dweller, here in the early decades of the 21st-century. It doesn't take a radiation bomb to destroy a city: a breakdown in the supply of lettuce and tomatoes and drinkable water can be enough to do it. Cities are very fragile things.

But out here in the boonies there was at least the illusion that no real upheaval had occurred. The land was unharmed; looked better, in fact, than it had since the 19th century, perhaps. The forests were taking over again. You still could see where farms had been, and where suburbs had been carved out of former farmland; but population was off by sixty or seventy percent from the 20th-century peaks and a lot of those places had been abandoned. The world was a green shield below. Jansen could still see an isolated farm, or even the occasional small town; but the general look of the triangle bounded by Louisville, Lexington, and Cincinnati was, he thought, pretty much as it had been in the days when the Indians held the land.

He was getting near the river, now.

The copter flew steadily: *chunk-a-chunk-a-chunk*, the rotors going round and round and round. Machinery wasn't very trustworthy any more, but the technicians of the Provisional Federal Government's air force knew what they were doing. A lot of competent people had settled in Kentucky once the Provisional Government got going. Competence attracts competence; the sort of folks who know how to do maintenance work on helicopters didn't much like to live in the chaos of the Anarchy, and they had come wandering in from south and east once word of Ben Thurston's organization got around. Jansen had come in that way himself. He had been a very junior member of the staff of Senator Robinson of Pennsylvania originally; but Pennsylvania wasn't there any more, Senator Robinson had gone up with the rest of the Washington government, and only by the flukey luck that he had been vacationing in North Carolina at the time of the Blowup had Jansen survived the war himself. Getting from Cape Hatteras to Ben Thurston's Kentucky headquarters had taken him two years; but things were a little easier now. A little.

Now the river was in view: timeless, lovely, a bright blue ribbon giving off sun-glints. A few of the bridges were still standing. That seemed almost miraculous. They said the radiation levels were way down, these days, that it was safe to go fishing in it again. No longer did all manner of hot poisons come blowing out of the destroyed territories whenever the east wind got going. No longer did the blizzards curving down past the Great Lakes carry a burden of radioactive menace. Things were getting cleaner. The world was purifying itself.

He crossed into Ohio.

It looked just the same on this side. Greenness everywhere, the faint scars of highways and towns just barely visible. But even from a thousand feet up it *felt* different. Ohio wasn't part of the Anarchy now, not any more, but so far as anyone in Kentucky knew it wasn't much better, just a disorganized mess of little independent towns scarcely meriting statehood. At least in Kentucky there was a central government that had some ability to keep things together. Little independent towns couldn't do proper maintenance of roads and bridges and power plants. Little independent towns couldn't do much about the roving companies of bandits who prowled the countryside. Little independent towns had no really reliable mechanisms for exchanging goods and services with one another. That was why, Jansen thought, human beings had begun grouping themselves into nations ten thousand years ago along the Nile and Tigris. And that was why some people were trying to do it all over again now in Kentucky. He felt a little chill, looking down on leafy Ohio, as though he were looking backward across time into some ancient prehistoric land. And he began to see himself as a kind of missionary, coming to bring the benefits of civilization to this place. The trick would be to restore civilization without restoring the kinds of craziness that had destroyed everything before.

There was some hope for that, he figured. It was going to be a long time before anyone would have the technological capacity to build atomic weapons again, let alone the motive or the desire to use them in warfare. When you had scarcely any idea what was going on across the next river, you didn't allow yourself the luxury of getting into abstract political squabbles and power struggles with people who lived ten thousand miles away. And perhaps by the time the world got itself back up to pre-Blowup technological levels the human race would have outgrown the need to toss bombs around. Perhaps. Perhaps.

Meanwhile the problem was not how to defend the American way of life against the warheads of external enemies, but how to patch up what was left of the country so that it could attain something better than a subsistence-level existence. Having a central government would help. So the Provisional Federal

Government that Ben Thurston had pasted together was extending its feelers, now, up from its base in relatively undamaged Kentucky into the more or less intact parts of Ohio, Indiana, Delaware, Maryland, Virginia, North Carolina, Tennessee. Time to move farther southward and westward later. There wasn't much point in going in the other direction: everything northeast of Harrisburg was gone, apparently, unless something still was ticking up around Maine and New Hampshire, and who was going to cross five hundred miles of hot wasteland to find that out?

When he was about eight miles north of the river he spotted a town—one main street with shops fronting a highway, three or four smaller streets parallel to it, seven or eight streets of houses crossing it; maybe a thousand or fifteen hundred population at most. It looked intact and inhabited. He began to guide the chopper down for a landing.

His wheels were still a couple of yards above the ground when he saw that stopping here was a mistake.

Intact, yes. Inhabited, yes. But not exactly ready to set up the voter-registration booths. Reestablishing constitutional democracy was pretty much beside the point here, Jansen suspected. All the signs indicated that what he had chosen for the first stop of his tour was a town of crazies—an outpost of superstition-ridden backwoodsmen permanently thrown off balance by the heavy burden of the doom that had come over the world.

In the bright summer sunshine he saw images of death and the fear of death wherever he looked.

They had fallout rods mounted on every building—groups of three narrow metal dowels, one red, one green, one yellow, rising out of little steel domes painted with bright lightning-bolt patterns. About as effective for warding off fallout as a parasol would be, but try to tell a crazy that. At the end of the main street, in front of a squat little bank building with shattered windows, they had set up an atom shrine, a sprawling pile of rubble held together with iron hoops and topped with the nuclear symbol fashioned out of strips of steel hammered into interlocking circles. At its base was a refuse-heap of wilted flowers, bits of rotting meat, fly-specked vegetables, torn-off branches: offerings to the atom gods. Jansen shivered. A prehistoric land, yes. Or posthistoric; it amounted to the same thing. He turned. Banners dangled from the roof of the Seven-Eleven Shop, long snaky strips of fabric, red, green, yellow, the sacred colors of the fallout cult. There were skull-and-crossbones emblems painted in every window. Outside the post office they had erected something that looked like a canoe with wings, a crudely carved object that was supposed to represent, he guessed, an intercontinental ballistic missile. It had an American flag painted across its nose, the Soviet hammer-and-sickle on one of its wings, a rough drawing of Christ on the cross on the other. Figure that one out, Jansen thought.

He realized he was being watched. Eyes, beady, suspicious, peered from every dismal dingy window. He let his hand rest lightly on his hip-holster.

Three men were coming from the Seven-Eleven now. They were thin, scraggly-bearded, dressed in faded jeans and patched shirts. They didn't look friendly. As they approached him they were making signs with their left hands, like medieval townsmen trying to ward off the devil, but the sign they were making was that of interlocking nuclear shells. They were making clicking sounds with their tongues, weird, spooky. Pretending they were Geiger counters, maybe? Jansen had heard a little about these crazies. Each town was said to have its own mythology, its own set of home-made rituals and idols and taboos. It would all be worth studying some day—the bizarre cults born of overwhelming terror, the strange new superstitions. But he wasn't here to study superstitions. He wondered if it would be smarter just to jump back in the chopper and get the hell out of this place fast.

When the three men were fifty feet away they paused. The only weapons they seemed to be carrying were hunting knives thrust through their belts. Jansen stood with his back against the helicopter, waiting.

Amiably he said, "My name's Jansen. I'm here to talk to you about an election."

He gave them a good warm smile. Smiling at them was important, he knew. *Rule One. In every way, try to dispel hostility toward the Provisional Federal Government and its representatives.* Even a sour sullen paranoia-ridden crazy would understand a smile.

"You from Broderick Territory?" one of them called.

He shook his head. "I'm from Kentucky," he told them. "I'm a delegate from the Provisional Federal Government."

"What's that?"

"The new United States. We're starting to put things back together. There's going to be a presidential election under the Constitution of 2012, and then a Congress will be chosen, and after that—"

His voice trailed off. He could have been speaking Chinese or Turkish for all the understanding he saw in their eyes.

"You gonna build the bombs again?" the tallest man asked.

"No bombs. There won't ever be any more bombs," said Jansen.

"You're gonna make another United States. That means bombs. They say demons walk the land, setting up ways to bring back the atom. You're a demon, right?"

Jansen smiled. "No."

"If you're not a demon, make the Sign of the Shells."

"I don't know it. I told you, I come from Kentucky. We don't have that sign there."

"Everybody knows the Sign of the Shells," said one of the others. His eyes were small and hard and gleaming with anger and fear. "You get your ass out of here. Fast. We don't need no demons in this town."

"And we don't need no Congress," the first one said. "We don't need no President. We don't need no atoms. You get your demon ass back to Broderick Territory and keep it there."

"I don't know anything about Broderick Territory," Jansen replied. "I'm from Kentucky." He pointed. "Back there, on the far side of the river. We've started to put the United States back together, over there."

"That's devil country, isn't it?"

"Not that I know of."

"Devil country. Sure." They were beginning to click their tongues again and make strange signs. He didn't seem to be dispelling much hostility here. They moved slowly toward him, glancing at one another as though working out some kind of strategy for attack. Maybe they burned demons at the stake in this part of Ohio. He wondered if he would have time to use his gun, if they all jumped him at once.

He said, "Stay back. I didn't come here to make trouble, but I'll sure as hell give you trouble if you make any for me. Just stay back, you hear? I want to know if there's anybody in town I can talk to about the Presidential election that's going to be held this fall."

"We don't want to hear about no devil election."

"Who's in charge in this town?"

"That don't matter." They stirred again.

"Stay back," Jansen warned.

"He's got atoms," one of them said. "He's going to spray atoms all over the place!"

"No," Jansen said. He drew the gun from the holster and let them see it, and then he cocked it. "I don't have atoms. What I have is a gun, and it's full of real bullets, and it'll make real holes in you if you come any closer. You aren't going to let me tell you about the election, are you? No. No, you aren't. I didn't think so. All right. Walk over there and stay there, all three of you. I'm going to leave. Maybe some time later on somebody will come back and try to explain to you what the United States is all about."

They were glowering at him, making new signs at him now, moving their hands in faster and more intricate patterns, murmuring what sounded like charms or incantations. Spooky stuff, he thought. They were acting as if they expected him to conjure up a burst of hard radiation and skewer them with it. To have gone so far backward in so short a time—yes, they probably would burn him at the stake if they got the chance. But they wouldn't have the chance. The Provisional Federal Government could get along without this weird little town for the time being. He hopped up into the helicopter. They eyed one another as if they were thinking of making some last-minute onslaught, but he had the rotors turning before they could get anything started, and the brisk wash of air sent them leaping backward, chanting and making signs as quickly as they could. The chopper rose. They shouted, brandished their fists, threw pebbles at him; but in a moment he was beyond their reach. When Jansen looked down he saw them with their hands linked, dancing around their radiation shrine. He shook his head sadly. Welcome to Ohio, he thought.

3.

The next town he came to, eleven miles or so farther up in the direction of Chillicothe, was more
promising. It was bigger than the last one, though
not large, a compact, huddled-looking place situated
in the heart of a patch of pleasant farmland that
seemed to be in a decent state of upkeep.

Jansen brought the helicopter down in the middle
of the town, a broad square with an old wooden
bandstand at one side. Even before the rotors had
stopped moving, little groups of townspeople were
beginning to collect, peering uneasily at him from
the far side of the street. Their faces were chilly with
suspicion. Well, nothing very surprising about that,
he thought, considering what sort of stuff was going
on in the neighboring towns and what the general
state of civilization had been for the past ten or
fifteen years. Probably they didn't get to see many
strangers around here these days, or any at all. Especially strangers who arrived by helicopters. He wished
Thurston had let him take the jeep after all. For all
Thurston's shrewdness, he wasn't right *all* the time;
and even though the roads around here were a mess,
Jansen still felt he would have been better off coming
in by jeep than dropping down out of the sky like
this. But at least these people weren't clicking their
tongues or making signs at him, and he saw no fallout rods, no radiation shrines.

He dug his thumb into the towering stack of election posters in the back of the cabin, peeled off about
a dozen of them, picked up the spraytite tube, and
jumped down from the copter. He had gathered an
audience of about twenty now—saying nothing, just
watching him frostily from a safe distance.

Jansen smiled at them, hoping it came across as a

straight Howdy-folks-glad-to-be-in-your-sweet-little-town kind of smile.

Rule One. In every way try to dispel hostility toward the Provisional Federal Government and its Representatives.

Rule One didn't seem to work any better here than it had in the last town. Nobody smiled back. Jansen had thought small-town people were supposed to smile back at you when you smiled at them. Not these folks. Well, they lived in difficult times. Maybe manners had changed some. Everything else had certainly changed some. These folks seemed, at any rate, more civilized than the last ones.

He walked across the square toward a lamppost, put down his stack of posters, took off the top one, positioned it at average eye level, and squeezed the handle of the spraytite tube. He put a few drops on the back of the poster. Pardon me for defacing your pretty little town with our political announcements, he said silently, and stuck the poster in place.

NOTICE!

Pursuant to the articles of the Provisional Constitution of the United States of America, an election for the office of President of the United States will be held on

Tuesday, November 4, 2013

The candidates duly selected by properly constituted nominating conventions are:

America Revival Party—
Benjamin V. Thurston for
President
Nicholas C. Ryan for
Vice-President

National Progress Party—
Thomas C. MacIntyre for President
Noel Parr for Vice-President

*Election is to be by direct popular vote and by
secret ballet. Your local Provisional Federal Government representative will explain the details of
election procedure. Participation in this election is
a prerequisite for readmission to the United States
of America under the terms of the Constitution of
2012. Election of a National Congress will be sched-
uled at the order of the President-elect within eighteen
months after his inauguration on January 1, 2014.*

*Given by my hand this 3rd day of
August, 2013
Benjamin V. Thurston, Acting President
Provisional Federal Government
Louisville, Kentucky*

Jansen stepped back, surveyed the poster, nodded,
and moved on. A couple of the townsmen wandered
over to inspect it. One began to trace the letters with
his fingertips as though examining a magic scroll. I
hope they still know how to read here, Jansen thought.

He put up a second poster against the bandstand
and a third half a block away, in front of the bank.
There were fifty or sixty people in the town square
now, and more were filtering in all the time. And,
yes, they did seem able to read the posters. He heard
them muttering to each other: "Election . . . Provisional Federal Government . . . President . . ."

Then Jansen saw a boy of about twelve who was
wearing nothing but a pair of ragged jeans cut off at
mid-thigh reach up and begin to scribble with a
piece of charcoal on the first poster.

"Hey!" Jansen yelled, rushing across the square.

"Cut that out! That's a government sign you're defacing. You can't mark up a government sign like that!"

The boy glanced up, grinning. "I can't? Why not? Who says?"

He had drawn a quick sketch of Jansen, crude but definitely recognizable, more than a little obscene. Despite himself Jansen felt amused. But he couldn't allow his amusement to show.

Sternly he said, "It's against the law."

"What law?"

The crowd was snickering now. This is not starting off well at all, Jansen thought.

He gestured at the defaced poster and said, "Are this boy's parents here?" No one replied. He went on, "Isn't there anyone here who'll explain to this boy why you can't just go scrawling on signs like that?"

More snickers. They weren't buying his outrage. All he was accomplishing, he saw, was making himself look foolish. Quickly he wiped out the sketch with his handkerchief and turned away, going back across the square to continue putting up posters.

Behind him someone sang out, "Hey, mister, what's an election?"

Jansen looked around. "Who said that?"

"I did." A tall straw-haired fellow stepped forward—about twenty, so he had never known any kind of world but this one. There was the glitter of intelligence in his eyes, though, and Jansen knew he was being baited.

He said, frowning, "An election is the free choice of a government by the people. We get together and pick the people we want to govern us."

"You mean I can pick between this Thurston fellow and this MacIntyre fellow for who I want to be President of the U-Nited States?"

"That's right."

"But suppose I don't want either of them. Suppose I want Ned Ludlow here to be President."

Jansen managed an uncertain smile. "Well, sure, it would be a neat thing if we could all pick our best friends to run the government. But it doesn't really make a whole lot of sense, does it, except as a joke. Running the government's a tough job. We have to be sure the man we choose is the one most qualified."

"And Thurston and MacIntyre are qualified?"

"Yes."

"Who says so?" There was no real truculence in the question, just a slow, unshatterable obstinacy.

Jansen held up a poster and pointed to the official seal. "The Provisional Federal Government says that they're qualified."

The other man guffawed. "Come off it, mister. That thing's signed by Ben Thurston! You're gonna stand there and tell me that Ben Thurston declares that Ben Thurston is qualified to be President, and have me swallow it?"

The crowd began to snicker again. Jansen, reddening, realized that he hadn't prepared himself in any way for this sort of impromptu debate. He had assumed simply that he'd go among the Ohioans to welcome them back into the new United States and spell out the mechanism of the election procedures and they'd jump in line right away, out of sheer delight that the country was putting itself back together. Sure.

He said, "Ben Thurston didn't write that poster. He just issued it, because he's temporarily in charge. The candidates for President were picked by conventions of the people, held in Kentucky last month."

"Yeah. And who picked the convention people?"

"Why—" Jansen found himself on the verge of sputtering. "They were chosen by the whole electorate of Kentucky."

"Terrific for Kentucky. How come we wasn't asked?"

"The next time, you will be. Kentucky's where the government relocated after the Blowup. Now we're reaching out, trying to draw our neighbors into the system that we're putting together. But we had to start somewhere, didn't we? The important thing is to get the government functioning again, and not just in Kentucky. Once we've rebuilt communication channels, once we've linked the country up again, we can hold a real nationwide nominating convention. Until then, we just had to pick the best men we had, and put them up for your approval. But nothing's being put over on you in the dark. You'll get your chance to hear both Thurston and MacIntyre. They'll be touring this way late next month to explain their programs for reconstructing the country."

Silence.

Jansen rocked back and forth on his heels, waiting for the next challenge. None came. He smiled broadly at the crowd, hoping to get at least one smile in return. But a solid row of sullen faces continued to stare at him without warmth.

And then the crowd seemed to lose interest both in him and in his posters. By twos and threes they drifted away until there was hardly anyone left, and soon there was no one at all except a boy of four with curly red hair who stood by himself, looking at Jansen, at the helicopter, at Jansen again.

"What's your name?" Jansen asked.

The boy put his finger in his mouth and said nothing.

"Come on. What's your name? Mikey? Jimmy?"

Silence.

"You want to take a ride in the chopper?"

A flicker of interest, just for an instant.

"My name's Lloyd," Jansen said. "I'm with the government. You aren't old enough to vote, I suspect.

But maybe we can make an exception for you. We need all the support we can get, Mikey, and I'm here to tell you that if Ben Thurston carries the election, his supporters in these Ohio towns will be well thanked. We could find a post for you in the diplomatic service, I'd say. How'd you like to be ambassador to Indiana, Mikey? Or maybe we could find some cabinet-rank post that you might—"

"Paul? Come away from there, Paul! Stop bothering that man!"

A woman, twenty, twenty-five years old, stringy carrot-colored hair, pale weary red-freckled face. Jansen nodded toward her. "He's not bothering me, ma'am. I don't think he's much interested in politics, though. But he seems to be the only audience I have right now, so I'm trying to find out where he stands on the big issues of the day."

She gave him a tentative smile, the first he had seen all day. "You from Kentucky?"

"That's right."

"You fly around in airplanes a lot over there?"

"This thing's a helicopter, ma'am. And no, we don't use them a lot. We're just beginning to get our transport equipment back into shape."

"Things are real good on the Kentucky side, are they?"

"Better than they've been, but not as good as they once used to be. We're getting there. And Ohio will get there too. Tomorrow I mean to talk to the people of this town about what the election really means. And then—"

"Tomorrow? You still going to be here tomorrow?"

"So I planned. Why?"

"Broderick's supposed to be visiting this town tomorrow, or maybe the day after," she said. "He comes around regular, you know. And I don't think he's going to be wanting you talking about any elections. I'm downright sure of it."

"Broderick?"

"Sam Broderick. Boss of Broderick Territory?"

"And where's that, exactly?" Jansen asked.

It was the second time this day that he had heard that name. The crazies had asked him if he came from Broderick Territory. It hadn't meant anything to him then. Now he began to understand. Probably all sorts of local strong men were setting up little principalities out in the Anarchy states: it stood to reason.

She waved her arms. "Broderick Territory, it's all around us. Don't you know? You're in it. *This* is Broderick Territory. From here to Chillicothe, maybe even farther. You really don't know about Sam Broderick over in Kentucky?"

Jansen shook his head.

"He's a big man. A mighty big man in all ways."

"I'd like to talk to him," said Jansen. "We'll need his help. I'm glad he's coming to town."

4.

Without really meaning to, he found himself getting invited to spend the night at her house. He wasn't quite sure what the invitation really meant, but it turned out to be nothing more than old-fashioned country hospitality: she realized that he had nowhere else to sleep except in the chopper, and so she brought him home with her.

Her name was Mary-Claudelle. She lived in a rickety little gray-green frame house with a badly sagging porch, up at the north end of town almost at the edge of the new forest. Four or five other people seemed to live there: some young men named Nick or Jim or Tim, one of whom was very likely little Paul's father, and another woman, a girl, really, who obviously was Mary-Claudelle's younger sister. She had the same reddish hair, the same freckled face, but she was a lot heavier, plump with the cheerful unabashed fleshiness of a hearty sixteen-year-old. There was a garden plot behind the house. An assortment of cats and dogs wandered about, and a goat was tethered on the forest side. Two battered, rusty old cars that looked as if they hadn't been functional since the week of the Blowup were visible, just barely, in the underbrush beyond.

"This is Lloyd," Mary-Claudelle announced. "He's here from Kentucky. There's gonna be an election."

"Do tell," said Nick or Jim or Tim coolly. But his coolness wasn't meant to convey sarcasm or scorn, evidently. It didn't seem to be meant to convey anything at all. He shrugged blandly, vaguely, and looked away, losing interest in Jansen almost at once. He was wholly incurious about the election, about Jansen, about Kentucky; so were the others. But at least they were friendly, in their fashion. They smiled, they offered him some of their potent home-brewed beer, they made room for him to sleep on a pile of more or less clean blankets on the porch. The oldest of them, Jansen guessed, must have been no more than eight or ten at the time of the Blowup. They would have only the haziest memories of the world that used to be, that long-lost dreamlike place of computers and airlines and movies and color television sets. But they seemed cheerful enough. They gave no sign of knowing that they lived in a greatly diminished world scraping by on minimal resources. He was hardly more than a decade older than they were, but he felt like a visitor from some other epoch, or even some other planet.

Dinner that night was commendable: a rich vege-

table soup, fresh corn, some sort of stewed meat, and
plenty of the sharp, tart home-brewed beer. The plump
sister—her name was Jondalla—was the cook, and
she obviously enjoyed her tasks. Jansen chose not to
ask her what sort of meat they were eating. Beaver?
Badger? Porcupine? Made no difference: he was hungry, and he didn't expect filet mignon here.

After dinner he sat on the porch by himself, watching night close down over the forest. The beer had
made him light-headed; it was strong stuff, dark and
foaming, with plenty of kick to it. One of the men
began to sing—quietly, badly, accompanying himself
uncertainly on an out-of-tune banjo. The boy played
with the goat, scampering around and around it until he ran out of energy; then Mary-Claudelle gathered him up and swept him inside, and they were not
seen again. Jondalla and the other two men were
talking softly in the kitchen. This could be 1830,
Jansen thought, but for the plumbing fixtures and
the old cars decaying in the woods. Pioneer settlers,
getting along, making do. Well, in some ways it *is*
1830 all over again, he realized. No telephones here,
no stereos, no electricity, no jets overhead bound for
Chicago or New York or San Francisco. The Blowup
hadn't exactly knocked the whole world back into
the Stone Age, the way some had predicted, but it
had turned the clock back more than a little.

Jansen lay awake a long while, listening to sounds
in the night.

Had he accomplished anything today? Not much.
An abortive visit to one town, some posters stuck up
in another. Election Day was three months away.
Did anyone out here care? They had been isolated so
long; they had probably forgotten what it had been
like to have a nation, a government, a world beyond
the horizon. It might be harder to get them inter-

ested in getting things started again than Ben Thurston suspected, Jansen thought.

The election, he told himself, was a wonderful thing—a sign that the decade and a half of disruption and chaos was ending, and that a real rebirth of the old United States was at last under way. True, things were off to a slow start. First the nucleus in Kentucky taking shape—the surviving members of the old government and the new post-Blowup leaders coming together, reaching general agreements, holding the Constitutional Convention. The new Constitution was a lot like the old one in its general principles, except that it made provision for more gradual federalization: a strong central government was pretty much impossible just now anyway, with communications and transportation still such a mess. Gradualism had to be the keyword. It was foolish to go about behaving as though everything could be put back to normal overnight, not when the country was still this badly splintered, whole regions uninhabitable, others apparently reverted to savagery, some altogether unreachable. No one this side of the Rockies had any idea, for example, of what was happening on the West Coast, whether they had survived at all out there, what shape they were in. There had been no contact with California or Washington or Oregon in fifteen years. The same for Alaska and Hawaii. Some kind of government had apparently been established in western Texas and New Mexico, but nothing was known about it: the border was closed. Minnesota and Wisconsin were mystery lands also. The Provisional Federal Government's reach was a terribly short one. But it was reaching, at least. The election was a big move forward.

No doubt of it, Thurston had worked wonders in organizing Kentucky. The physical damage done to this part of the country by the Blowup hadn't been all that great, but the psychological havoc had been enormous, as it was everywhere. Pulling the state up from the Anarchy required intense effort and dedication; but Thurston had managed it. Kentucky's rebirth was no illusion.

Kentucky today, Ohio tomorrow, Indiana, Tennessee—

But first an election. Thurston was deeply troubled by the illegitimacy of his power. He was Acting President only because he said he was; it was a self-assumed mantle, which he had donned because he was plainly the right man to put it on, but he fretted endlessly about going down in history as a mere dictator. He wanted the election to confirm him in office, and if a true national election was still impossible he insisted at a minimum of holding one that extended beyond Kentucky. Of course, the outcome of the election was preordained. Nobody seriously thought Tom MacIntyre stood a chance of winning, and certainly Tom himself had no desire to take the job away from Ben. But there had to be two candidates, to keep the old forms alive. A one-candidate election would be worse than none at all: a mockery, a farce.

After the election Ben Thurston's Provisional Federal Government would have some sort of legitimacy. Thurston would call for the election of a Congress, would appoint judges, would help the nearby states reconstruct their governments, would send out ambassadors to the distant states still lost in the Anarchy. Gradually the old web of law and tradition and custom would be spun anew. A Government of the United States of America would again be supreme from coast to coast—before the twenty-fifth anniversary of the Blowup had passed, so Thurston hoped.

It was a glorious thing, Jansen thought, to be alive at the same time Ben Thurston was, and to be taking part in the rebuilding of the United States. It was giving his life purpose and meaning. He had spent his whole adult life in political activity of one sort or another, starting when he was still in college and working in Ned Robinson's first senatorial campaign; but in those days it had simply seemed like fun, an intellectual challenge, a stimulating and exciting career. He had seen politics then, he realized, as a thing in itself, an activity distinct and apart from government. But of course in a rational society the two, politics and government, had to be indivisible: the political process was merely the potentiating aspect of the governmental process. Jansen hadn't examined that notion very closely, except to the obvious degree that if he helped to get Ned Robinson elected to the Senate he would to some extent be helping to further the ideas and programs that Ned Robinson stood for, or claimed to stand for. Well, now there was no Senate, no State of Pennsylvania, and no Ned Robinson; and Jansen understood that by helping to get Ben Thurston elected President he was not merely aiding one man in his consolidation of power but he was in fact helping to solidify the structure of society: politics in the original Greek sense of the word. It felt like a noble cause. He would not easily have been able to maintain, in the old days, that working as a minor administrative assistant on Senator Robinson's staff was anything that could be called noble.

Darkness had come. Owls hooted in the night. Dogs howled far away—or were they coyotes? Jansen kicked off his shoes and stretched out. He felt a vast weariness sweeping up over him. His first day's contact with the citizenry beyond Kentucky hadn't been encouraging. But he had known all along that it would take a hell of a lot of patient toil to undo the damage of the Anarchy, to persuade these people that they *needed* to join in the effort to rebuild.

They were really only peasants, he thought. A patronizing word, an un-American word: but it was the truth, he told himself. They lived close to the land here, they toiled from sunrise to sunset, and if they ever lifted their eyes to the stars it was only to find out whether it was likely to rain the next day. The big issues of philosophy and politics and history didn't matter a damn to them, and why should they? They weren't philosophers. Most people never had been; but after the Blowup philosophy had become even more of a luxury than before. A Federal government was an abstract concept. "We must all hang together, or assuredly we shall all hang separately," Benjamin Franklin had said. Sure. In Franklin's time it would have been easy enough to understand why a single united nation stood a better chance of survival than thirteen small colonies. But was that true any longer, Jansen wondered? The world these people lived in was a shattered one, and what had shattered it, if not the overwhelming power of great nations acting to safeguard national interests? Why rebuild the nation, these farmers might ask? Just so that we can smash ourselves up all over again?

It would be no simple job to get them to overcome that fear. But they would; he was certain that they would. They'd come to see that a reunited nation did not necessarily mean an unavoidable second Blowup a century or two down the line. They would join in the rebuilding, yes. And some day these people would bless the name of Ben Thurston. Maybe even bless the name of Lloyd Jansen.

He grinned at his own presumption. I refuse to speculate about my own place in history, Jansen thought. For Christ's sake, what damnable idiocy! What supreme arrogance!

He closed his eyes and slipped off into sleep.

5.

In the morning he went back down to the town center to find out whether the mysterious Sam Broderick was really due to arrive here this day.

Jansen's basic assignment was to hit as many towns as he could in a ten-day swing and in each one to speak with the mayor, the town council, anyone who might be in charge. Not even small towns like this could simply run themselves on automatic pilot: somebody had to make policy and carry out the things that needed to be done. It was Jansen's task to find that somebody, spell out for him the practical advantages of affiliating his town with the Provisional Federal Government, talk to him about the arrangements for the election campaign and the election itself. And then he would move on to the next town, and the next—

But already the job was starting to look a bit more complicated than that. Evidently some kind of pseudo-state, maybe even a little feudal kingdom, had already taken shape here in south-central Ohio. Broderick Territory couldn't be any vast domain, Jansen figured, since not the slightest rumor of its existence had reached across the river into Kentucky; most likely it was just a loose league of five or six small towns much like this one. But any sort of political entity at all was a big step up from the conditions that had prevailed in the Anarchy, and Ben Thurston would need to be informed about it, its size, its power, its intentions. For all anyone knew, Broderick Territory meant to set itself up as a direct rival of the Provisional Federal Government; maybe this Sam Broderick intended to be President himself, or king, or emperor, or whatever. Jansen couldn't leave here until he had found out.

There was hardly anyone in the town square when

he reached it. That surprised him a little. He realized that he had expected to find an impromptu town meeting going on, hundreds of aroused citizens milling around holding a vociferous discussion of the pros and cons of the election. But he saw at once how silly that notion was. For one thing, any town meeting that might be taking place would be happening behind closed doors. For another, this was a bright sunny morning and there was work to do in the fields: these people were too busy to spend their mornings milling around in the town square. This wasn't the Fourth of July, after all. Assuming that anybody remembered in these times that the Fourth of July was supposed to be a holiday.

His posters were still up, at any rate. And his helicopter did not appear to have been disturbed during the night. But three men were leaning against it, obviously waiting for him. They looked disagreeable—lean, all three, raggedly dressed, with uneasy flickering eyes and stubbly faces. They weren't any friendlier-looking than the trio of atom-fearing crazies who had confronted him yesterday in that other town. Trouble comes in threes in these places, Jansen thought.

"Mind if we have a word with you, mister?" one of them asked.

Jansen regarded them calmly. He crossed his arms and let his left elbow rest against the butt of his holstered gun.

"What can I do for you?" he said.

The man in the middle came forward. Forty, forty-five years old, hollow-cheeked, wearing old faded overalls. He thrust out his hand. "Name's Chuck Webster. I seen your signs put up. I come to tell you I'm with you one hunderd percent. Lots of people around here don't like this election thing, but I'm old enough to remember what a wonderful country the U-Nited

States of America used to be, and I want to tell you that I'm with you all the way. All The Way."

"Yeah," one of his flankers said. "Me too. The election's a damn fine idea. Long overdue, us having a President again. You got to have a government. A great country like this, yeah. You got to have a President. That's e-ssential."

"E-ssential," echoed the third.

Jansen allowed himself to relax just a little. He wasn't at all sure what these three were up to, though it plainly was something other than this earnest native flagwaving stuff. But he felt he had to take their pious statements of support at face value until he saw what lay behind them. How sincere were they? He'd find that out soon enough, he supposed; but whatever their game, at least there were three men around here who didn't react with blank-faced apathy to the idea of restoring the federal government.

He gave them a Rule One smile.

"Glad to hear I've got a few people standing beside me in this part of the country," he said in his most resonant way. "We need lots more like you."

"We're here to help you get them," Webster said. "Like they always say, you scratch our backs, we'll scratch yours."

Ah, Jansen thought. Here it comes.

"And what is it that needs scratching, exactly?" he asked.

Webster stuck his thumbs into his belt. "We figure the Federal Government can help us out some with our problem. That's why we've decided to get behind you. This town's in a bad way, y'see. We got a dictator here who's trying to run the place. But the Federal Government, it don't allow no dic-tators, that's for sure. We figure if we can get the Federals in here, you'll bust him down to size."

"A dictator?"

"Name of Broderick. Sam Broderick."

"Right. I've been hearing a lot about him."

"Set himself up as boss right after the Blowup, in a little town seventeen-twenty miles north of here just outside Chillicothe. Then every year he's been moving out a little way, taking over other towns. We had some decent folk running things here—our own people, y'understand, not any damn outsider—but Broderick came in, he said we were messing up, he just tossed our people out and took the town over. Runs the place like he was born here. Tells us how much to pay in taxes and everything."

"Taxes? You pay taxes? Who to?" Jansen said.

"Why, to Broderick! Who else? There ain't no more I.R.S., you know."

"You use money here? Real currency?" That was startling.

"We do now. At first, you know, after the Blowup, there wasn't no money in circulation after the old U.S. bills wore out, and nobody was issuing new money on account of the government not being there. So what we did was swap things around, trade labor for goods, so much time in return for so many bushels of corn or cabbages, and then maybe swap the cabbages around for other things, you know, like in olden times. But now these days we got Broderick's new Corn Dollars—that's what he calls them—backed by produce. People decided they was safe, because you can take them to the market town and trade them in for corn if you want to, and then you can use the corn to buy things, but carrying the bills around is a whole lot easier than carrying a wagonload of corn, and corn spoils, besides. I guess that's why people started using banknotes in the first place. Broderick puts them out himself, his signature on every one. They's only good in what he calls Broderick Territory, but we don't travel around a lot outside

Broderick Territory, you know. Here. Here's what they look like."

Webster handed him a worn, folded piece of blue paper the size and shape of an old U.S. banknote. Jansen felt a tremor of astonishment. Currency? No doubt of it, the real thing. Crudely printed, probably run off in some rural newspaper office on God only knew what kind of creaking antique of a press. An intricate border of interwoven stalks of wheat, and bold smudgy lettering in the center. BRODERICK TERRITORY MONEY, it said. GOOD FOR FIVE DOLLARS IN CORN. And an engraving, some Greek-looking goddess holding a shield in one hand and a bolt of lightning in the other, most likely the first stock cut that had come to light in the print-shop. The bill was signed—in ink, by hand—with a bold jagged scrawl, *Sam Broderick*. Amazing, Jansen thought. They've reinvented currency, and this stuff is actually a lot more solidly backed than the Provisional Federal Government's banknotes. Or, for that matter, the greenbacks that the U.S. Treasury used to put out before the Blowup. You couldn't take a Federal Reserve Note down to the bank and trade it in for a bushel of corn on demand, and you sure can't do it with one of our bills. But you can do it with one of these. BRODERICK TERRITORY MONEY, it says. And it is: legal tender. Amazing. Amazing. Real money. Issuing money is a prime mark of sovereignty, isn't it? They've got an entire little republic going out here.

And in that case we have big troubles ahead, Jansen told himself gloomily. Ben Thurston isn't the only one who's been slicing away at the Anarchy in this part of the world. And it looks like this Broderick has been doing a pretty fair job, except that what he's been putting together here isn't the United States of America, it's more like the United Towns of Sam Broderick.

"Tells us how much to pay in taxes," Webster went on, "tells us who has to come and work on the highways a certain number of hours a month, tells us how much lumber we can buy from the sawmill that they've got going out by Circleville—"

"A regular dic-tator," said one of the other men. "Runs this town like he owns it, and he don't even come from here."

"But you accept his money?" Jansen asked. "You obey his orders?"

"It's the only money around, ain't it? If we put out our own, why should they take it at the sawmill? There ain't no government money we can use, no real U.S. money."

"But there's Broderick's money. *He's* the government. He's the boss."

"Won't let decent people speak up with their own ideas," said the third man, scowling. "A regular dic-tator."

"What would happen if you said you weren't going to listen to him any more?" Jansen asked. "Does he have an army? A police force? Can he *make* you do what he wants?"

Webster said, shrugging, "Not really an army, no. Maybe some police. We aren't talking force here. He's got the people bulldozed, is all. Two thirds of them, they just don't give a damn. Like sheep, you know? You make sure they get enough to eat and they're satisfied. They're willing to let Sam Broderick tell them what to do because it makes them feel like there's some sort of government again. It don't matter that he comes from someplace else. You don't expect the government to come from your own town anyway."

"You expect the mayor to come from your own

town," said one of the others. "We don't even have no mayor. Broderick decides everything for us."

"A regular dic-tator," Webster muttered.

"What about the third of the people who don't want Broderick running things?" Jansen asked. "Why don't they get together and toss him out of here? It can't just be that it's convenient to use his banknotes. Or are you three the only ones in town who really don't want him?"

"There's lots who don't," said Webster sullenly. "Lots. But we ain't organized right. He's too strong for us. He controls too much stuff all around—the mills, the warehouses. People are afraid he'll just cut us off if we go against him, and we'll have to live like the crazies do, in falling-down old shacks, eating whatever we can raise ourselves or catch in the forest. A few years back I tried to push him the hell out of this town, but it didn't work. I'm not giving up, though. I got my men. Lots of people round here think *I* oughta be running this town instead of him, and maybe not just this town. A lot of Broderick's own people think that way too. Deep down inside they know they'd rather have me in charge than him, but they're too scared of Broderick to admit it."

It seemed like the moment to score a political point or two, Jansen thought. "This is exactly why we have to get the central government working again," he said. "Can you imagine some private citizen setting himself up as the boss of a couple of counties, just like that, in the old days? It couldn't possibly have happened. But if it had, the government would have moved in on him in five minutes. But now there's no organization. There's no way of enforcing anything. We aim to fix all that."

"Yeah," Webster said. "A-men, brother. We understand each other."

"And the election will be the first major step in reconstructing—"

"Absolutely," said Webster. "We're behind you one hunderd percent. *Three* hunderd. I'm going to get out there and tell the people they got to vote, they got to join in with the new government. Broderick, he don't want no elections in Ohio, but I aim to see that we have one." Webster paused. "Provided that the new Federal government recognizes me and my men as the legal government of this town, that is."

Of course, Jansen thought. What else but that?

Cautiously he said, "You know I can't give you any definite guarantees."

"You can't?"

"I don't have the right, for one thing. For another, even if I did, would you expect me to hand the place over to you just on your own say-so? I haven't even been in this town twenty-four hours. But I tell you this: once the authority of the Federal Government is reestablished in this district, we'll conduct a thorough investigation of what's been going on around here. If the constitutional rights of the citizens have been violated, we'll take steps to reestablish democracy and law and order here—which is bound to mean throwing Broderick out."

"And replacing him with—?"

"Well, that remains to be seen. But I think I can say that we'd be likely, all other things being equal, to want to turn the town over to someone who has proven himself to be a staunch supporter of the Provisional Federal Government, someone who has helped us to bring this town into the United States, rather than to someone who might have hindered and opposed our efforts to put this election on."

"All other things being equal," Webster said. "Yeah."

"We understand each other, I think," said Jansen.

"Yeah. Yeah. We sure do. You got yourself a deal,

Mr. Provisional Federal Government. You go right ahead and run your election, and we'll give you all the help you need, you hear? All the help you need."

6.

He spent the next two hours closeted with Webster and five or six of his friends in a cluttered little office behind the barber shop on the far side of the square. They wanted to know all about the new government—what kind of powers it had, what policies it was planning, what the relationship between the Federal administration and the local authorities was going to be. Would there be states again, and counties? Who would collect the taxes? Who would rebuild the roads? What about industry—how was that going to be started up again? With Federal money? Where would the Federal Government get money?

They weren't foolish questions. These weren't foolish men, Jansen realized. They were an unsavory bunch, sure—rough, slovenly of manner and speech, blatantly looking to feather their own nests—but however crude and obvious they might be, they were no mere hayseed dummies. It would be dangerous to underestimate their shrewdness.

They were looking to gain power. No surprise there. In any polity, no matter how small, there's a modicum of power to be had and people of the power-seeking type will invariably seek it: Aristotle had remarked on that little tautology twenty-five centuries ago. Somehow these men had been pre-empted in their own town by a power-seeker more effective than they, but that hadn't caused them to give up. They understood that they couldn't get what they wanted without the help of the Provisional Federal Government; that was why, and probably the only reason why, they were willing to support reaffiliation with the United States and to help put on the election. All right. No surprise there, either.

But the Provisional Federal Government needed them, too. The only way it could survive and establish itself across the land was with the cooperation of the local power-holders. Sam Broderick sure as hell wasn't going to cooperate with the Thurston administration; but Chuck Webster and his friends might. If Sam Broderick's hold on this town could be broken, these surely were the men who were going to move in and take things over. Jansen knew that it would be unwise to risk alienating them at this stage. It wasn't his aim to ally himself necessarily with the saintliest people in town, just with the ones who could make things happen the right way. Saintliness could wait till later.

"So it's understood," Jansen said finally. "The week before the candidates come through this way, you'll hold a series of three town meetings at which the outline of the structure of the United States under the Constitution of 2012 will be fully explained, and the rights and responsibilities of citizens in a democratic society will be discussed, and—"

There was a knock at the door.

"See who that is," Webster murmured to one of his companions.

A short red-cheeked man with peculiarly intense greenish eyes came in. He glanced curiously at Jansen, frowned, and looked toward Webster, who nodded and said, "It's okay. What's up, Clyde?"

"Broderick's not getting here till tomorrow."

"You sure of that?"

"Yep," the red-faced man said. "The word just came in from the relay post. He ran into some kind of squabble two towns up the road and he's staying the night to iron things out. He'll be here by lunch-time tomorrow."

"Man here waiting to see him," said Webster.

"So I see. Who is he, Chuck?"

"Kentucky man," Webster said. "From the Provi-sionals." He turned to Jansen and said, "You going to stick around here another day, then?"

Jansen shrugged. "I damn well have to, don't I? My whole mission to this area won't make any sense if I don't manage to come to some sort of under-standing with Broderick." He felt a rising sense of annoyance. Stuck for three days in this little town—far behind schedule, the undistributed posters gath-ering dust in the back of the chopper—

The red-faced man said, "What mission is he talk-ing about?"

"Election," Webster told him. "For President. The Provisionals are starting up the U.S. of A. again around these parts. Didn't you see the posters, Clyde?"

"I came straight here," Clyde said. "Election, huh? What's Broderick going to say about that?"

"That's what I need to find out," said Jansen.

"I bet he'll run," said Clyde. "I'll bet he wants to be President so bad he can taste it. That bastard. President Broderick, huh? I bet he'll go for that real big."

Jansen said, "Broderick's not going to be a candi-date. The candidates have already been chosen."

He had a sudden flashing image of last month's nominating conventions, ten or twelve men and three or four women sitting around on rickety chairs in the Oval Office, trying to figure out who would be will-ing to stand up and run for President against Ben Thurston and what the name of the opposition political party was going to be. It was Thurston, finally, who had come up with the opposition party name him-self, National Progress Party, and talked Tom McIntyre into taking the nomination. Nobody in Kentucky had so much as heard of Sam Broderick then. A national nominating convention, and nobody knew the name of a boss who was big enough to be issuing his own currency just on the far side of the Ohio River! It had seemed like a grand thing, deciding to hold a real election and taking the campaign to the people who lived outside Kentucky; but nothing about it struck him as very grand at all, right now.

"Not going to nominate Broderick?" Clyde said, looking amused. "Well well well. I'd like to see that bastard's face when you tell him you come in here to make somebody else President over him. Who's your President going to be, anyway?"

"The election will decide that," Jansen said quietly. "Ben Thurston's the likely winner, though. You know him? He's Acting President now. Put the Provisional Federal Government together practically single-handed."

"Never heard of him," Clyde said. He turned to Webster. "Tony O'Neill's in town already, by the way. Broderick sent him on ahead and he got here maybe fifteen minutes ago. He's having breakfast at the Crawford place right now."

"You could talk to O'Neill about your election," Webster suggested.

"O'Neill?"

"Broderick's Number Two man. The main trouble-shooter, sort of."

"The chief hatchetman, you mean," said Clyde.

"That too. A very shifty character," Webster said. "Real smart, lots of book learning, talks a little the way you do. I'd watch my step around him, if I was you. Anything you say to Tony O'Neill, it goes straight to Broderick, only it gets a little twisted along the way. Maybe the smart thing is wait for tomorrow, just talk to Broderick."

"No," Jansen said. "O'Neill must have seen my posters on his way into town. He'll be thinking about them. I think I'd better meet with him today, before he can form a lot of wrong impressions to pass along to Broderick tomorrow. Will somebody take me down to see him?"

"If you want," said Webster. "Whatever you say."

7.

O'Neill was unexpectedly elegant and courtly: a small dapper man of about sixty, with a thick head of gleaming hair swept straight back from his forehead. His movements were economical and graceful, his voice was soft and cultured, his gaze was keen and thoughtful. He seemed more like a senator or at least a professor, Jansen thought, than like any sort of hatchetman.

"So there will be an election," O'Neill said serenely. "The first, I think, in quite a long while, eh? The return of a vanished American custom. Of course, they may be holding elections in California or Texas or Minnesota already, for all we know. But I doubt it, don't you? I think yours is very probably the first. Wouldn't you say?"

"I'd welcome a return to traditional democratic procedures in any part of the country," Jansen said. "I know Ben Thurston would. And if it turns out that other Constitutions have been written, that there are three or four United States with their own Presidents in charge, I'm pretty sure that the passage of time will straighten that out. Reasonable people will work out reasonable solutions to the problem of putting the country back together."

"Naturally. There's something in the human spirit

that abhors the increase of entropy. Wouldn't you say?"

Despite himself, Jansen laughed.

O'Neill's eyebrows lifted. "I don't understand. Did I make a joke without being aware of it?"

"No joke, no. It's only that—well, just last night before I went to sleep I was lying there thinking that I couldn't expect to find philosophers over here, that philosophy was a luxury that most people couldn't afford in times like these. And the very next day I find myself getting into a discussion of the human attitude toward entropy. I was laughing at the irony, that's all."

Smiling, O'Neill said, "I think you'll find, if you take a closer look, that we're all philosophers today. The difficult nature of existence requires us to define the way we intend to live, day by day, in every action we take. Simply getting out of bed in the morning is an act of existential courage. Of course, I suppose it always was. You understand, philosophy is a professional interest of mine. Was."

"Professional?"

"Before the Blowup I was an instructor at Ohio State. Spinoza, Descartes, Hobbes, Locke—" He shook his head. "Several geological epochs ago. What was your school, Mr. Jansen?"

"Penn," he said. "Several geological epochs ago, yes. I remember those names. And the others. Kierkegaard, Schopenhauer, Nietszche, Sartre—"

"Hegel?" O'Neill asked.

"Hegel, yes."

"One of the greatest masters, so I thought then. And still do, I suppose. Thesis and antithesis—who could deny the force of that simple idea? A rational man: the most rational of men. But I began to talk of entropy. The measure of chaos, yes? Would you agree with me that the struggle against increasing entropy is the defining trait of human civilization? Yes, of course. And in our poor sad post-cataclysmic world, the rolling back of entropy must be our highest priority. This election of yours—"

"Restoration of traditional forms is part of the war against entropy, isn't it?" Jansen said.

"In a sense. But the return to democracy? Is the democratic system part of the war against entropy or merely one aspect of its unceasing increase? As one 20th-century philosopher—was it Claude Shannon? I do forget—said, "Absolute entropy is cosmic democracy." Each atom of matter spread out neatly equidistant from the next, no distressing aggregations and congregations of substance—"

"If by democracy you mean setting up a legislature that consists of the entire population," said Jansen uneasily, "then democracy would indeed produce a high-entropy state. Chaos. But nobody's talking about doing that. The former United States operated on a system of representative democracy—vertically organized hierarchies of authority, an elaborate structure through which the needs of the entire population could be channeled in a systematic and productive way so that—"

"Ah," O'Neill cut in. "We have no disagreement. Government is order, tending in its pathological forms toward utter rigidity; democracy is disorder, tending in its pathological forms toward chaos. The task is to find the point of equilibrium at which we will fall neither into absolute totalitarian control on the one hand nor into complete uncontrollability on the other. A society will cease to grow—eh?—if everything is locked firmly into place. But it is stultifying also to have utter anarchy. A message that is all redundancy contains no information; a message that is all information is unintelligible. We must find a balance, Mr.

Jansen. We must always find a balance. Remember your Hegel: thesis, antithesis, synthesis."

"Indeed. We have no disagreement."

"This election of yours—"

"Will bring us back a certain distance from fragmentation and disarray toward order and control."

"Prematurely, perhaps?"

"I don't think so," Jansen said. "How long can we go on living as a bunch of separate villages that have little or no communication with one another?"

"The human race lived that way for millions of years."

"And saw fit to evolve gradually toward a society of city-states and then toward one of nations and then toward imperial mega-states."

"And then toward chaos again. The Hegelian antithesis, yes?"

"No. The Blowup wasn't inevitable. It was stupidity, sure, but not destiny."

Again O'Neill shrugged. "Perhaps. Still, we live with its consequences. Our society was shattered. Now we attempt to put it back together. By what means, though, that's the question we're trying to answer! By what means?"

"Gradual restoration of the democratic process, which I think and I hope you think is the most effective method of government that humanity had managed to devise before the Blowup."

"It was effective then," O'Neill conceded. "Up to a point."

"And now?"

"I'm not so sure."

"What then? Continued fragmentation? The village as sovereign unit?"

"Not really workable in the long run. The villages must coalesce once again. That process is already under way."

"And how are the coalesced villages to be governed? Autocracy? You think Louis XIV is a better idea than Abraham Lincoln?"

"Under certain circumstances, perhaps. The enlightened despot can sometimes—"

"And it goes without saying that Sam Broderick is a truly enlightened despot, or otherwise—"

"Please," said O'Neill. "I thought this was a purely theoretical discussion."

"Among philosophers?" Jansen managed another laugh. "I think I should return to my orignal position, then. Philosophy is a luxury we can't afford in the present state of the world. Let's talk about the election, shall we?"

"Very well. I think when you meet with Broderick you'll find that he believes your election is a premature step."

"Because it gets in the way of his own ambitions?"

"I think his position is a little less shameless than that. But let him explain it to you himself when you speak with him two or three days from now."

"Two or three days?" Jansen's eyes widened. "I understood that he'd be getting into town tomorrow!"

"So we all thought. He'll be delayed a little longer, as it turns out."

Irritatedly Jansen said, "I can't sit here all week waiting for him to turn up. I have a tremendous territory to cover—something like half of what used to be Ohio—and I'm due back at the Kentucky White House in eight days. If—"

"I think it would be a good idea for you to wait here until Broderick arrives."

Jansen shook his head. "That's impossible. But look: we don't have to stand on ceremony, do we? Tell me what town he's in now and I'll fly over there this afternoon."

"He's quite fully preoccupied in dealing with the problems that have arisen there."

"Then I'll go on with my tour and come back here in three days and meet with him then."

"We prefer that you wait here," said O'Neill smoothly.

"I've told you. I can't do that."

"We think it's best that you discuss the matter of the election with Broderick before you carry your campaign to other towns of this area. And since he's currently preoccupied with emergency matters, that would require you to wait here the additional day or two until he—"

"Require?"

"Yes."

"I'm a prisoner in this town, is that what you're saying?"

"We regard you as an ambassador from a friendly neighboring state. We could scarcely detain you against your will. But if you intend to discuss these things with Broderick, you'll have to do it on the terms that are offered, Mr. Jansen, or else I doubt that it will be possible for you—"

"In effect, I'm a prisoner until I've spoken with Broderick," Jansen said. "You deny it and admit it in the same breath."

"When an envoy is forced to wait until the prince with whom he must parley arrives, is that detainment?"

"I see. Broderick's a prince, is he?"

"I use the word metaphorically. Come, Mr. Jansen. It will be only a day or two. We can spend our time discussing Hegel, if you like. Fichte—Kant—Hume—even Plato, if you wish. Do you know *The Laws* of Plato? A useful corrective to *The Republic*, I think. What do you say? To devise a constitution not for an ideal state, but for a society of average human beings—

the balance between *eleutheria* and *monarchia*, popular control and autocratic authority—ah, so much that we can discuss, Mr. Jansen, so long since I've had the opportunity to explore these matters with an intelligent opponent! You'll stay, won't you? Of course you'll stay!"

"Of course," said Jansen bleakly.

8.

Broderick said, "I think you better take those posters down and put them back in your whirlybird and go on back where you came from, son. We ain't going to have any election here."

He said it very softly, almost gently. But there was no mistaking the force behind his words.

It was the third day after Jansen's arrival in town. Broderick had turned up about noon, riding in an old jeep with an entourage of six or seven men in jeeps even more dilapidated than his. Tony O'Neill had met him and conferred with him; and now Jansen, restless after what had amounted to three days of house arrest, stood before him in the town square.

Broderick was in his late forties or maybe early fifties, an enormous man, six feet four at the least. His face had power in it to match his size. A huge black mustache drooped below a savagely beaked nose. He wore an easy smile, but there was a subtle grimness about it, a hidden quality of some sort that was not at all ingratiating. Jansen was surprised and dismayed to realize that this man offered a presence as commanding as that of Ben Thurston himself: maybe more so.

"It's up to the town authorities to decide whether the election will be held here, isn't it?" Jansen said.

"*I'm* the town authorities," Broderick replied cheerfully. "No election. I won't even try to be diplomatic about it. I don't want you boys getting the slightest foothold here. Is that clear enough for you?"

"Very much so. But I want to remind you that I'm a representative of the government of the United States, which has overriding sovereign power throughout its territory."

"Sure it does," said Broderick. "But this ain't its territory."

"Do you really believe that?"

"You bet. The United States got dissolved on the day of the Blowup. It hasn't been around to exercise its sovereign power ever since. I don't recognize a bunch of fellows over Kentucky way as the United States."

Jansen nodded slowly. Broderick didn't sound angry or blustering, only firm, very sure of himself. Jansen warned himself to proceed carefully, to keep this discussion from heating up. As calmly as he could he said, "And by what right is recognition or non-recognition up to you, Mr. Broderick?"

"I'm in charge here. Which means that whenever there's trouble, they send me out to take care of it. I didn't particularly ask for the job, but I got it, and I'm doing it. And you're trouble, mister."

"I'm not here to cause trouble. I'm simply here—"

"To tell us about the elections. Sure, I know. And that means trouble." He pointed toward the other side of the square. "Come over to the town hall with me. There's an office that I use when I'm being mayor. We can talk better there."

In silence Jansen followed Broderick across the square into the gray, dumpy two-story building that was the town hall. He was troubled by Broderick's manner—stolid, unhurried, unyielding, immensely confident—and even by the mere physical massiveness of him. Breaking this local strongman's hold by force would be a tough job, maybe an impossible job, certainly a foolish thing to attempt; but co-opting him into support of the Provisional Federal Government might prove even harder.

The ground floor of the town hall had once been a post office—dusty now, drawers open and empty, sacks of undelivered and undeliverable mail lying around in a corner where they probably had been heaped for a decade and a half. Broderick led him upstairs and into a small office. He opened a desk drawer, took out a clay jug, two small clay cups. He uncorked the jug and poured about two inches of whiskey into each of the cups.

"Drink hearty," Broderick said.

Jansen took a hesitant sip. It was fiery stuff, leaping at his tongue.

"What is it?"

"Applejack. Don't they have applejack where you come from, mister?"

Jansen smiled. "I suppose they do. I'm not really much of a drinking man." He set the cup down. "Now, about the election—"

"Yeah. The election."

"Tell me this. Are you opposed in principle to the idea of restoring the United States Government?"

"Well, not in principle, no."

"But you decline to accept the Provisional Federal Government that's currently based in Kentucky as the legal successor to the former Washington government, is that it?"

Broderick toyed with his great comb of a mustache. "Side issue. We can get to that later. The basic thing is that I know what'll happen after we recognize the Provisionals by holding your election here. The Federal Government will come in here and decide it doesn't like the way this territory is being run, and next thing I know I'll be mixed up in a power struggle. This town and the towns around are all full of power-hungry fools who're eager to bamboozle the Feds into putting them in control here, and quite capable of doing it. You see that?"

"I see that some kind of regularization of local government would be necessary, yes."

"A fancy way of saying that I'd be pushed aside and some nitwits would take over."

"Perhaps. Perhaps not."

"I don't want to risk it. I happen to think that I've been doing a better job than anyone else could have done around here. That I'm the man who ought to be running the show."

"How did you come to be running the show in the first place?" Jansen asked.

"Nobody else was. And then some were who were incompetent. We'd all have starved to death. So I had to do it. And I found out that I was good at it. So I mean to continue."

"If you're that good an administrator, won't the people vote to keep you in office?"

"If they had any sense they would. But once you bring Federals into the area with authority to rejigger things, things might get rejiggered the wrong way."

Jansen laughed. "I haven't heard anyone arguing in favor of the divine right of kings in a long time, Mr. Broderick."

The remark didn't seem to annoy Broderick. He simply shook his head in a slow bemused way and poured out two more cups of applejack.

Then he said, "You mind if I try a few questions on you, Mr. Jansen?"

"Go ahead."

"How come there has to be an election in the first place?"

"Why, to reestablish formal legal authority in the

United States. To end the condition of anarchy that's prevailed since the Blowup. To replace self-appointed regional leaders with people chosen by the will of the people."

"Uh-huh. That's what I thought. Okay, you want to reestablish the legal authority of the United States government, and put the Constitution back in effect, and all that kind of stuff. What for?"

"What *for?*"

"That's what I said. Why bother restoring all that goddamned broken-down machinery?"

"That's how you perceive it? Goddamned broken-down machinery?"

"You still haven't told me why we should bother setting it all back in place again."

"Didn't you say five minutes ago that you weren't opposed in principle to restoring the government?"

"More or less, I'm not. But I want you to tell me why you think we ought to do it right now."

"All right. We need a national government because we want to build ourselves back to where we were before the war, and we can't do it as a lot of little separate villages. If we're going to get our national strength back, we have to be a nation again politically, we have to be guided by a single vision, we have to have a *union*. It's so obvious that I feel silly explaining it like this. In union there's strength. If some enemy should attack us—"

"There ain't no enemies left," Broderick said. "We *won* the war. If you can call that winning."

"If we're in better shape than most of the rest of the world, someone's likely to want what we have. We don't know that we don't have enemies."

"Anybody who wants to take away what we have, such as that is, has to do a hell of a lot of work before he gets even as strong as we are now," Broderick said. "And we ain't very strong. But you're ducking my main question. What's all this need for a Federal Government, for a United States? Assuming there's no outside enemy, and anybody in his right mind would know that there ain't, what will a national government give us that we don't have now?"

Jansen hadn't expected to find himself challenged on this level. If Broderick had simply stuck to his original position—that this was *his* territory and he didn't mean to tolerate anybody from the outside coming in and telling him what to do—it would be easy enough to understand where he was coming from. But evidently the boss of Broderick Territory had picked up a little of the spirit of philosophical inquiry from his henchman O'Neill. And it appeared that Broderick meant to toy with him, play devil's advocate, shift the issue from one of simple power-grabbing to some higher ground.

He said, "A national government would restore travel and communications across the land. It would offer a comprehensible set of laws that everybody shares. It would provide markets for your produce, and products from other parts of the country. Do I really need to spell all that out? Can you honestly say that it's better to remain as an isolated bunch of scattered little towns than to be part of a nation?"

"We got laws here," Broderick said. "When two people in this town have an argument, they come to me. I settle it. We got contact with our fellow Americans, right in the five towns of Broderick Territory. We got trade between the towns. We got currency. Did you know that, that we issue money? Corn Dollars, I call them. Legal tender, properly backed. And everybody accepts it. We got everything that we need that an old-time nation could offer. And more: I got a hundred men I love and trust like brothers. Did you have that many friends when you lived in some big city? And we got communication, too. When I want to see Jimmy Lyons, I go over to his place. If he ain't there, I leave word. Or he comes to me. And what do we need markets for our produce for? We make what we need. And we've got everything we want. So what do we need your election for, mister?"

Jansen felt a dull throbbing in the pit of his stomach. These arguments were so simple-minded that he hardly knew where to begin fighting back. He took a quick gulp of the apple brandy, but it didn't make him feel more calm.

He said, "Okay, I grant the fact that you feel happy living in a little self-sufficient self-contained clump of towns. But the human race can't make progress that way. There's got to be a going out, a seeking for bigger things."

"Why?"

"If we stand still, we'll stagnate and die."

"Says you."

"It's a law of human nature!" Jansen retorted. Broderick's bland assurance was infuriating. "Since the Greeks, the Romans, the Assyrians, however far back you want to go. We strive. We make voyages. We don't just sit back and shut out the rest of the world and tell ourselves that that's just fine."

"Why the dickens not?"

"Progress—"

"Where did progress get us the last time? Where's all the progress of New York? A bubbling slagheap, that's all. Where's Washington? Where's Cleveland? Where's every goddamned big city in the world? Where's all your progress, mister?"

"We made mistakes," Jansen said.

"Big ones."

"Real big. They destroyed the world. But now we have a second chance."

"To make the same mistakes all over? Uh-uh, friend.

We tried your kind of government and it didn't work. This time we've got to try something different."

Jansen scowled. "Like a country made up of a bunch of independent towns run by strong-fisted bosses? Is that your idea of how things ought to be? Yeah. Yeah, I suppose it is."

"You must think I'm a real bastard," Broderick said casually. "A power-hungry villain, a grasping monster. Listen, if I was what you think I am, I'd just have told my boys to slit your throat the minute I heard about your election posters."

"The fact that you didn't doesn't get around the fact that you run this territory as if you own it. You don't even pretend to be observing democracy here."

"Damned right I don't. But do you think I *wanted* this goddamned job? You think I want to listen to damnfool quarrels when I could be fishing? You think I want to spend my good time deciding produce quotas, or keeping no-good crooks from stealing everybody blind, or talking to idiots from Kentucky who want to have elections?"

"Right. You really don't care for power at all. That's why you call these towns Broderick Territory and travel around from one to another as though you were Caesar handing out the law."

"I didn't say I minded doing what I do. But I didn't go out of my way to get the job. Things were in a bad way in my town after the Blowup, and I had to do something about it for the sake of my family, my friends, for my own sake as well. So I did. I started to put things to rights. Somebody had to, you follow me? Then a little while later a bunch of people from around here came to me and said, 'Sam, you've got to come on in and straighten things out the way you did in your own town. Chuck Webster and his pals are screwing everything up.' I ran them off my farm. They came back. 'Sam, we need you.

Sam, help us.' Sam this and Sam that. You forget how it was, right after the Blowup. Everybody was crazy out of his mind. Some people still are. After a while I got the idea that if I didn't take over everything around here, the crazies might. So I put myself in charge, and a couple of other towns invited me to help out, and people started calling this district Broderick Territory. All right. In union there's strength, you say. I agree. But what we got here is big enough to suit me. It works."

"You wouldn't want to have another five or ten towns?"

"What for? It's just that much more goddamned work. I don't even want this much work."

"Am I really supposed to believe that?"

"You can believe any damn thing you want. I'm just telling you how things are around here."

"You must think I'm awfully naive," Jansen said. "What I believe is that you love bossing these five towns, that you mean to pull all of Ohio into Broderick Territory as fast as you get the chance, that you'd take Kentucky too, that you'd like to be President of what's left of the United States, and that you don't want us to have the election because you're afraid Ben Thurston will get in the way of your plans. That's what I believe."

"That I'm jealous of Thurston. That I'm hungry to be President myself. That's what you think."

"You bet I do."

"Well, what you say makes a lot of sense, son. Anybody with some power always wants more power: that's a rule of human nature, right? Right. Except you're wrong. It happens not to apply in this particular case. You really think I want to be President, huh?"

"Or king, or emperor, or some other title. Of as much territory as you can grab."

"Wrong. Very wrong. You don't understand me at all, boy. Any time somebody around here shows me he can do the job better than me, he can have it—with my blessing. Truth. God's own truth."

"Someone like Chuck Webster, say?"

Broderick laughed harshly. "That slippery snake? He had his chance, right after the Blowup. Put himself in charge, gave all his friends soft jobs, collected graft right and left, told everyone what to do, didn't do a damn thing himself. Well, this town couldn't put up with that. Nobody's fitten to boss other people if he can't even boss himself. So after I saw that if someone didn't stop Webster he was going to run the town into the ground, and that if I didn't do the stopping no one else would, I walked in here and threw him out. He's been scheming to get back in, ever since."

"And you're completely sure that your way of doing things is the best way."

"Look, this town was like a runaway engine with a moron at the wheel. So I grabbed the controls myself, because I didn't want to get run over. I think most people will agree that I'm doing it the right way. If they didn't, they wouldn't let my currency pass here. They wouldn't ask me to judge their squabbles. Now you come along with your election. So Webster and his scalawags try to cook up a deal with you. Oh, I know all about it, don't worry! They come and say to you, you look after us and we'll look after you. Right. So the Federals will march in here and turn the town over to Webster. You think that's a wonderful idea?"

"We're simply interested in restoring democracy."

"Democracy's only a word," Broderick said. "What ought to interest you is restoring law and order. Which is what interests me."

"Suppose the people really prefer Webster?"

"Wouldn't be surprised if they did. Even the ones who say they admire what I've been doing. Admire, yes, but they know things would be sweeter for them with Webster in charge. For a little while, anyway, until the damage he was doing started to show up. Then it would be too late, of course. But they'd want him at first if they got the choice, most likely. People always want damnfool things. Never know when they're well off."

"So you admit that you're ruling here by force, then!"

"Never said any such thing. Only that if we had a town election, chances are Webster'd come out on top, being that he's a local man and I'm not, and he'd know how to rig things the right way with his friends. You give people a chance to vote for crooks, half the time they will. More than half. Even one like Webster that they had to throw out once already. He'll come promising them the moon, and they'll say, Sure, sure, he's one of us, his cousin is married to my sister's brother-in-law's boy, and they'll vote him in. That's what elections do."

"You don't trust your own people. I wish they could see how much contempt you have for them. You think they're like children. You're the only one who knows what's really good for them, is that it? Big Daddy Broderick? You don't dare let any sort of election be held. You know it wouldn't go the way you like."

Broderick chuckled. "All right, friend. You like elections? You want democracy? You'll get it." He stood up abruptly, looming over Jansen. "I'll call a town meeting. You can have your chance to tell the people what your Federals have to offer. And then we'll see what they want to do."

9.

All afternoon they came drifting into town by twos and threes, until at least four hundred of them were gathered in front of the old wooden bandstand. Jansen saw the red-haired woman out there, holding her little boy, and her plump sister beside her, and the men from the house. But he saw no one else he knew, not Webster nor any of his people. "Okay," Broderick said. "Let's go." He stepped into the bandstand and clapped his hands for attention. "This here is Lloyd Jansen. He comes from the Provisional Federal Government over in Kentucky. Wants to talk to you."

It took twenty minutes for Jansen to say what he had to say. He gave them everything he had: fragments of Ben Thurston's speeches, bits of the old Constitution and the new one, whole chunks of American history. He wheedled, cajoled, even bribed and threatened a little. He explained, half a dozen times in half a dozen ways, how necessary it was that everyone in what had been the United States get behind the reorganized government. They listened in silence. A very chilly silence, Jansen thought. It was like addressing an audience of statues.

He finished with the strongest stuff he had:

"... and we here highly resolve that this nation under God shall have a new birth of freedom, and that government of the people, by the people, for the people shall not perish from the earth. One nation—indivisible—with liberty and justice for all. The choice is yours. Will you help us forge the new America?"

He stepped back. There were no whoops of applause, no patriotic outcries. Just more silence, plenty of it.

Broderick came forward again. His towering form dominated the platform. "That was a mighty fine speech, young fellow," he said amiably. "You really know how to orate. Let's give the boy a good hand, folks!"

A moment of light applause. Then silence again.

Jansen scowled. In three patronizing sentences Broderick had wiped out whatever effect his speech might have had.

The big man went on, "I just want to say one little thing before we vote. I don't like this Federal business much, myself. I think we're doing okay running ourselves. I think the Federals might mess around with us in a way we won't like.

"Let your consciences guide you. But keep this in mind: there are still plenty of crazies out there, and hungry people from the cities, and a lot of other wanderers who go around raiding farms. I've put together a pretty tough little corps to protect this territory. But anybody who wants to vote for joining this Federal Government, well, I figure he'd rather be protected by them, not by the territorial militia. So I'll pull back my men from guarding the land of anyone who prefers to have the Feds running things here. That's fair enough, ain't it?"

"Wait a second," Jansen burst out. "That's outright—"

Broderick went right on. "And now it's time for voting. We're all friends here, so we don't need to fool around with paper ballots, right? Just stand forward and lift your hand. Everybody here who wants us to have these elections so Ben Thurston's government can come in here and run us, raise your hand up good and tall."

Broderick paused. No hands went up.

"Kinda looks like you lost," Broderick said easily. "The other side of it, now. Anyone who don't want no elections, suppose you sing out loud."

The deafening *Nay* from four hundred throats almost blew Jansen off the platform.

"Okay, folks," Broderick said. "Meeting's over. You can all go about your business now."

"Nicely done," said Jansen. "I'll never see a more beautiful job of rigging the vote."

"I just put the realities to them, son, and let them stand on their hind legs and state their democratic preference."

"You blackmailed them. Would you really have withdrawn protection from anyone who voted to hold the election?"

"Maybe not quite like that. But if they meant to repudiate the territorial government they ought to realize that there won't be anybody else to protect them. You Feds can't go policing every small town. I just put it to them in a slightly different way."

"I should have known you'd connive," Jansen said bitterly. "The meeting was a farce. You wouldn't have let it happen if you thought it would have gone against you."

"They have to be pushed a little sometimes," Broderick said. "Deep down, a lot of them would love to toss me out and put somebody like Webster in. Leave them be and they'd be likely to do just that. And he ain't fit to run the town. I am."

"You're pretty cocky about your qualifications."

"I've got sense," Broderick said. "Pretty near the only man around here who does."

"Where was Webster at the meeting?"

"He wasn't. You think I was going to let him and his pals come in to make trouble?"

Jansen applauded. "Bravo! Bravo! So that's your idea of a free and open meeting! Keep your opponents out and threaten the voters. Nicely done, Broderick!"

"You know any better way? I don't." One of Broderick's massive paws tightened on Jansen's arm. "Does that whirlybird of yours fly by night?"

"It can, yes."

"Good. Suppose you get in it now and fly it away, yes? That's a lot better than having you sticking around here stirring up more problems for me. Come on. I'll walk you over to it."

It was getting dark, now. Jansen saw townspeople ripping down the election posters. He heard someone say, "Elections! Governments! What the hell for?" And someone else said, "We had one once, and all it did was blow everything to bits, right?"

"They don't understand," Jansen murmured.

Broderick smiled sadly. "You look awful hurt, son. Don't take it personal, okay?"

"I'm not hurt. I'm angry. Sheer dumbness makes me angry."

"It isn't dumbness," Broderick said. "It's fear."

"Fear of having a real national government?"

"Fear of making bad mistakes twice. Look, you go back where you came from, hear? Next town you stop at, you might get yourself lynched. Won't happen to you in Broderick Territory, not unless you try to make a nuisance of yourself, but I can't speak for the towns beyond. They're real wild folk out there."

"I'll take my chances," Jansen said. "One of these days the Provisional Federal Government will be a real thing in Ohio. And then we'll come back here and clean this place up."

"You still harping on my wickedness?"

"You're a small-time dictator," Jansen shot back. "You want me to pat you on the back and tell you what a wise ruler you are?"

"Wouldn't be a bad notion," Broderick said, showing no sign of offense. "Maybe I look like a dictator to you, but I like to think I'm a sort of philosopher-king, the kind Plato talked about."

"Plato again? That's what you use O'Neill for, I guess. To write your lines for you."

Now Broderick looked genuinely angry for the first time. "How dumb do you think I am? We still got a library here. My grammar's not so fancy, but I can read. And think. And what I've been thinking is that we've got to change this country around a little. Sure, we need a central government, if we're ever going to amount to anything again. I told you right off, I'm not against that in principle. But I don't think we're ready to set one up. And I won't ever speak out in favor of the government of fools by fools."

"And you think Ben Thurston's a fool?"

"Probably he isn't, but he's trying hard to act like one. Him and his bunch in Kentucky are trying to do a Humpty Dumpty act with this country. He's got a right to try, sure, but I know it's a dumb thing to do right now, and I'm not going to support him." Broderick yawned. "Thurston's a good strong man. I've heard a little about him, over here, not much, but what I hear ain't bad. I respect strong men. But he's full of a lot of crazy ideas. So are you. This ain't no time to go around with fancy-pants frills like elections and congresses and political parties."

"It's fifteen years since the Blowup. How long do you think we ought to wait? Five hundred years? A thousand?"

'The Blowup," Broderick said, "set this country back three hundred years at least. What got blown apart takes a lot of time to grow together. No matter how hard you Kentucky people want to put back the good old days of television and advertising and Republicans and Democrats, you better learn that it can't be done. Maybe even *shouldn't* be done. Look at those people over there." Broderick gestured at the men pulling down the last of Jansen's posters. "Those people are scared shitless of anything that looks like the old kind of government. Those governments built the bombs. Then they got into the damnfool arguments that made it seem right to start throwing the bombs back and forth. If things stay split up this way, there won't be any more bombs and there won't be any more big wars to use them in. These people don't want wars."

"Who does?"

"And they figure that if there's no government that can make a war, there'll be no wars. You heard them. They been there once. What good did it do them? The government sits on you and tells you how to run your life and takes your money away and uses it to build bombs and then it blows up the world. With bombs that it built with your own tax money. That's crazy."

"It sounds crazy when you say it that way, sure. But it isn't *necessary* to get into wars. The next government won't make the same mistakes."

"You think so?"

"What do you think is better? Village life? Letting things slide right back into Stone Age barbarism?"

"Of course not. We'll be a country again, and we'll do it right, the next time around, just like you say. But not yet. You can't bring on a new golden age just by proclaiming an election. The time ain't fitten for democracy, yet. That's Ben Thurston's mistake. He wants the whole extinct shooting match, conventions and parties and secret ballots and everybody standing around yelling for the special things he wants for himself, and the politicians falling all over themselves to win votes by handing goodies all around. Well, all that stuff's nice enough, I guess. But right now what we need is somebody who'll lead, who'll do what needs to be done, not somebody who'll do what feels good to the voters. Because we're all smashed up, see? We're still bleeding from our wounds. Those wounds have to heal. Right now this country is made up of a lot of weak, scared people. They just want to be left alone, to hide their heads like ostriches. We got to cozy them along, to get them up out of the sand, to guide them the way you'd guide children."

"That's been the excuse dictators have been giving for thousands of years. That the ordinary people are like children, that they don't know what's really good for them, that they need a strong man to tell them—"

"I don't aim to be a dictator, friend."

"You sure sound like you do."

"In Broderick Territory, yeah. Because Broderick Territory is where I live, and I want things to make sense right where I live. I don't really give a damn what goes on in California or Minnesota or even in Kentucky, really. You think I'm hungry for power, don't you, but no, no, I just want my kids and their kids to grow up in a decent quiet place. Let somebody else have the power. But if he's going to have power over me and mine, he damn well better have some sense in his head if he wants me to support him. I say we aren't ready for elections and such yet. If Thurston wants to set up shop as Emperor of the United States, I might go for it. But a constitution? An elected President? No. No. The time ain't ripe for such things yet."

"Thurston thinks it is."

"Well, he's *wrong*," Broderick said. "Let him try it. He'll see what happens. Sooner or later some guy like Webster will get himself voted into office. Fools like that know how to get other fools to vote for them. In times like this, there are lots of fools. The Blowup took the starch out of people. They need a leader."

"Thurston's a leader," Jansen said.

"Yeah. Yeah, very likely he is. But he's leading you down the wrong track, with this election stuff. If he'd

take the other track, maybe I could go for him."
Broderick frowned. "But I suspect he wouldn't see
what I'm driving at any more than you do. He's got
his head so full of old-fashioned nonsense about democracy and whatnot that he can't see the changes
that have happened. So he'll think I'm an evil tyrant,
just like you do. An enemy of society. In the name of
democracy he might have to come in here and wipe
out the fascist dictator Broderick. Eh? Eh? Don't you
think that could happen?"

Jansen stared.

Broderick went on, "You know something? I might
have to start a little political movement of my own. I
swore I never would. I swore I wouldn't get mixed up
in politics. But O'Neill's right. He said to me, Everything's politics, Sam, there's no hiding from politics,
it's politics just to say hello in the street. I might just
have to get involved a little in what goes on outside
Broderick Territory. And if I have to, I will, just like I
pushed Webster over when I had to."

Jansen said, "How would you feel about meeting
with Thurston in some neutral territory before the
election?"

"I might. I might." He didn't make it sound likely
that he would.

"I think it could be useful."

"Useful for who?"

"For the people of the United States," said Jansen.

Broderick laughed. "There ain't no United States,"
he said. "But let me think about it, okay? Maybe I'll
do it. Maybe Thurston'll see something in my ideas
that'll make sense to him. Maybe I'll see something
in his. Who knows? I'll think it over."

"Yes," Jansen said. "Think it over."

He started to climb into the helicopter. Broderick
looked up. "Let me have one of those posters, son."

"What for?"

"A souvenir. A souvenir of Ben Thurston's government. I got a feeling it ain't going to last too long. These posters, they're going to be valuable, eh?"

Silently Jansen took one from the stack and handed it down to the big man. Broderick nodded in thanks. Jansen switched the engine on.

Broderick said, "When you get back to Kentucky, you tell Ben Thurston everything I said, hear? About how the time ain't ready for bringing back democracy?"

"I have a feeling he won't want to listen."

"Don't be too sure of that, son. I bet Ben Thurston's a smart man, to be where he's gotten. Pretty soon he's bound to see that he's trying to move down the wrong track." Broderick winked. "Take it easy, son. Have yourself a good flight home."

The rotors whirled. The copter went straight up.

Jansen hovered for a moment at five hundred feet. Far below, in the dark square, he saw the shadowy dot that was Sam Broderick. The poster fluttered in Broderick's hands. Jansen was sure that Broderick was laughing.

It had all sounded so glib, so easily plausible. The old rationale for elitism, for oligarchy, for dictatorship: the people are children, the people can't be trusted to do the right thing. One thing seemed certain: Broderick was perfectly sincere. When he said he wasn't out for power for power's sake, Jansen believed him. But could he be *right*? Was constitutional democracy really an unworkable idea in the post-Blowup world?

Maybe it was, Jansen thought. This may be the 21st century, but in some ways it's more like the 12th. The network of instantaneous communication and virtually all but instantaneous transportation that had held the modern world together was gone and would be a long time rebuilding. How well would constitutional democracy have worked in the 12th century? How well could it work in the shattered 21st? Jansen's head began to throb. Could it be that Broderick was right? He wondered whether he ought to fly back to the river and dump his stock of election posters over the side.

No. No. No. How can I quit just like that? I'll head up north a little, and try another town, he told himself. Two or three more. Maybe half a dozen. Broderick's got these people bull-dozed, sure, but outside his territory they may see more need for our kind of government. Maybe. Maybe. And then we can put things to a test.

The copter droned northward. Now and then he saw the glow of some town's hearth-fires rising out of the darkness. When it was close to dawn he decided he was safely clear of Broderick Territory, and he picked a town and prepared to land. His head was still aching. "I'm from the Provisional Federal Government in Kentucky," he heard himself saying. "I'm here to tell you about the election that's going to be held in November." And then what? Would they rush to sign up? Or would they back off as if he were carrying some kind of plague? "Election, mister? We don't need no election around here. We been there once already. We don't feel like going back for more."

But they would—sooner or later. Sooner or later, Jansen knew, we'll crawl all the way back up out of the rubble and rebuild and make the world whole again. And when we do—when all these fears and doubts and confusions have disappeared—things will be better than they ever were before. Democracy isn't just an obsolete aberration, he told himself, something that had had its chance and had failed and now was to be discarded together. It wasn't because of democracy that the Blowup had happened. We made some mistakes, sure. But even so, the system we had was still the best one that human beings had ever devised to cope with the job of living together in a rational society. Even Broderick knows that. Our argument with him is just about timing, not about basic ideas. And democratic government will come back. Broderick knows that, too. It's our job to bring it back—and set it up in such a way that we won't make all the same old mistakes. Do I really believe that, he asked himself? Yes. Yes. I really believe it. I wouldn't be able to go on at all, if I didn't. But maybe it's going to be later rather than sooner, eh? Maybe we're going to have to put together a lot of little Broderick Territories, and then put all the separate little territories together into larger ones, retracing step by step the path from the beginning, instead of just declaring the United States back in business with a President and a Congress and all. Maybe. Maybe.

The first light of morning began to slip into the sky. He saw a town beside a small placid lake and looked about for a place to land. "I'm Lloyd Jansen," he would say. "I'm from the Provisional Federal Government, and I'm here to tell you about the election that—"

Somehow he had a feeling that he was going to be back in Kentucky, trying to explain things to Ben Thurston, a lot quicker than anyone expected.

"If there is a Bible—or even a tribe of savages—that lacks a General Deluge it is only because the religious scheme hadn't any handy source to borrow it from." A dark mood overtook Samuel Clemens in his old age, and he must have written this on a day when cynicism outweighed his good humor. His 1906 essay "Reflections on Religion" attacked the truth of the Old Testament. But he might just as well have been chiding those who believe a modern Deluge would have a more permanent effect than did Noah's.

It's fairly obvious that the Great Flood did not sweep all wickedness from the Earth. If worldwide disaster could guarantee a superior product, we could start Armageddon with a clear conscience. Make a fresh beginning, with room for brand-new ideas. Banish the Enemy in the East, and build a new planetary society conceived in liberty and dedicated to the proposition that all men are created equal.

But war rooms—and common sense—show us the truth. Every simulation leads to disaster, and the figures are so persuasive that the major powers have vowed never to set off this particular Deluge. Whether we can believe promises made in fear, we may not rest assured. Strategists have predicted that the proliferation of warheads means an almost unavoidable nuclear "accident" sometime within the next twenty years—a detonation set off by a terrorist group, perhaps, or on the orders of a vicious despot.

Norman Spinrad faces this possibility squarely, yet manages to make it funny, in "World War Last." So what else can we expect from the author of The Iron Dream and Bug Jack Barron?

WORLD WAR LAST

Norman Spinrad

Six weeks before Election Day Elmer Powell, the famous pollster, got a phone call from an anonymous someone at the Korami embassy who made him an offer he could hardly understand, let alone refuse.

Hassan al Korami wished a private consultation, for which he would pay the equivalent of one million dollars in a currency of Powell's own choosing.

There was only one catch: Hassan wanted to talk to him *right now*, meaning that Powell had to fly to Koramibad within the next four hours, take it or leave it.

Powell took it. Three hours later a limo from the Korami embassy picked him up at his downtown Washington office, an hour and a half after that it had managed to fight its way through the traffic to Dulles International Airport, and fifteen minutes later he was aboard a Korami Airlines Concorde on his way to the tiny Arabian sheikdom.

He seemed to be the only passenger aboard, though

it was hard to be sure, since the plane's interior was done up as a series of little private tents. He was served an excellent five-course French meal but no wine or other alcohol was available, though the hookah alongside his luxurious couch was provided with a chunk of hashish the size of a baseball.

After dinner, instead of a movie, a stunning and scantily clad young woman appeared, announced that she was his houri for the flight, and proceeded to transport him to an impressively realistic Earthly version of Moslem paradise for as long as his body could take it.

So by the time the plane began its descent over the sere desert wastes approaching Koramibad International Airport, Powell was stuffed to the gills, fried to the eyeballs, and screwed silly. He had read the stories on Hassan which appeared now and again in *People, High Times,* and *The National Enquirer;* now he was beginning to believe them.

The Sheikdom of Koram was a desert principality about the size of Los Angeles County, floating like a cork atop an immense pool of oil. The mild earthquakes which rocked the sheikdom from time to time were not, as the bedouins wandering the dunes in their Land Rovers and mobile homes believed, manifestations of the so-called Sacred Rage of Hassan al Korami, but manifestations of the fact that the entire state of Koram was slowly subsiding as the forest of wells which covered it sucked up the oil table below into Swiss bank accounts.

Hassan the Assassin, Sheik of Koram, practiced and enforced his own stoned-out brand of Islam, which indeed made the Iranian ayatollahs and Shiite mujadin seem like the effete liberals he often enough called them.

No alcohol. No movies. No TV. No newspapers. No jails. Even minor transgressions were punished by public beheading, unless Hassan was feeling particularly mellow that day, in which case a traffic offender might get off with a mutilation and a stiff warning.

Hashish, however, was legal to the point of being mandatory. Hassan al Korami, as the third son down and not figured ever to inherit the throne, had spent his early manhood playing a hippie Ali Khan in the more disreputable flesh and dope pots of the decadent West until one day, while supposedly reading William Burroughs on acid, he experienced the mystic revelation which made him a Born Again Moslem.

He suddenly began appearing on sleazy cable TV talk shows declaring himself to be the reincarnation of Hassan i Sabah, the legendary Master of the Hashishins. Soon thereafter, his elder brothers expired under rather suspicious circumstances, after which his father was conveniently trampled to death by a herd of camels.

Upon assuming the throne Hassan began preaching a stoned-out form of Islam in which he was the Pope and hashish was the sacrament. All his government functionaries and troops were required to be stoned during duty hours in order to maintain the purity of their fanaticism. Random urine checks were done from time to time, and any soldier or official whose piss was found wanting in the residues of tetrahydrocannabinol was given a choice between castration and execution.

He also nominated himself all Islam's destined leader in a *jihad* he declared against Israel and periodically proclaimed his intent to drive the Jews into the sea. Since the entire adult male population of Koram was less than 50,000, no one took this bellicosity very seriously except, of course, for the international arms merchants, who supposedly took north of three billion dollars a year out of the bottomless Korami treasury.

Powell, like most westerners, had discounted much of this as stoned hyperbole. But upon debarking from the Concorde onto the broiling tarmac, stoned as he was, he had to admit that seeing was believing.

A soaring Bauhaus terminal highlighted with incongruous minarets and a great golden dome was the centerpiece of Koramibad International Airport. Surrounding this monstrosity and seeming to occupy every square foot of the huge airport save the main runway was a veritable junkyard of jet fighters of all nations, bleaching and rusting in the cruel desert sun.

American F-16s, F-15s, F-21s. Russian Mig 21s and 27s. French Mirage 3000s and Super Entendards. Swedish Saabs. British Super Harriers. Good lord, there were even Israeli Kfirs, as if Hassan just *had* to complete his collection.

It must have been the third largest air force in the world after the Russian and American, and surely the Israelis would be in deep shit indeed if Hassan ever found enough pilots to put half of it in the air before it rusted away to rubble. Fortunately, mercenaries avoided Koram like the clap despite the high wages, since they were required to live under the draconian laws of the self-styled Scourge of the Infidel and fly stoned as well, and the few Korami natives who tried their hands from time to time bought the farm after a month or two.

An air-conditioned Rolls waited at the foot of the ramp presided over by two of al Korami's Hashishins, replete with kafiyahs, Kalashnikovs, and enormous spliffs, and Powell was ushered into the back seat, handed another of the gigantic joints, and treated to a wild ride to the palace.

Koramibad, such as it was, had been built from

scratch in a few years at unthinkable expense in order to provide a sheikdom with a population of no more than 100,000 with Hassan al Korami's version of a world-class metropole and capital.

A huge lakebed had been excavated, lined with concrete, and then filled with water which by now was as brackish as the Dead Sea. Koramibad itself was built on an artificial island in the middle of Lake Korami. The city could be reached only by air, since there were no bridges over the lake, and the island was encircled by a fifty-foot-high concrete wall studded at ten-meter intervals with machinegun emplacements; Hassan al Korami had no intention of suffering the fate of Hussein or his own father.

An eight-lane freeway circled the city, replete with electronic slogan boards and access control systems at the numerous on-ramps, though the only traffic on it were tanks and armored personnel carriers whenever Hassan's whacked-out troops managed to get some of them moving. Another freeway, somewhat more functional, connected the airport with the palace.

The rest of the city was one vast empty Potemkin Village. Broad radial avenues lined with huge parched-looking cedars kept barely alive with sprinkler systems at hideous expense converged on the central palace compound. Huge empty luxury apartment towers in perfect repair stood along most of these spotless and deserted streets. Other avenues sported ornate branches belonging to every major bank in the world. There was a Hilton, a Sheraton, a Meridien, a Ramada Inn, and a replica of the Waldorf Astoria, all subsidized and kept afloat by the Korami treasury. Similarly, the empty Macy's, Bloomingdales, Harrods, and GUM branches owed their survival to government subsidies, though Gucci, Tiffany's, the Rolls Royce dealership, and Frederick's of Hollywood managed to survive on their own.

As the Rolls careened crazily towards the palace, Powell caught glimpses of what lay between the vast aisles of empty monolyths, to wit enormous car parks choked with Hassan al Korami's impressive accumulation of tanks, armored personnel carriers, mobile artillery, Katushka rocket launchers, anti-aircraft guns, Jeeps, and assorted armored cars.

Powell found himself sucking nervously on his spliff and wishing for a few good stiff drinks as the Rolls crossed the drawbridge over the moat that surrounded the palace, for the moat swarmed with huge hungry Nile crocodiles and the spikes that studded the top of the palace compound wall were decorated with the rotting heads of minor criminals.

Inside, however, was a fair version of a desert-dweller's vision of paradise. The palace compound was built around a central garden done up as an Amazon rain forest. Scores, perhaps hundreds, of naked and splendid houris wandered about entertaining the troops. Parrots screeched, monkeys flitted through the treetops, and as Powell was ushered towards Korami's personal residence, he could hear a nasal version of Ravel's *Bolero* playing endlessly from hidden speakers.

Hassan al Korami's manse itself was a fifth-scale replica of the Taj Mahal replete with reflecting pool, and the throne room was a large round high-ceilinged chamber dripping with gold filigree studded with rubies, sapphires, and emeralds.

On a black marble dais in the center of the chamber, a vibrating skeletal figure in a white silk burnoose heavily embroidered in gold reclined on a vast cushioned golden throne sucking avidly on the ivory mouthpiece of an enormous hookah. Flanking the throne were a brace of Kalashnikov-toting Hashishins gumming the standard-issue spliffs. A semicircle of huge plush cushions faced the throne, each provided with its own hookah. On one of these reclined an elegantly coiffed silver-haired man in a tan Yves Saint Laurent suit chewing nervously on the mouthpiece of his hookah as the man on the throne ranted and raved at him.

"Nukes, Armand, *nukes!*" demanded Hassan al Korami. "Me want me *nukes!* It's not as if I were demanding Trident submarines, or Stealth Bombers, or SS-25s, or even MX missiles! A few dozen Tomahawk cruise missiles will suffice, a brace of Pershings ... by the beard of the prophet, I would even settle for some of those ancient B-52s which the Americans are planning to sell for scrap anyway. I would even pay well for a few Vulcans, if worse came to worse; surely at least the bankrupt British cannot afford to turn me down!"

With his long wild black hair, great flowing black beard, and huge glowing brown bloodshot eyes, the Scourge of the Infidel reminded Powell of nothing so much as a speed-freak Rasputin.

"Were it up to me, mon ami," said the urbane silver-haired man, "I would be pleased to provide your Sacred Cause with all the megatonnage and delivery systems you can afford. But alas, you have declared the Americans the Great Satan, the Russians Godless Atheistic Devils, the British effete limey bastards, the Germans krautheaded sons of bitches, the Chinese opium-eating degenerates, and the French a nation of frog-eating faggots. This, unfortunately, does not quite entice any of them to be cooperative. . . ."

"What!" screamed al Korami. "You dare to blame my courageous declarations of Allah's truth for your own failures, you effete krautheaded limey frog-eating degenerate devil running dog of the Great Satan!"

The guards cocked their Kalashnikovs eagerly. The

silver-haired man coughed out a great lungful of smoke, trembling.

"Non, no, nein!" he exclaimed. "For who can deny the truth of your words, O Lion of the Desert! Only spare this worthless servant, and I shall redouble my efforts in your behalf, for there may be a way.... Naturellement, it will be somewhat expensive...."

"Nukes!" roared Hassan al Korami. "Me want me *nukes!* Move your ass you perfidious infidel, and do not return without them!"

"I hear and obey, O Scourge of the Infidel," the silver-haired man declared, rising to his feet, and bobbing his head in an endless series of bows as he backed out of the throne room past Elmer Powell, who stood there transfixed, sweating in his socks.

He favored Powell with a little smile and a wink en passant. "You are in luck, mon ami," he whispered sotto voce. "He's in a good mood today."

"Elmer Powell?" demanded Hassan al Korami, glaring at him with his great hash-reddened eyes.

"The same, your Majesty, your Magnificence, your ah . . . ah . . ." Powell stammered in no little terror.

"Be seated, Elmer Powell," Hassan commanded. "Toke up! Get your shit together with this primo Afghani!"

Powell collapsed onto the nearest cushion and sucked in a great lungful of smoke.

Hassan al Korami glowered at him. "One question you will answer, O pundit of the infidels! Speak truly, and I will shower your Swiss bank account with tax-free hard currency; speak falsely, and I will add your head to the collection on my palace wall!"

"Trust me...." Powell muttered fearfully, wondering what was coming next. Some cryptic sufi riddle? Some deadly zen koan? Some Koranic conundrum?

The Scourge of the Infidel puffed thoughtfully on

his hookah. "Who," he finally demanded, "will be the next President of the United States?"

"What?"

"I have not yet torn out your tongue, have I? You are the same Elmer Powell who conducts the Powell Poll, are you not? Speak! Who is going to win the American Presidential election?"

Elmer Powell let out a great sigh of smoke, befuddlement, and relief. "Samuel T. Carruthers," he said.

Hassan eyed him peculiarly. "You are certain?" he said. "That asshole? On this you stake your life. . .?"

"Popular vote 60% to 40%, plus or minus five points, minimum of 300 electoral votes, unless he drops dead or turns into a raving maniac on the tube before Election Day, and even then it would probably be no worse than even money," Powell said confidently. "It's a lock. America loves Uncle Sam."

Hassan al Korami broke into raucous laughter. "America loves Uncle Sam!" he howled as if it were the punchline of his favorite joke, and then he broke up again, rolling his eyes, shaking with mirth and spraying spittle, a wired Rasputin indeed.

Still fairly gibbering with laughter, he waved a negligent hand in Powell's general direction. One of the guards yanked Powell to his feet and began escorting him out of the throne room.

"That's it?" Powell exclaimed. "A million dollars? An eight hour round-trip plane ride? Just for—"

"Mysterious are the ways of Hassan the Assassin," said the guard, jamming another spliff into his mouth. "Be cool, and don't make waves."

Only three weeks to go until Election Day and Samuel T. Carruthers was riding high and wide if not exactly handsome towards the apotheosis of his American Dream, a success story such as was possible only in the Land of the Free and the Home of the

Brave! Where else but under the Red White and Blue could the proprietor of a seedy used car lot in Santa Ana California rise in glory within a decade to become President of the United States?

After serving his country in the crummy jungles of Central America for three years as a supply sergeant, Carruthers had skimmed just enough capital to leverage the purchase of a tacky used car lot in Santa Ana and its unsavory inventory of ancient clunkers. Shortly thereafter, while cruising along the Santa Ana Freeway in his five-year-old Buick, he had driven by a billboard near Knotts' Berry Farm and been Born Again with the inspiration that was to change the course of history.

A cartoon Uncle Sam stood knee-deep in a sea of red ink glowering at the passing motorists and pointing an admonishing finger. Plowing through the waves around his kneecaps were a series of Chinese-type ships flying Japanese flags and piled to the gunwales with cars, VCRs, TV sets, and robots.

"Buy American!" shouted Uncle Sam in red white and blue letters, and lest anyone miss the point, the boats on the billboard also flew banners proclaiming "Cheap Jap Junk."

"That's *it*, Margot!" Carruthers exclaimed, slapping his wife on the thigh with such distraction that he almost sideswiped the Toyota in the next lane.

"Up yours, you unpatriotic asshole!" he shouted at the Toyota driver when that worthy had the temerity to honk at his 100% red-blooded Detroit Iron. "Praise God and our massive trade deficit, I've seen the light!"

And so, as it turned out, he had.

Carruthers sold off every foreign-made car on his lot at a dead loss, took out a third mortgage on his house, and restocked with the cheapest collection of crummy old American gas-guzzlers he could find. He renamed the establishment "Uncle Sam Carruthers'

Red White and Blue One Hundred Percent American Used Car Lot." He bought himself a fraying Uncle Sam suit at a costume shop, had Margot let it out to more or less encompass his paunch, stuffed himself into it, bought commercial time on a local TV station, and, in the grand tradition of Southern Californian superstar used car salesmen, began starring in his own TV commercials, introducing the world to the spiel that, ten years and one bankruptcy later, was to make him President of the United States.

"Come on *down*, come on down to Uncle Sam Carruthers' Red White and Blue One Hundred Percent American Used Car Lot!" he would declare as he stood before his clunkers in his Uncle Sam suit. "Wouldn't you rather buy an *American* used car from your old Uncle Sam than some overpriced piece of unpatriotic crap from a traitor to the American Way of Life? If you can't trust your old Uncle Sam, then *who can you trust?* Come on down, come on *down*, lookee here, lookee here, my fellow Americans, why here we have a 1985 Dodge Van, AM-FM stereo, power everything, and only 55,000 miles on the clock or fry me for a Rooshian, and the first five thousand takes it. Now I'm only willing to let this one go at such a loss because this cherry little darling was previously owned by a *genuine* American hero serving his country in Patagonia who was forced to put it on consignment due to war wounds which necessitate trading it in on a hand control model, and this brave lad can't get back on the road until I move this one off the lot and into the loving hands on one of your lucky patriots. . . .

"Come on down, come on *down*, and drive away with this 1980 Cadillac Seville, a mere 75,000 on the clock, and every last mile put on driving to church by a Gold Star Mother forced to sell it off and go on *welfare* when her husband lost his job at the Ford plant to coolie labor in Korea. . . ."

Well what with the temporary oil glut of those years, and the rekindled sense of American patriotism, and the Buy American movement, and the unemployment, Uncle Sam Carruthers struck a chord in the public psyche. Not only was he able to move a lot of old Moldy Detroit Iron at premium prices by wrapping his clunkers in the flag, he became as much a media hero as Ralph Williams or Cal Worthington ever had and then some, and was even invited from time to time to make the local LA talkshow circuit.

It was on one of these talk shows that he met the Reverend Allan Edward Wintergreen, and was Born yet Again as a franchiser.

Wintergreen was one of the most successful TV preachers in the country and certainly the richest, for he not only solicited contributions on his syndicated TV hour like all the others, he was the only one who sold *commercial time* between the sermons and the disco choir.

"God has brought us together to save the Nation and make mucho dinero in the process, my boy," he told Carruthers, and once the silver-tongued preacher and his accountant laid it out in dollars and cents, Carruthers Saw the Light again.

Why not *franchise* a nationwide chain of Uncle Sam Carruthers' Red White and Blue One Hundred Percent American Used Car Lots? For 10% of the gross, the franchisee got to use the name and reap the benefit of the commercials that Uncle Sam Carruthers did on the Rev. Allan Edward Wintergreen's nationally syndicated TV show.

And since Carruthers was already mortgaged up to the eyeballs, the Rev. Wintergreen, who was rolling in dough, easily enough persuaded himself to put up the necessary capital in return for a mere 49% of the action.

All went swimmingly until the Great Oil Famine, when the oil-producing countries wised up, suspended production entirely for three months, and then doubled the price.

All at once, Red White and Blue 100% American gas-guzzling old Detroit Iron became virtually worthless and not all the patriotic appeals to national honor could move it off the lots, and franchisees went belly-up all across the country, soon to be followed by the home office itself, whose bankruptcy even threatened to drag down the Rev. Wintergreen's Church of Revealed Wisdom.

Broke, famous, without a pot to piss in or any prospects, what else could Uncle Sam Carruthers to do but run for the United States Senate? It was an easy transition. He just continued to run more or less the same commercials on the Rev. Wintergreen's TV show peddling his own ass instead of used cars, and made his live appearances in the same Uncle Sam suit, railing against the A-rabs and the Nips and the Rooshians who had done his business and the national enterprise in.

When the long-retired Johnny Carson refused to run against him, his election as junior Senator from California was assured, and he hit Washington already a national hero. His picture was on *Time* and *Newsweek* and *People* and he even made the cover of *Rolling Stone*. He refused to waste his time with boring committee assignments, and instead concentrated on using the national TV coverage of the Senate floor to best advantage, rambling on for at least an hour a week for the next four years, so that by the time the Presidential Primary season approached, he had twice the face and name recognition of his closest rival in the polls.

So too did the election turn into a Red White and Blue Cakewalk, for Uncle Sam was the most seasoned TV performer Presidential politics had seen since Ronald Reagan, and not even Reagan had had the chutzpah to do his act in costume.

To clinch it, Rev. Wintergreen had twisted enough arms in the party hierarchy to make them hold their noses and nominate his fellow TV preacher, Fast Eddie Braithewaite, for Vice President.

Fast Eddie had first intruded upon the public consciousness as "The American Bob Marley," whose disco reggae records may never have climbed very high in the charts, but whose Reformed Rasta rap was good enough to launch him on a second career as a TV evangelist of a peculiar sort when his pipes began to give out in middle age.

"Lack of cash is the greatest evil in Babylon," he told his viewers. "All men are green in the eyes of Jah! No peckerwood's about to call you a nigger if you got a wallet full of credit cards, mon! Cast your bread upon the waters of Zion, and ye shall for sure be saved! It's *your* love donations that lets me loan out money at 2 points under the prime! Together, we build our Zion in the Belly of the Beast, and together, we make the First TV Bank of Babylon a Fortune 500 company!"

It was a stroke of genius, for while most blacks viewed Uncle Sam Carruthers as a honkie asshole and while more blacks than not viewed Fast Eddie Braithewaite as a con artist, how many of them, in the privacy of the voting booth, could refrain from voting for the first *black* con artist to make the national ticket?

Moreover, this was also a dream ticket that rednecks and bigots could vote for with pride; they could vote for Uncle Sam Carruthers' Red White and Blue jingoism and feel smug about displaying their nonexistent American sense of racial fair play in the bargain.

As for how either of these boobs could be expected to function as President, well, that was the sort of situation that the pros behind the scenes and the moneymen behind the pols knew could be professionally managed.

Three weeks from Election Day, riding high in the polls, Samuel T. Carruthers, accompanied by two Secret Service Men, went into the men's room after gorging himself on rubber chicken at a fund-raising speech at the Century Plaza Hotel.

Five minutes passed, ten, a quarter of an hour, while the Press Secretary and the Campaign Manager fidgeted nervously, hoping Carruthers hadn't come down with the trots again, but somewhat fastidiously reluctant to interrupt the Great Man on the pot to inquire after the state of his bowel movements.

But after half an hour of this, there seemed nothing for it but to drag him off the crapper in time to make the plane to Minnesota.

The men's room was empty aside from two pairs of legs visible in adjacent toilet stalls. These proved to be the two Secret Service men, bound and gagged with their pants down around their ankles. The last thing they remembered was entering the men's room and being assailed by a horrible stench. When they woke up, they were tied and gagged on the toilet seats, and the next President of the United States was gone.

Just as they were all about to dash out of the john to raise posse and pandemonium, the Press Secretary's pocket phone rang.

"This is the Mendocino Liberation Front, running dog of the Drug Enforcement Agency, and we've got Carruthers stuffed in a gunny sack on the way to our secret headquarters in the Sierras," said a shrill, nasal, female voice. "Now listen carefully, here's the deal. We just want to like *educate* the next President of the United States for 24 hours. If you do what you're told, you can have the asshole back after that and no one's the wiser. But if a word of this gets to the press or any police agency, we'll feed him feet-first into a tree-chipper, and mail his head to the *Washington Post*. Power and profit to the Pot Farmers of America and our national trade balance! Boycott Colombian Imports! Buy American-grown Dope!"

The Press Secretary and the Campaign Manager did some fast hard professional management thinking. If these maniacs did kill Carruthers and mail his head to the press, they'd be left with *Fast Eddie Braithewaite* at the head of their ticket. If they lost, they'd all be out of jobs, and if they won, they'd be out on the streets anyway, because that crazy nigger hated their guts. If they did as they were told, there was at least some chance they would get their meal ticket back.

Bottomlinewise, the smart money said keep your mouth shut and manage the situation as best you can as long as you can, like the Russians had been doing with the corpse of Pyotr Ivanovich Bulgorny for at least five years. After all, they were sophisticated professionals, and Uncle Sam Carruthers had not yet even croaked. Surely if the Russians could pull it off for all these years, American known-how could manage such a situation for at least 24 hours!

Fast Eddie Braithewaite had smelled the unmistakable odor of bullshit since the closing weeks of the campaign. For one thing, while he and Carruthers had never exactly partied together, now neither he nor anyone he had talked to had even been allowed in the same room with him by the Campaign Staff. They flooded the air with a blizzard of old taped commercials, they cut old footage into a phony live interview show, and Samuel T. Carruthers made only a dozen or so more live appearances, the news coverage of which made it seem that he was luuded out and badly lip-syncing a tape.

His victory speech had been broadcast late at night from his hotel room instead of in front of his loyal supporters and he had nodded off halfway through it and had to be elbowed in the ribs not quite off camera.

Between election night and the Inauguration, they kept him closeted on some private estate in Palm Springs putting together his government, and sure enough the expected gang of the usual suspects was rounded up for the Cabinet and the pros on the Campaign Staff segued into the White House.

Samuel T. Carruthers' Inaugural Day performance was more than Fast Eddie could finally pretend wasn't happening. He had taken the oath like a zombie on methadrine, babbling the whole thing out twice before the Chief Justice could more than open his mouth. During his speech, his mouth was hidden by a badly-placed podium, and he stood there staring motionless into space as if his feet had been nailed to the floor.

The day after that, Fast Eddie had stormed into a White House Staff meeting and demanded to see the President on threat of going to the press and telling them that he was taking over under the 23rd Amendment because the President had been captured in a palace coup.

"Don't say you didn't ask for this then," the White House Chief of Staff had told him with a peculiar expression, and he and the entire inner circle stuffed themselves into helicopters which took them to Camp David.

The main lodge had been transformed. Half of it had been turned into an elaborate television studio and the other half of it was now some kind of medical facility.

"Where you got the fat boy stuffed?" Fast Eddie demanded.

"In a nice safe place."

They took him down a hall towards what had been the master bedroom. The wooden door had been replaced with a steel slab with a wire-barred window.

The Press Secretary whistled *Hail to the Chief*.

"Mr. Speaker, Members of Congress, Distinguished Guests, my fellow Americans," said the National Security Adviser, inviting Fast Eddie's attention to the window, "The President of the United Skates."

The entire bedroom has been turned into a huge and luxurious padded cell. Within, Samuel T. Carruthers sat naked on the pale beige matting, babbling to himself and jerking off.

"Pussy, One Hundred Percent American Made Pussy in Red White and Blue cheerleader skirts put out for Uncle Sam as American as Apple Pie no cheap Jap junk. . . ."

"As you can see," said the Press Secretary, "we are having temporary technical difficulties."

"But nothing that can't be managed in a professional manner," said the Chief of Staff, and before Fast Eddie could even get his gaping mouth to close, they had hustled him off into a nearby cabin to talk bottom line.

"Be special nice to me, turkeys," Fast Eddie told them, " 'cause I'm going to be the President of this Babylon in about the next two bars, mon! I mean, you got yourselves a crazy man in there, first time you need him live, they farm him to the bughouse and throw away the key."

The interchangeable faces of the White House Staff had the same smug interchangeable smiles of bureaucratic patronization painted across them as the

White House Staff sat there in their interchangeable conservative business suits looking down their thin little noses at the nigger who unfortunately for them was about to become President of the United States.

Velveeta and Cool Whip on Wonder Bread, mon! Fast Eddie was going to enjoy kicking their tight white asses out onto the end of the long unemployment lines where they belonged!

"What happened to the man? How long have you guys been sitting on this?" he demanded. "Speak true, or when I take over and lift the lid off this garbage can, you'll all have free unpaid vacations in Allenwood!"

"The President has merely been the victim of a terrorist act, from which the doctors assure us he will soon recover, if they want to keep their jobs," said the Chief of Staff.

"Terrorist act?"

"Something called the Mendocino Liberation Front had him for 24 hours."

"We found him on one of those chicken ranches in Nevada in a pretty heavy bondage scene," said the Press Secretary.

"To hear Uncle Sam tell it, they pumped him full of amphetamine, LSD, and L-dopa, and let him run wild in a roomful of jaded hookers for a day and a night. . . ."

"Disgust you to hear it. . . ."

"But nothing, Mr. Vice President, that we can't *manage*. . . ."

"Media techniques are much more sophisticated than you might suppose these days," the Press Secretary said. "We have enough audio and videotape we can computer process to have Uncle Sam up and spouting brightly on the tube anything we want him to say. We have three actors undergoing plastic surgery to do live appearances. We can manage with a President who's crazy as a bedbug—"

"—After all, the Russians are still managing with Pyotr Ivanovich Bulgorny—"

"And everyone knows he's been dead for at least eight years."

"This may be Babylon, but it ain't Russia yet, my man," Fast Eddie said. "If the Vice President of the United States goes on the tube claiming the President is nuts, you're gonna have to show the fat boy doing his thing live in public. I'll demand fingerprint tests, I'll have dentists do a hologram of his teeth with lasers, and when he gets thrown in the bin, I'll be President and your asses are grasses."

"I don't think you're going to want to do that," said the National Security Adviser. "I mean, that might compromise national security, if you get me, and you might have to be terminated with extreme cement overshoes."

"Mon, you think you can snuff the Vice President of the United States before I get the people to listen to me?"

The Press Secretary laughed. "Credibilitywise, your Neilsen will be zero, kiddo," he said. "*No one* will believe that Uncle Sam is a drooling sex maniac because no one will *want* to. Because if Uncle Sam is a drooling sex maniac, then they've got themselves *you* for President. . . ."

"Besides," said the National Security Adviser, "there's always the Bulgorny option for the likes of you if you become too much of a problem."

"The Bulgorny option . . .?" Fast Eddie said, suddenly quite sure that this dude meant some very extreme business.

"I mean, if the Russians can trot out Bulgorny to stand on Lenin's Tomb twice a year and make a speech to the Supreme Soviet just when people are getting to think he's gotten too moldly, you think we can't stuff and wire a Vice President the same way to stand like a stiff at funerals?"

"And the first funeral you perform at if you open your mouth will be your own, Mr. Vice President," said the Chief of Staff. "We'll trot you out before the cameras and have you tell the Nation your ridiculous charges were the result of drinking too much cheap port wine and you won't feel a thing. You won't even be there."

"See, Mr. Vice President, it's all under control," said the National Security Adviser. "We've done a run on every possible scenario, we've covered all the angles. I'm sure that you'll now agree that we can manage just fine with a maniac in the White House and an audioanimatrated stiff for Vice President if we have to."

"Well, when you put it that way," owned the Vice President nervously, "it's kind of hard to argue with your logic."

Purchasing hashish in Moscow, like everything else, required stable secure connections, connections with a class self-interest in never selling you out to the authorities. Since no Soviet citizen could reliably predict when or whether he might find himself in Lubianka negotiating his own survival, finding a hashish connection with a minimal risk was no mean feat.

And indeed, by very virtue of being free market profiteers in the hashish trade, all such connections were both anti-party elements by definition and employees, if not agents, of the KGB.

The Red Army had not only lost considerable clout on the Presidium over the Afghanistan fiasco, they had so bungled the economic situation that Sergei

Polikov, the Czar of the KGB, had come out of it with all-but-total control of the whole hashish trade.

Now all the caravans led straight across the border into Turkestan where 250,000 Soviet troops lurked conspicuously, ready to blitzkrieg their way back into Afghanistan, should the Mujadin violate their part of the bargain.

Under these conditions, the Red Army could more or less keep their troops free of hashish dependency as long as they were stationed far away from major cities; the Soviet Union secured desperately needed hard currency; and the KGB could control the supply, set the prices, and limit the amount of hash that filtered into the domestic market from the vast re-export trade.

No doubt, having secured control of the total supply, the KGB could have entirely eliminated the vast population of hash smokers that had blossomed in the Soviet Union during the period when 200,000 soldiers rotating in and out of Afghanistan every year had gone into business for themselves as free market profiteers.

But by the time they cut the deal to end the war, Sergei Polikov saw that there were political as well as economic advantages to allowing the domestic trade to continue. Every dealer had to get his supply from someone else who sooner or later had to get it from the KGB. So the KGB could access the identity of any one of the thousands of petty economic parasites involved in the trade, which meant that any one of them could be induced to inform when required. The dealers, in turn, knew the identity, collectively, of several million Soviet citizens who were guilty of an infraction punishable by 5 years' internal exile.

Never before had the KGB succeeded in extending its fine tendrils this far into the tender flesh of the masses. Somewhere in that Great Interrogation Cell in the Sky, Joseph Stalin and Lavrenti Beria were no doubt turning green with envy.

Ivan Igorovich Gornikov, however, had found, or been found by, a source with the mystical power to render itself invisible to the KGB.

Mustapha Kamani was a cultural attaché at the Korami embassy, and seeing as how Koram had no culture to speak of to export, Kamani's true business in Moscow could be only one thing—purchasing agent for the government of Hassan al Korami, the largest single customer the KGB had.

No doubt the hash Kamani sold to a few favored Russian friends was skimmed from shipments headed back to Koram, and therefore already signed, paid for, and disposed of on the KGB's books. But not even Sergei Polikov, indeed especially not Sergei Polikov, would arrest a golden goose with diplomatic immunity.

And indeed even if he did, Kamani knew what would happen to him if he stooled on his Russian contacts, for his Russian contacts—at least the ones that Ivan had met—were all, like himself, comrades in the Computer Underground. There would not have been a Soviet Computer Underground were it not for the Korami involvement. While Hassan al Korami was reputedly quite able to pay for the tons of hashish he bought each year from the KGB out of petty cash, he had contrived to force the KGB to accept a portion of the price in rubles, and these rubles were acquired by smuggling in computer equipment in return diplomatic pouches, and selling the stuff to hardware-starved Russians at obscene prices. An ancient MacIntosh could fetch 15,000 rubles, the latest IBM mini would set you back 50,000, and people had been known to shell out 5,000 for a 16k Sinclair. As for dot-matrix printers, these were worth their weight in caviar, since one could distribute samizdat on disks and print out copies at 200 cps.

There was only one thing that the KGB hated more than the Computer Underground, and that was the thought of losing the billions of hard dollars that Koram spent on hash in the Soviet Union each year.

But Ivan knew that if *he* were ever exposed as a member of the Computer Underground, if the KGB learned that *he* was being supplied with hash by the embassy of Koram, the whole game would be up for everyone.

For Ivan Igorovich Gornikov was the day shift operator on the Bulgorny—one of the select few with access to the software that was the Chairman of the Central Committee of the Soviet Communist Party and President of the Union of Soviet Socialist Republics.

And Ivan had taken great care to inform Mustapha Kamani of the hacking he had done on the Bulgorny, the better to motivate him into hoping he was never exposed as the foreign agent who had known this and had continued to get him stoned.

Which was why there was no real tension in the apartment that Kamani maintained across town from the embassy, for everyone there knew each other, they were all desperate characters, and everyone had every reason not to betray anyone else.

There was Boris, the night shift operator on the Bulgorny, and Tanya, who worked on the team that compiled the statistics at the Ministry of Agriculture, and Anatoly, who wrote programs that set production quotas for TV sets, cars, and toilet paper, and Grishka, who ran the computer that dealt with the waiting lists for apartments for all of Moscow. Among them, they had put enough bugs, practical jokes, and random noise into the software of state to send them all to Siberia for a million years if anyone found out, and they spent their stoned-out seances here in Mustapha Kamani's apartment vying with each other to do more.

". . . so the half share in a one-room flat went to the professor of astrophysics, and the bubba who used to sweep the street outside got the luxury penthouse. . . ."

". . . which is why when next you crank him up to address the Supreme Soviet, Comrade Bulgorny will be able to boast that we lead the world in the production of toilet paper, though most of the people will still have to use *Pravda* since it has all been shipped to Novosibirsk. . . ."

"If only we dared to really have him say that!" Boris exclaimed as Kamani wrapped up a take-home for him in toilet paper, as if to boast of his unlimited access to such luxury items.

"Why not?" said Ivan. "All we have to do is mail-merge some old speeches on toilet paper production quotas with the stock attack on distribution ineffi-ciencies when they ask for something to have him boast about and something with which to belabor the petty bureaucrats who are responsible for every-thing that goes wrong."

"Low toilet humor, if you ask me," giggled Tanya. "Boys will be boys."

"Perhaps one of you would care to part with 2,000 rubles in return for *this*?" Mustapha Kamani sud-denly said theatrically, pulling a floppy out of a pocket.

"2,000 rubles for a piece of *software*?" Grishka scoffed. "Come off it, Mustapha, we can all write our own, thank you."

"Perhaps you are right, I am far from versed in such matters, though those who are have told me that there has never been such an insidious little bedbug as *this*," Kamani said, toking on the commu-nal hookah.

"Oh?"

"What does it do?"

"It is called the Joker, my young friends, all the rage in western circles, according to the bourgeois press. It is written around a random number generator that as you might say disappears into the system without a trace and overlays the interface of everything with everything. And once you've introduced it, there's no way of getting it out, short of wiping all the data and programs in the memory bank. . . ."

"Hashish for computers!" exclaimed Boris. "Why shouldn't they have some fun too?"

Ivan laughed. "Why shouldn't *Pyotr Ivanovich* have a chance to get stoned?" he said. "The poor bastard probably hasn't had any fun since he died."

"The Bulgorny?" exclaimed Boris. "You would randomize the programs and garble the memory banks of our beloved Party Chairman? You would have the Bulgorny begin babbling like Khrushchev on vodka?"

"Even better than that," Ivan said. "Remember, if the forces on the Central Committee hadn't been in such perfectly balanced deadlock all these years, they would long since have have buried Bulgorny in Lenin's Tomb where he belongs and agreed on a live successor. . . ."

"The decision-making program!" exclaimed Boris.

"That's right, this little bedbug would randomize that too!"

"I love it, Ivan, I love it!"

"What are you two *talking about*?" Tanya demanded crossly.

"The deepest darkest secret of the Soviet State," Boris said, pulling on the hookah. "Shall we tell them, Ivan?"

"Are we not all comrades of the Computer Underground, Boris?" Ivan said, filling his lungs with smoke.

"The Central Committee, as you can well imagine,

is frequently deadlocked," he told them. "In the old days, when you had a live Party Chairman and no one could muster a majority against him, that was that. Now they ask the Bulgorny to break deadlocks."

"*The Bulgorny*!" exclaimed Grishka. "But Pyotr Ivanovich has been dead for four years!"

"Eight."

"Six."

"Whatever. The Chairman is just an embalmed corpse wired for motion and sound, how can such a thing decide anything?"

"Each member of the Central Committee has a weighted vote calculated by the computer according to his current rating in the power struggle as determined by secret polling of his rivals. These are tabulated statistically via an Australian ballot system until a mathematical consensus emerges. This is interfaced with the memory banks via an index program which selects and edits old Bulgorny speeches so that the Chairman can announce his decisions in his own familiar deadly prose."

"Bulgorny can write his own speeches?" Grishka said.

"Better than he did when he was alive," said Boris. "The computer that controls him remembers every boring word he ever uttered, and if he were alive to suffer that, it would surely kill him!"

"And if this Joker program inserts random interfaces between the statistical data and the tabulation. . . ."

"And between the decision-making program and the memory banks, where the index program should be. . . ."

"Then decisions of the Soviet State will be made by rolling the software bones. . . ."

"And Pyotr Ivanovich Bulgorny will deliver them in gibberish. . . ."

"Which no one will dare point out. . . ."

"Which everyone must therefore pretend to understand. . . ."

"And they won't be able to fix it without finally burying the Chairman. . . ."

"Which they'll never do until the corpse starts to rot!"

Mustapha Kamani had been lying back and sucking on his hookah during all of this, nursing a secret little smile. Now that smile became a supercilious grin. "Ah, you Russians are such a marvelous people!" he said. "In the effete West, this Joker program is used for mere sport—practical jokers insert it in each other's video games and scramble the data of collection agencies—but here in mother Russia, it becomes a weapon against the state."

"Come on, lighten up, Mustapha!" Tanya said. "We're not enemies of the state."

"We're hackers, not anti-Soviet elements."

"And hackers just want to have fun."

Armand Deutcher slurped down another oyster with a hefty swallow of Muscadet, then leaned back in his chair expansively, as if to wrap himself in the aura of La Coupole. Once, long ago, this noisy barn of a Saint Germain cafe had been a gathering place for somber Parisian existentialists, later a show business hangout, then a tourist trap, and now it was a huge house of assignation for the arms dealers, foreign agents, and American political exiles who were said to make up a quarter of Paris's current population. It was a place one went to for ambiance, not haute cuisine nor noble vintages, but there was little the chef could do to ruin raw oysters in season.

"Surely you would not wish to see this contract go to East Bloc sources, Zvi," Deutcher said. "You're my last hope. Unless you agree to supply the warheads, Hassan will turn to the Soviets, and we'll lose the delivery system deal as well."

"Even from you, I can't believe this," Zvi Bar David said, spooning a gooey dark morsel of profitrole au chocolat into his mouth. "Even the Russians aren't crazy enough to sell nuclear missiles to a maniac like Hassan al Korami, and we both know it. *Israel* should sell him nukes? As if he'd buy them from us in the first place!"

"Ah, but naturellement, he is never to know that his warheads are Israeli," Deutcher said. "You will deliver them to the South Africans, who will allow them to pass over to Zaire, who will sell them to the Angolans, who will assure the Koramis that they were made in Czechoslovakia and bartered to the Cubans through East Germany in return for mercenary troops to fight the Rastafarian resistance in South Jamaica."

"What can you possibly imagine would induce us to do such a thing?"

"What else?" Deutcher said good-naturedly. "Money!"

"Surely you cannot expect us to sell nuclear weapons to that anti-Semitic maniac at any price!"

"You sold him those Kfirs, didn't you?"

"We sold them to Singapore, who sold them to Taiwan, who moved them to the Chinese through Hong Kong, who bartered them to the Iranians for oil, and the Iranians told Koram they had picked them up when the Brazilians overran Paraguay."

"Come, come, Zvi, be all that as it may, the Mossad certainly knew where they were going!"

Zvi Bar David shrugged. "Who could resist?" he admitted with a grin. "They were Yom Kippur War vintage junk. Not even the Haitians would buy them. If we had surplus Spitfires, we'd be happy to unload the mess on Hassan too! But we're certainly not going to sell Koram ordnance that they can really use against us, let alone nuclear warheads!"

"But of course, mon ami," Deutcher said slyly. "Au contraire, what I propose is that we together sell Koram twenty nuclear missiles for ten billion dollars that *you* can use against *him*."

Bar David eyed him narrowly now, wiping chocolate sauce from his chin. Armand Deutcher nodded.

"From Senegal via Algeria, I have acquired twenty truly moldy American F-llls that the Vietnamese appropriated way back when they overran Saigon," he told Bar David. "At ten percent over scrap prices, since their airframes and engines have only a few thousand miles left in them and not even a kamikaze pilot would dare to try to fly them. . . ."

"They were dreadful dogs even when they were new, as I remember," Bar David observed critically.

Deutcher nodded. "A shining example of American over-complication," he agreed. "But bon chance for us, for the Americans equipped these aircraft with low-level terrain-hugging radar systems, the immediate forerunner of the cruise missile systems they developed later. . . ."

"I seem to remember some small problem with the swing-wings falling off. . . ."

"Ah, but that is not *our* problem, now is it, Zvi?" Deutcher said airily. "As fighter-bombers, they may be disasters, but imagine them as big, cheap, fast highly unreliable cruise missiles!"

"I think I'm beginning to get your drift, Armand. . . ."

"But of course! Stick some kind of crude nuclear device in the bomb bay, wire it up with remote controls off your supersonic reconnaissance drones, and voilá, twenty cut-rate supersonic medium-range cruise missiles that should cost us about half a million apiece at worst to sling together, and which we can then unload on Hassan al Korami for *five billion dollars*, and frankly, as you have already surmised, my ass is in a sling on the warheads, so I'll split the profits right down the middle, meaning Israel's balance of payment situation is improved by $2 billion courtesy of the Scourge of the Infidel!"

Bar David scooped up a spoonful of his dessert and savored the heavy dark chocolate sauce thoughtfully. "It certainly is tasty . . ." he admitted. "But unthinkably dangerous! Three billion for us, one for you."

"Only to Hassan al Korami," Deutcher told him, knowing that this was the clincher. "For *you* will be supplying the remote guidance systems, n'est ce pas. 55-45."

"So we will," Bar David said slowly. "So we will . . . 60-40. . . ."

Armand Deutcher laughed. "Make it 57-43, and I'll also throw in a consignment of third-hand Japanese game-computers I bought in Shanghai complete with a cartridge called *Cruise Missile Commander* which is good enough to convince hashish-sodden maniacs who have never even seen a video game before that they're playing with the real thing."

"We could build a big fancy console around the video game computer for the controllers to play with, projection TVs, joysticks, maybe even stereo sound. . . ."

"And then jumble a great heap of junk with a lot of flashing lights and LCD readouts in the cockpit and hide the real control circuit on a chip somewhere in the works. . . ."

"So if they ever launch the things, we just take over. . . ."

"And drop them harmlessly into the sea!"

"Perhaps . . ." said Zvi Bar David.

Deutcher laughed. "You wouldn't be thinking of having the Scourge of the Infidel aim at Tel Aviv and hit, peut etre, Mecca?"

"What a delicious notion, Armand!" Bar David exclaimed. "He would then be honor-bound to declare Holy War against himself!"

"Being First Lady certainly hasn't been anything like what Sam promised so far," Margot Carruthers whined.

"Why are you bitching about it to me, moma?" Fast Eddie Braithewaite demanded. "You think I like this shit any more than you do?"

"No, Mr. Vice President, I don't," Mrs. Carruthers said coldly. "That's why I think you and I can make a deal."

For the first time since she had called him from a pay phone and insisted he meet her in the Watergate garage, Fast Eddie started to take the First Lady seriously.

For sure, what with her old man confined in a padded cell by his staff and unable therefore to throw the White House parties and take her on the helicopter rides he had promised her, she had her reasons for being pissed off.

And as for himself, Fast Eddie was grinding his molars into stubs as he was constrained to attend funerals and keep his mouth shut, while all the while he should have long since moved into the Oval Office where he belonged.

"A deal?" he said. "What do you and me have to dicker over?"

Margot Carruthers slithered a little closer to him across the back seat of her rented Mercedes. "I thought *you'd* understand, Fast Eddie," she said breathily but hesitantly. "I mean, you people invented rock and roll, didn't you, you're in tune to the . . . ah . . . jelly roll vibrations. . . ."

"Say what?"

She-yit, was Uncle Sam Carruthers' old lady *com-*

ing on to him? He didn't know whether to laugh or puke.

"Sam and I hardly got it on together for years," she told him. "It got so I finally forgot what it felt like to be really turned on, so I hardly even missed it any more."

She sighed. She smiled blissfully. "But then, after Sam came back from whatever those terrorists did to him, before those White House staff creatures threw me out of our bedroom and turned it into a padded cell, Sam fucked my brains out. All night long. Over breakfast. On the toilet. I haven't had it so good in twenty years."

Fast Eddie goggled at her in amazement.

"Don't look at me like that!" she said. "I may not look like it now, but back when Sam was slogging around in Central America for three years, I had my little fling as a queen of the singles bars, I even turned a trick or two in my time for the hell of it. So when boring old Sam turned into a bright green pleasure machine, I had juicy enough memories to be re-awakened, and now I'm so horny all the time I could scream."

Aghast, Fast Eddie sidled across the seat away from her until his back was pressed up against the door handle. *"Mrs. Carruthers,"* he said, "what *are* you trying to tell me?"

"Look at me," she told him, "Not so bad for 55 if I do say so myself, but I'm not going to make out with the beautiful people at my age, and the First Lady of the United States would be a little conspicuous in a disco. Besides, it was like a Second Honeymoon, not that the first one was any great shakes in bed."

She gritted her teeth in determination. "I don't care whether Sam is competent to be President of the United States or not, I want him in my bed, not in a padded cell, and I *don't* want him cured. I *prefer* my husband as a sex maniac."

"All right, moma, what did you have in mind?" Fast Eddie exclaimed. "I always was a sucker for true romance!"

"You get to fly around on Air Force One," Margot Carruthers said, creeping up on him again. "I get to visit Sam. I get him out of his cell and into a helicopter, and you have the plane ready and waiting at Dulles. We'll fly him to Los Angeles and put him on 'America Tonite.'"

"And they'll toss him right back in the bin!"

"But you'll be President, Fast Eddie. And if Ford could get away with pardoning Nixon as part of his deal, surely you can let us ride off somewhere into the sunset together. All I want out of this is my man."

"How you gonna get him out of the cell?"

"With a few twists and turns. . . ." Margot Carruthers said, wriggling her thighs against him.

"And what about the Captain of Air Force One . . .?" Fast Eddie, said leaning toward her.

"Oh, he wasn't bad for someone who wasn't exactly my type," she said with a feral grin. "What about the next President of the United States? I mean, don't be insulted, but I always had this thing about the back seats of cars and black men."

"Funny you should say that. I always had this thing about married white women who had a thing about black men."

"Today is the day, now is the hour, now will the Scourge of the Infidel kick Zionist ass!" declared Hassan al Korami.

TV lights outshone the desert sun, befuddled reporters muttered idiot commentary into their mikes like color men in the fourth quarter of a very one-sided football game, and the palace guards surrounding the little reviewing stand upon which stood the Scourge of the Infidel stroked their Kalashnikovs nervously and hazed Hassan in a cloud of smoke from their spliffs, so that the cameramen cursed under their breath as they tried to keep sharp focus on the figure before the huge makeshift tent.

Korami troops and officials and the foreign press corps alike eyed each other paranoiacally across the tarmac, the former scandalized at the unseemly sight of hundreds of running dog mouthpieces of Satan polluting the purity of scared Korami soil with their evil machineries, and the latter eying the drug-crazed, red-eyed, machinegun-caressing troops with no little dread, and wondering why the Lion of the Desert had opened his borders to the foreign media for the first time in his reign for the purpose of staging this airport press conference.

Three days earlier, the major European, American, Soviet, and Japanese news networks had been invited, indeed all but commanded, to produce their minions here in Koramibad International Airport for an announcement modestly promised to "change the course of world history."

One by one their planes had landed, and been surrounded by heavily armed and even more heavily loaded Korami troops. The reporters and crews were allowed to deplane with their equipment, and they were all hustled out here, where bulldozers had piled up rusty fighter planes in great heaps to clear an area in the great aerial junkpile large enough to erect the enormous tent which apparently concealed Hassan's big surprise.

"Hear O Israel!" the Scourge of the Infidel shrieked into his mike, sucking on the mouthpiece of a large hookah, and apparently beginning to work himself up into a proper rage. "Hear the words of Hassan al

Korami, O ye bloodsucking Zionist camel-fuckers, and despair! Within four days and four nights, you shall remove your unclean presence from all of Holy Jerusalem and withdraw all your troops to the east bank of the Jordan River. Every Jew, every synagogue, every kosher delicatessen, must be cleansed from Jerusalem by the dawn of the fifth day, so commands Hassan al Korami, Sheik of Koram, Lion of the Desert, Scourge of the Infidel, Master of the Holy Hashishins!"

Mutters of astonishment, raucous laughter, and then an ugly growl of ire issued forth from the press. The crazy son of a bitch had finally OD'ed on his own hash! He had been issuing asshole demands on the Israelis since he had assumed the throne, and now here he was standing the midst of hundreds of junk fighter planes toking up and demanding their surrender!

That much was funny, but good enough to make the nightly half-hour news it was not, and that wasn't funny at all, because the crazy bastard had dragged them all out here into this miserable desert at great expense to themselves for a story that didn't exist. And there wasn't even any booze.

"You dragged our asses all the way out here for *this!*" The News Director of NBC roared in outrage to a chorus of guttural agreement. "You can't treat the world press this way, you bedsheet-wearing little pissant! Believe me, you're going to pay heavily, imagewise, for this stupid little joke!"

The Scourge of the Infidel regarded him expressionlessly. He puffed on his hookah. He smiled thinly, and pointed at the Senior Network Figure with the little finger of his left hand.

Five palace guards forthwith trained their Kalashnikovs on him and blew him away.

"Do I have your attention now, mouthpieces of the

Great Satan?" Hassan al Korami asked sweetly. "Here is what you came for," he said as the flaps of the great tent behind him began to fall away. "If one Israeli remains in Jerusalem or west of the the Jordan River on the morning of the fifth day, I shall use *these*!"

But when the tent was down, the TV cameras found themselves recording the sight of nothing more earth-shaking than five more of Hassan's vast collection of moldering fighter-planes, notable only for the fact that they were even more ancient and decrepit than most of the rest of them.

"Jeez, those are F-111s!" someone exclaimed. "Thirty years old if they're a day!"

"You will observe their markings, infidels," said Hassan al Korami.

The five antique F-111s had been given new coats of Korami green which were already starting to blister and flake off the rusting metal beneath. On the wings of rear fusilages, the Korami ensign—a marijuana leaf crossed by a machinegun—had been inlaid in gold leaf.

On the noses of the F-llls, a white circle bore words in Arabic, English, and Hebrew lettered in Israeli blue:

Tel Aviv.
Haifa.
Eilat.
Beersheba.
Galilee.

"Those are the targets we will destroy: Israel's population centers and its Jordan River Irrigation System," declared Hassan al Korami. "We will turn the Zionist state into a radioactive desert cemetery where no one lives and nothing grows unless our commands are followed promptly and with perfection."

"With those?" a hidden voice called, and the press

corps had to choke back giggles for fear of arousing further admonitory gunplay.

But Korami ignored the lése majesté this time. "You are now invited to come forward and examine the triumph of Korami military technology, the Sword of Hassan Supersonic Nuclear Cruise Missile," he said, his bloodshot eyes gleaming with the collector's true passion. "With a range of 2000 miles at a speed of a thousand miles an hour, with terrain-following radar that allows it to come in right down on the deck like an Exocet 3000, the latest in computer control technology, and a quarter-megaton nuclear warhead."

For the better part of an hour, the reporters and technicians were allowed to pore over the aircraft. Whether half of these wrecks could fly from here to Israel before their wings fell off was problematical, but if they could go the distance, it would certainly seem that they could zip in under any radar, for the ancient original terrain-hugging guidance systems still seemed more or less functional, and that was what they had been designed to do.

They were handed Geiger counters and allowed to probe the bomb bays with them amidst much clicking and moaning. The cockpits were crammed with enough electronic bric-a-brac to mix a record album, and there was a control van with enough monitors and keyboards and joysticks to impress the hell out of the reporters and air personalities and make wonderful high-tech footage.

But the camera and sound technicians were less than totally impressed, though they kept their amusement to themselves.

For the educated eye could detect that all this had been jumbled together out of crazily-mismatched modules of this and that cannibalized from bits and pieces of Commodore game computers, Japanese TV sets,

Build-A-Robot kits, and what looked like the innards of old Moog synthesizers. As to what it all did, one would have had to have been a member of the Russian Computer Underground to be crazy enough to try to trace the circuits out.

"Tell the world that Hassan al Korami speaks truly," the Scourge of the Infidel told the thoroughly shaken world press when these examinations were concluded. "If the Zionist oppressors do not obey my commands to the letter, in five days I shall nuke them into extinction!"

Then he nodded to his palace guard commander. "Remove these verminous mouthpieces of Satan from our Sacred Soil now," he said negligently.

And, with a disdain that would have made many a former American President rub his hands and chortle, the ladies and gentlemen of the world press were booted and prodded back to their planes at gunpoint, and sent on their way in a barrage of ink bottles and random automatic weapons fire.

"Come on, Sam, get serious, just do what I tell you, and we'll get you out of here," Margot Carruthers said, as the President of the United States felt her up in his padded cell.

"Kiss my wienie and I'll follow you anywhere," he said, offering up the selfsame frankfurter of state for her inspection. "They haven't let me have any nookie for weeks! Old Oscar Meyer wants some sesame seed buns!"

"All right, all right, we'll play hide the banana," Margot told him, not at all displeased with the thought. "But when we do I'm going to scream and yell like you're forcing me to do it!"

"Oh boy, oh boy, oh boy!" said the President. "Can I tie you up with your nylons too if I promise to use slip-knots?"

"No, Sam! Not *now*!" the First Lady said. "Wait till we get to Burbank. When the guard comes in, leave everything to me, and do what I tell you. . . ."

"Rape! Rape! Ooo! Eee! Aaah! Aaah! Aaah! *Aaah*!"
Sergeant Carswell was under strict orders not to enter the Presidential Padded Cell, but when he heard the screams and grunts and sounds of struggle coming from within, gentlemanly instinct intervened, and he found himself dashing inside before he could think about it.

The President of the United States, naked, had the First Lady's dress hiked up over her stomach, had her panties tied around her neck, and was humping away at her grunting "Hail to the Chief" as she scratched and bit at him.

The sight of this obscene state of the union shorted out a synapse in Sergeant Carswell's Christian and patriotic brain. Which is to say that Supreme Commander or no, no god-fearing patriotic American could allow this shit to continue.

He dashed across the floor matting and grabbed the President in a half-nelson, yanking him upwards and backwards off the First Lady, then spun him around and flung him into a padded wall.

He felt something move up behind him, and turned around just in time to see Margot Carruthers' haymaker as it collided with his jaw.

"Remember, Sam, you're *the President*, don't let these flunkies push you around, show them who's boss," Margot Carruthers told the President when she had gotten him out into the corridor. "Don't take any lip."

Hand in hand with her stark-naked husband, the First Lady walked down the corridor towards the first checkpoint, where two young Marine guards stood blocking their passage standing at ease.

"Aten-*shun!*" bellowed the ex-Supply Sergeant and used car salesman.

The two befuddled Marines popped to attention reflexively and then started fumbling with their holsters and staring at each other uncertainly at the sight of their naked Commander in Chief standing suddenly before them with an enormous erection.

"What are you fruits staring at?" the President demanded. "Haven't you ever seen a Supreme Commander before?"

"Uh . . . ah . . . Mr. President, we have orders . . ." stammered the white Marine.

"*I* give orders around here!" bellowed the President. "I'm the President of the United States ain't I, and all those communists who didn't let me have any nookie are all fired as of now!"

"C-communists!" exclaimed the black Marine.

"That's right," said Margot Carruthers, "the White House Staff has been taken over by Albanian agents and they've tricked you into believing my husband is crazy by taking away his clothes, feeding him Spanish fly, and forcing him to watch hour after hour of Russian soap operas."

"And they didn't let me have any nookie either, men," the President said petulantly.

"Help us to escape, and you'll both be heroes," said the First Lady.

"Better than that, I hereby make both of you four-star generals as of now," said the Commander in Chief. "Now who do you say is crazy, boys?"

"Four-star generals?"

"Can he do that?"

"If he's still President."

"Shit man, *is* the dude still President?"

One Marine smiled at the other.

"He is as long as we say he is, now isn't he?"

"Where to, Mr. Prez . . . ?"

"The nearest helicopter," said Margot Carruthers.

By the time the Presidential party had reached the helipad, Camp David had been at least temporarily secured. The non-coms had been promoted to general, the privates had suddenly made Sergeant, the officers had been busted and arrested for treason, the doctors and shrinks were assured of lucrative Medicare payments, and all the TV personnel were promised Presidential letters of introduction to big time Hollywood producers.

The President, bundled into a blanket, and the First Lady, doing most of the talking, boarded a helicopter which speedily conveyed them to the airport, where it landed directly beside Air Force One, already warmed up on the runway and cleared for takeoff.

Once safely in the air, they were greeted in the plush Presidential cabin by Vice President Fast Eddie Braithewaite and Captain Bo Bob Beauregard, the crew commander and pilot, a big beaming blonde hunk, who winked at the First Lady, saluted the President, and fixed his noble visage in his best heroic fly-boy expression.

"Don't worry, Mr. President, as of now you're safe in the hands of the United States Air Force," he said. "Margot here told me all about how those Cuban agents secretly replaced the White House staff with East German clones who kidnapped you and forced you to endure unspeakable perversions with Russian diesel dykes, makes my blood boil to think of it, but let me assure you that the Air Force of the United States is behind you one hundred percent! Why don't you have us take 'em all out with our Gorilla Killa mini cruise missiles? Shit, we can fly those sweet little sons of bitches right up their assholes!'

Fast Eddie looked as if he had fallen down a rabbit hole. The President stroked his erection reflectively as if considering it.

"Wait a minute, Bo Bob . . . er, Captain Beauregard," the First Lady said. "You just fly us to Burbank."

"Aw come on, Margot," the President whined, "let's have some fun."

"We'll have plenty of fun, Sam, when we get to Hollywood!"

The President's expression immediately brightened. "We're going to Hollywood?" he exclaimed. "Oh boy oh boy! I'm gonna get me some movie stars just like John F. Kennedy!"

"Better than that, Sam," Margot Carruthers told him, choking down her irritation. "You're going to go on *television*. You're going to address the Nation."

"I am?" said the President. "What am I supposed to say? Do I have to read a speech?"

"*Uncle Sam Carruthers* don't need no jive speechwriter, now does he?" Fast Eddie told him, grinning. "You're the *President*, mon, you can say anything that comes into your honkie head, all you gotta do is let it all hang out."

"That's right Sam, you just go on as if you were still selling old Buicks and tell the American people whatever you think they ought to hear," Margot Carruthers said, giving him a little goose. "We'll see about movie stars later." *And when they see what a horny old billygoat you've become, Sam Carruthers*, she thought, *I'll have you all to myself.*

Somewhere over Colorado, Captain Bo Bob Beauregard reappeared in the Presidential cabin, scratching his head. By now, Margot had gotten the President more or less into his Uncle Sam suit, though there was no way she could get him to keep his fly zipped up.

"Mr. President, there sure is some weird traffic on the air from down below," Captain Beauregard said. "Some crazy A-rab has got himself hold of some cruise missiles, and he's threatening to nuke the Hebes if they don't give up Jerusalem, and now the Israelis are sayin' screw you, Charlie, everybody knows we have no nukes, but if you lob one at us, we could acquire 50 Slings of David mobile ICBMs with one-megaton warheads faster'n hot baboon shit through a tin horn, and your entire ass is radioactive glass."

"Sure you're not listening to Radio Free Gonzo and doing spliffs up there?" Fast Eddie said. "Sounds like you've got some spaced-out dj thinks he's Orson Welles."

Captain Beauregard frowned. "Hell boy, I've been on the horn to the button room, and they're freaking out. They sure as shit want to go on Red Alert, batten down, and get our SAC B-1s in the air just in case, but all they can get from Washington is 'No comment' from the White House Press Secretary and 'It's not my job' from the Secretary of Defense."

"You tell them not to listen to anything those Commie spies tell them!" the Commander in Chief shouted. "Uncle Sam Carruthers is back in charge now! You tell my generals that I'm going on the air to address the Nation, and when I do, I want my Air Force to be ready to vaporize the Godless Atheistic Rooshians and the crazy Arabs and the smart-ass Jews and anyone else who gives us any crap when I tell them to!"

"Yessiree, Mr. President!" Captain Beauregard enthused, saluting. "That's just what the United States Air Force has been waiting to hear!"

"Wait a minute!" shouted Fast Eddie. "You can't do that!"

"Why not, boy?" demanded Bo Bob Beauregard.

"Because . . ." *Because the fat boy is bugfuck bananas*, Fast Eddie had been about to say, but one look at the granite set of this peckerwood's patriotic jaw disabused him of any such notion. "Because . . . because . . . because they won't believe you, mon!" he finally blurted. "The White House staff has got half a dozen actors who can fake the President's voice! They'll countermand the orders! They'll have the Secret Service grab us as soon as we get off this plane!"

"Can they do that, Captain?" the President said fearfully. "Can they lock me up again and take my nookie away?"

"You don't worry none about *that*, Mr. President," Captain Beauregard said triumphantly. "We're always prepared in the United States Air Force."

He went into a cabinet and came back with a bright red mobile phone. "This little sucker goes straight to a secure satellite in geosynchronous orbit, and then right down into the button room by tight laser-beam. They got a voice-analyzer on the other end that will tell them it's you, and all I've got to do is verify it's a live broadcast. You just get on the horn and tell them to go to Condition Black. That means they put all strategic forces on full Red Alert, seal up the control center, and accept no orders that don't come right through that phone in the authenticated voice of the President of the United States."

Beaming, the President took the red phone.

"Sam, I don't think you should do this," Margot Carruthers said nervously as he played with the phone with one hand and himself with the other.

"You're always telling me what to do, Margot!" the President whined. "Don't you have another Martini, Sam, Sam you're driving too fast, you keep your eyes off those cheerleaders, Sam! Well I'm the President of the United States now, and no one's going to tell me what I can't do, not my mother, not the Rooshians, and not you!"

"Give 'em hell, Mr. President!" Captain Beauregard said brightly, as he showed him how to get an operator.

"Hello, hello, this is the President . . . What do you mean I should hang up and dial directly myself?"

"This is Radio K-RAB, the Rockin' Voice of the A-rabs, beamin' a hundred thousand watts of Good Vibrations right at ya, all you crazy Shiite and Sunni mamas and papas you, from our Ship of Rock and Roll Fools out here in the Gulf, and here's the Big Number Twelve on Radio K-RAB today, "Jihad Jump" by Abou Abou and the Hashishins, right after this word from Kalashnikov, the state of the art in automatic rifles, and at a price you don't have to be an oil sheik to afford!"

Armand Deutcher turned off the air feed before the commercial could come on, and returned his attention to the world news monitors he had had jury-rigged in the control room of the seaborn pirate radio station.

Even as Zvi Bar David had predicted, Hassan al Korami had not waited for the full shipment of Sword of Hassan cruise missiles to arrive before he did his dingo act. So far, so good.

Now NBC was reporting that the Israelis had issued their own ultimatum. Hassan had four days to surrender his nuclear cruise missiles to Israel or they would take them out with their mighty high-tech air force without the need to resort to nuclear preemption. Since Koram had threatened Israel with nuclear annihilation, they could hardly be blamed by world opinion if they launched at all-out air attack against the miscreant as long as they righteously kept their own nukes hidden under the rug.

And now Radio Moscow was reporting that Hassan al Korami was falling right into the trap. He had just declared that the moment an Israeli aircraft crossed his borders, he would annihilate Tel Aviv, Haifa, Beersheba, Eilat, and the Jordan River Irrigation System.

They were goading Hassan into it. The Israelis would probably wait till the deadline just to keep him getting hotter. Then they would hit the Skeikdom of Koram with about a thousand or so drone fighter-bombers firing Pitchfork metal-seeking missiles which would destroy Koram's forces utterly while the world stood on and cheered.

Deutcher only hoped that the Israelis wouldn't be *too* efficient. He had several billion francs riding on Hassan getting at least one of his cruise missiles off the ground before they were taken out by the Israeli luftblitz, and he would be a lot happier if the Israelis made sure Koram fired first.

After all, what difference did it make to them? Even if the Lion of the Desert managed to launch all five, the Israelis would just dump them all into the sea anyway, or so at least they should think.

Now there was danger of a major financial set-back. Deutcher had counted on the Israelis wanting to let Hassan get at least one missile in the air so they could make him hit Mecca, indeed he had given Zvi Bar David the idea free of charge.

Then, with the mighty hundred-thousand-watt trans-mitter of K-RAB, the Rockin' Voice of the A-rabs, *he* could take control of the missile that the Israelis took away from Hassan's controllers and use it where it would do the most good.

It had cost him good money to rent this pirate radio ship too, let alone how deep he had dug to leverage his real estate speculation, and now the Israelis threatened to throw a monkey wrench into the works!

*   *   *

Ivan Igorovich Gornikov had never seen the Central Committee in such a state, and he had seen plenty as the dayshift operator of the Bulgorny all these years.

When Hassan al Korami had issued his first ultimatum to Israel, the Committee had convened immediately, and when the Israelis had threatened to destroy his missiles by non-nuclear means, they had gone into permanent session, and when Hassan had declared he would launch his nukes on warning, they had panicked and repaired here, to the Dacha, to the emergency control center buried half a kilometer down in the heart of the Urals.

And that had been the only consensus these Heroes of Socialist Labor had managed to reach. Marshall Borodin conceived the notion that this was somehow the ideal time to blockade Berlin. The Foreign Ministry advised a peace offensive, that they should side with whoever was attacked first. Sergei Polikov insisted they side with Hassan to protect his best hashish customer. The Minister of Finance agreed. The Minister of Propaganda believed that they should side with Israel, who would have world opinion on their side if they were nuked. And by now all of them were hoarse with exhaustion and repeating themselves endlessly.

And all the time, Pyotr Ivanovich Bulgorny, his skin varnished and polymerized to a high gloss and rouged to a ruddy glow, sat there at the head of the table, silent, motionless, and imperturbable. Admittedly, the Chairman's failure to panic like the rest of them owed a certain debt to the fact that he was dead.

As for Ivan Igorovich Gornikov, his state of mind was anything but tranquil, for he knew the signs. The Central Committee was quite thoroughly deadlocked, and by now most of them were drunk. The moment they found themselves faced with an unavoidable decision, they would ask the Bulgorny to speak.

And Ivan, alas, had already fed the Joker program into Pyotr Ivanovich's memory banks and decision-making software. He had no idea what kind of gibberish would issue forth from the speaker behind the corpse's teeth when they told him to put the question to the Chairman of the Central Committee of the Soviet Communist Party. For better or worse, the Soviet Union would soon be at the command of a randomized collective decision-making process.

"This was just received from our embassy in London," said a minor Ministry functionary, handing a single piece of paper to the Foreign Minister. "It was called in from a pay phone by someone who claimed to represent the Mossad."

The Foreign Minister read it and went pale as a sheet.

"What is it, Nikolai?" demanded Polikov. "You look as if you have bitten into a turd."

"Apparently the Mossad is now afraid that their own government is about to go too far," the Foreign Minister said. "According to this, if any of Hassan's missiles should actually hit anything, they will use it as an excuse to destroy him using their own nuclear arsenal, announcing its existence thereby, and forcing the world to accept Israeli hegemony over the Middle East as a new nuclear superpower. The Mossad begs the Soviet Union to force Koram to capitulate to the Israeli ultimatum to prevent extreme Zionist elements from accomplishing this."

"They're right! We cannot allow the Israelis to rule the Middle East!"

"Pre-empt them!"

"Pre-empt *who*?"

"Israel!"

"Koram!"

"Berlin!"

They continued to scream and shout at each other, fortifying themselves with more vodka, but soon enough the unwholesome contumely began to run out of energy, and one by one, the Members of the Central Committee fell silent and turned their gaze to the tranquil and impassive leadership of Pyotr Ivanovich Bulgorny, who sat there like the corpse he was, loftily transcending this unseemly spectacle.

"Gornikov!" Marshall Borodin finally said. "It would seem we must consult Comrade Bulgorny on this matter. Boot him up, and load his decision-making program at once!"

Shaking, Ivan set to work at the control computer. "Be a good boy now, Pyotr Ivanovich," he whispered into the Bulgorny's ear. "For the sake of Mother Russia, and Ivan Igorovich's ass."

"It was *your* idea, Margot," the President complained. "*I* didn't want to make any speech, I just wanted to fly to Hollywood and boff me some movie stars!"

Air Force One had arrived at Burbank Airport without any Secret Service or FBI showing up, and it seemed they could have gotten Uncle Sam Carruthers to NBC's Burbank studios and on the air without being intercepted, as per the original plan.

But now neither the Vice President nor the First Lady could contemplate with any equanimity the notion of putting the President on the air with the command phone in his hand and the strategic forces gone to Condition Black. If Sam started raving about annihilating the Godless Rooshians or taking vengeance against the price-cutting Japs or even ridding Washington, D.C. of grafting pansy bureaucrats while the red phone was on, the Air Force would bloody well do it, and no one could get through to stop them.

And Samuel T. Carruthers kept stroking the damn thing and wouldn't let Margot take it away from him.

"It's too dangerous, Sam," she told him. "Once they know you've escaped and know where you are, they'll cut you off the air and send in the FBI and Secret Service."

"I got to admit the Little Lady's right, Mr. President," said Captain Bo Bob Beauregard. "You better stay right here on good old Air Force One where the Communists with the butterfly nets can't get at you." His eyes lit up. "In fact, just to be on the safe side, why don't I just get on the horn and get us some air cover? I reckon a couple dozen F-25s from Edwards would be enough to show the flag."

"I'm getting tired of sitting around on my ass in this airplane!" the President shouted angrily. "I want to go out and have some fun!"

"We could always nuke Washington," Bo Bob suggested helpfully. "The American people would understand. We had to destroy the city to save it from the Communist Conspiracy."

"It's full of nothing but pointy-headed bureaucrats, foreigners, and welfare chislers who voted against me, isn't it . . .?" the President said thoughtfully.

"You could say it's not a part of the real red-blooded U.S. of A. at all. . . ." agreed Captain Beauregard. "I'd recommend four low-level airbursts with five-megaton Widowmaker airborne IRBMs coming in on the deck from B-7 Penetrator hypersonic bombers. That should take out the White House Staff, wherever the slimy sons of bitches are hiding, six if you want to go for a little overkill. . . ."

"I'll show those ingrates what happens when they

take away my nookie!" the President said, holding the red phone to his mouth.

"Wait, wait!" shrieked Fast Eddie. "I've got a better idea!"

"A better idea?" said Bo Bob. "Maybe you're right, boy! Now *New York City* is someplace a lot of people have always wanted to see sawed off from the rest of the country. . . ."

"No, no, no," said Fast Eddie off the top of his head. "Why don't you just call them up and make them surrender?"

"Surrender?"

"Give it a try before you start World War III over this jive, mon! Let them know you've busted out of the bin, and tell them you'll go on the tube and whip up a lynch-mob if they give you any more shit."

At which point, the White House staff would have no choice but to finally turn over the Presidency to *him* in return for keeping their jobs, and he'd take considerable pleasure in punching out this crazy old honkie and getting hold of the phone to the button room himself.

"He's right, Sam, the snivelling cowards will give up without a fight," Margot Carruthers said, fondling his privates. *Or anyway they'll play along long enough for me to get you into the sack and away from the red phone.*

"Aw shit," said Captain Bo Bob Beauregard, "we're not gonna get to take out Washington?"

"I guess I would enjoy telling the bastards what I think of them first," the President decided.

"Don't look so sad, Bo Bob," said the First Lady. "You can still go play with your fighter-planes!"

"They say I am mad, but I am not mad," Hassan al Korami cackled to himself. He took another great hit from his hookah, and beamed happily across the throne room at his assembled officers and ministers, sprawled on the cushions before him, or standing at attention sucking on their spliffs.

Everything was falling into place exactly as his divine inspiration had foretold. The American President was locked in a padded cell masturbating, unbeknownst to the Israelis, who believed the Americans would protect them from his wrath. By now the Russian Computer Underground which he had created for just this purpose had blown electronic hashish into the computer that controlled the Russian corpse.

Now he was ready to kick over the anthill and watch the Satanic vermin scramble and stagger to their doom.

"Vizier," he commanded, "order the evacuation of Koramibad, for now will we return to the clean desert sands from whence we came!"

"General, hitch up our Sword of Hassan cruise missiles to the palace Rolls-Royces!" he commanded.

"Scribe, release this pronouncement to the international news media! We have evacuated Koramibad, and disappeared into the desert with our missiles where no Israeli aircraft can find us before we launch. I, the Scourge of the Infidel, now therefore issue a new non-negotiable ultimatum. The Zionist oppressors now have three days to evacuate their population to New York and Miami entirely, or we shall vaporize them all where they stand!"

Even in the court of Hassan al Korami, this pronunciamento was the cause for some concern, though of course no one present dared declare anything less than perfect comprehension of the Wisdom of the Lion of the Desert for fear of facing the Sacred Wrath of same. But no amount of hash could convince any of them that the Israelis would ever accede to such a demand.

Including Hassan al Korami.

It had all come to him in a vision last night.

Of course the Zionists would never give up without a fight to the death! They might be infidels, but they were no wimpish cowards! Instead, they would do what he was forcing them to do, openly brandish their own nuclear missiles, the Slings of David, and threaten to use them first on Koram.

And then, ah then, the Russian bear would finding itself twitching and stumbling out of control onto the stage!

"The frigging Israelis have gone and done it!" the National Security Adviser said as he came back from the can to the Cabinet room still zipping up his pants.

"Done what?"

"Whipped it out!"

"Whipped out what, you don't mean—"

"Their frigging nuclear strike force, that's what! They're displaying their Slings of David mobile ICBMs on television, and they say they'll take out Hassan's missiles if he doesn't surrender in 24 hours by the simple expedient of turning all of Koram into a two-kilometer-deep radioactive crater."

"That's nothing we can't manage, is it?" said the Press Secretary. "I mean, imagewise, it's not our problem, is it?"

The Cabinet meeting room, like the White House Staff, had certainly seen better days. Ever since Hassan al Korami had trotted out his cruise missiles they had been holed up in here, holding themselves incommunicado from the press, who wanted to ask them questions they couldn't answer, from the Pentagon seeking orders they didn't know how to give, and from the Cabinet members and Congressional Bigwigs demanding to see a President, who on the one hand was crazy, and who on the other, would now seem to have escaped.

So there was nothing for it but to live on take-in junk food and attempt to manage the situation, which, like the piles of old pizza cartons, chicken bones, and half-eaten greaseburgers which littered the big long table, was beginning to get overripe.

"It isn't fair!" declared the Chief of Staff. "Isn't this what we hire ourselves a President for, to make the decisions that can only come out wrong, and then take the blame? We're here to take care of business, not run this mess ourselves!"

Ivan Igorovich Gornikov was sweating like a pig, and he would have given half a year's wages for a single hit of hash. He was getting the shakes; if not from withdrawal, then certainly from what these vodka-sotted assholes were putting him through.

Every time he thought he had finally gotten the last update entered, some other little apparatchnik would appear with another disaster report on the rapidly deteriorating situation, and he would have to sit around and listen to them discuss it drunkenly for an hour and then enter a new round of decision input yet again.

He was almost tempted to tell them that it didn't matter, that Pyotr Ivanovich's software had been quite thoroughly randomized, so that additional data would only introduce additional noise into the system. But at least for the moment even the present situation was preferable to a log cabin in deepest Siberia or a bullet in the back of the head.

Which no doubt would come soon enough anyway, once the stuffed and wired mummy of Pyotr Ivanovich was ordered to speak.

*   *   *

"Broadcast my words to all the world!" declared Hassan al Korami. "Let the Zionist dogs piss unmanfully in their trousers!"

"You're not putting me on?" said the voice over his car radio. "This is really *the* Hassan al Korami, Lion of the Desert, Scourge of the Infidel, and you're *really* listening to K-RAB, the Rockin' Voice of the A-rabs, well *too far out*, tell all our mamas and papas out there in the mystic sands, if you don't mind, Hassan, you wild and crazy guy, what's you're fave rave of the month?"

" 'Jihad Jump' by Abou Abou and the Hashishins," the Scourge of of the Infidel found himself saying into his phone, which was only natural, since he owned the group that had made the charts with the heavy metal version of the Korami National Anthem.

"But I did not call to do record promos!" the Lion of the Desert roared when he caught up on what had happened. "I have a proclamation that will shake the world and set the flag of Islam flying over Jerusalem! Hear, O—"

"Hold on to your hookah, Hassan, we'll be right back to freak out on your Sacred Rage after this word from Harada, maker of fine samurai swords since before old Omar made his first tent, boys and girls!"

And the Scourge of the Infidel was constrained to wait through the commercial.

But he found to his own surprise that for once he did not at all mind this pause between contemplation and act. For the first time in his life, he was actually feeling mellow.

The moment was perfect, and perfect too was the fact that he was passing through it out here in the endless desert sands, free under the sun and the sky, wandering the wastes once more, in the manner of his ancestors, though of course, as befitted the Lion of the Desert, he had much the best of it, riding in the capacious air-conditioned cabin of his outsized Rolls, rather than humping about and broiling on the back of some camel.

"And now, Radio K-RAB, the Rockin' Voice of the A-rabs brings you a special treat, you spaced-out Shiites and Sunnis you, live, direct from the ass-end of nowhere, that heavy rapper that's got 'em all rockin' and rollin' in the aisles in Moscow and Washington this week, a K-RAB exclusive preview, you heard it here first, boys and girls, the latest unconditional ultimatum from the Scourge of the Infidel, *Hassan al Korami!*"

"Hear the words of Hassan al Korami, Zionist vermin," Hassan began mildly. "For behold your futile threats to destroy our Sword of Hassan cruise missiles with your Satanic Slings of David are as the fartings of camels! My Hashishins and I have vanished into the desert with our nukes from whence we will annihilate you! Fire your missiles at Koram, villainous kikes, as you will, for I defy you!"

He paused, smiled to himself, and went on more calmly. "But before you do, know this, O Israel, know this, American running dogs of Zionist imperialism, I have just received iron-clad assurance from the Soviet Union," he lied, "that the moment a single nuclear explosion pollutes the sacred soil of Koram, the Soviet Union will launch an all-out nuclear attack on the United States."

"Well *far out,* I'm sure we'll all be tuning in to see whether the world is going to hear the Big Bang before the weekend, and so while we're waiting, let's all get in the proper thermonuclear mood with 'Brighter than a Thousand Suns,' that golden radioactive oldie from The Four Horsemen of the Apocalypse. . . ."

Hassan al Korami turned off the radio, and sucked

at his hookah, giggling to himself. Left to their own
devices, the Americans would no doubt pressure the
Israelis into at least surrendering Jerusalem and the
West Bank now, while the Russians would be falling
all over themselves to deny that they had ever promised Koram such a thing.

But of course Hassan had not left the twin limbs of
Satan to their own devices! The American President
had been turned into a raving maniac by the Mendocino Liberation Front, and the computer that controlled the Russian Chairman had been confounded
to Babel by the Russian Computer Underground.

Between them, an insane American President and
a dead Russian Chairman animated by a thoroughly
garbled computer would surely contrive a way to
blow each other and the Israelis to bits.

If the Americans did not pre-empt the Russians,
the Russians would pre-empt the Americans' preemption, or the Israelis would pre-empt him, forcing
the Russians and the Americans to simultaneously
pre-empt each other.

It hardly mattered which Limb of Satan pressed
the panic button first. Russian missiles would annihilate Israel and America, and American missiles
would annihilate Russia, and then would the Lion of
the Desert declare Jihad and victory at the same
time, and march into Jerusalem as the Imam of all
Arabia and the Sultan of what was left of the world.

Admittedly, it was quite likely that in the process
Koram could expect to take some hits, but that was a
price that the Scourge of the Infidel was quite willing to pay. For what was there in Koram to be destroyed but an empty city and some scattered tribes
of bedouins? No amount of megatonnage could take
out the true font of his power, the bottomless pool of
oil upon which his sheikdom and his transcendent

destiny stood. Indeed, with most of the world in radioactive ruins, he could up the price of petroleum to anything he chose!

Marshall Borodin read the latest communique that had been handed to him and fainted dead away. The Foreign Minister set to reviving him by pour the remains of a bottle of vodka over his head and slapping his cheeks, while Sergei Polikov retrieved the communique, scanned it, went pale, and drank straight from the mouth of another bottle before summarizing it to those of the Central Committee who were still conscious.

"Hassan al Korami has announced that the Soviet Union will react to any nuclear attack by the Israelis on his territory by an all-out pre-emptive attack on the United States. Furthermore, we have promised him we will do this even if he launches a nuclear attack on Israel first! Which he would seem to have every intention of doing!"

"Sergei, you imbecile, how could you promise him such a thing?" demanded the Foreign Minister.

"*Me*?" said the KGB Director. "I never promised him any such thing. It must have been the Red Army."

Marshall Borodin, by now, had revived sufficiently to declare his indignation. "How dare you accuse the Red Army of such stupidity!" he roared. "*You* are the one who sells the maniac his hashish, Sergei Polikov!"

All eyes turned on the Foreign Minister.

"Don't be ridiculous," that worthy said. "Everyone knows I'm just a technician."

"What will we do?" wailed Marshall Borodin. "If we launch our missiles at the Americans, they will launch their missiles at us, and the truth of the matter is that we both have more than enough to annihilate each other."

"But even if we *don't* launch our missiles when

Israel responds to Koram's first strike, the Americans will still think we might, and then *they'd* launch first," pointed out Polikov.

"We must announce that Hassan is lying," said the Foreign Minister. "We must inform the Americans publically that we will not attack them no matter what Koram and Israel do to each other."

"Will they believe us?"

"Can we believe them if they say they believe us?"

"But if we let the Israelis get away with nuking Koram, it will turn all the Arabs against us, destroy our credibility in Eastern Europe and cause a mass uprising, and leave the Middle East in the hands of a new nuclear power we have spent the past half century supporting terrorists against!"

"Perhaps we should strike pre-emptively at the Israelis?"

"Better to destroy that double-dealing parasite Hassan!"

"Someone must get on the hot line to the American President," said the Foreign Minister.

"Who?" sneered Marshall Borodin. "Certainly not you!"

"The Red Army certainly cannot expect to negotiate directly with a head of state!"

"Comrades," said Sergei Polikov, "it is quite clear that both protocol and the fact that we will never agree on what to propose to the Americans ourselves requires that Pyotr Ivanovich, our beloved Chairman and official chief of state, be the one to deal directly with his American counterpart on a summit level."

Ivan Igorovich Gornikov could all but smell the alcoholic sighs of relief even now at the ultimate hour of impending Armageddon, as they gratefully reliquinished their responsibilities as the living representative of the Soviet People to the animating software of a corpse.

"Activate Pyotr Ivanovich immediately, Gornikov," Marshall Borodin ordered.

"Da, tovarish," said Ivan, sending the first jolts of current to the steel exoskeleton concealed within the voluminous folds of the Bulgorny's traditional ill-fitting blue suit. Pyotr Ivanovich began to jerk and jiggle, his eyelids flapped open and closed asynchronously, his lips began to mutter to themselves, as the audioanimatronics warmed up.

Then the software took complete control, and Ivan brought the Chairman to his feet, looming above the Central Committee in all his ponderous bulk, staring out at them unwaveringly through his unwavering glass eyes, dominating them utterly with his implacable and tireless visage.

Even if his software *is* randomized, even if he *has* been dead for ten years, Ivan suddenly perceived, Pyotr Ivanovich Bulgorny certainly cut a better of a figure of a man than any of this besotted collection of generals, Chekist thugs, and time-serving Party hacks! *Ironically enough,* he thought, *the anti-party elements, the Central Committee, and myself now all find ourselves in perfect agreement.*

The only good Party Chairman is a dead one.

"This is the President of the United States, you effete eastern communist assholes, and I'm really pissed off!" roared the voice on the speaker-phone, and a great moan of woe went up in the untidy smoke-filled Cabinet room.

"It's Uncle Sam all right, we checked it out," said the National Security Adviser. "He's speaking from Air Force One, which for some reason is parked at the Burbank airport, and there's a squadron of F-25s overhead putting on a display of supersonic aerobatics that's shattering every window from Pasadena to Pacoima."

"You bastards had no right to lock me up without any nookie!" bellowed Samuel T. Carruthers. "I'm horny as a billygoat and mad as an ayatollah, and I'm *the President of the United States*, and from now on, I'm in charge here."

"Get the Secret Service out there! Get the FBI! Get a SWAT team from Los Angeles! Someone's got to get a net over the son of a bitch before the press gets wind of this!"

"Now you listen here, you miserable flunkies, I want your resignations right now, or I'm going on the air, and by the time I've finished telling the American people how you kidnapped their President, held him prisoner, and tortured him with a case of the blue balls, you'll all be breaking rocks in Leavenworth!"

"Oh my god . . ." moaned the Press Secretary, dropping a phone like a dead fish and holding his head in his hands. "The Russians have threatened to nuke us if the Israelis attack Koram!"

"What'll we do?"

"We'd better put our straegic forces on Red Alert," said the National Security Adviser. And he picked up the phone to the button room.

"And don't try to send your goons after me, either!" said the President. "My air cover will blow them away. And if you give me any crap, I'll let Bo Bob nuke Washington."

"Holy shit!" shouted the National Security Adviser, dropping his phone like a hot potato. "They've already gone to Condition Black!"

"Condition Black? What the hell is *Condition Black*?"

"The button room is sealed off and running on internal air and power. All I can get on the phone from here is a robot voice telling me the number is temporarily out of service. There's only one active line in now, and that's the red phone on Air Force One."

"That raving maniac has personal control of our nuclear forces?"

"You got it! The lunatic has taken over the asylum!"

Ivan Igorovich held the Party Chairman at stiff attention while he keyed in the final update, exactly as he did on May Day and the Anniversary of the Revolution, when Pyotr Ivanovich stood heroically imperturbable for long hours in the dank breezes atop Lenin's Tomb. At least the exoskeleton controls would seem not to have been affected by the Joker program.

But now it was time to run the thoroughly barbled decision-making software, and when he turned matters over to *that*, it would be terra incognita, for even stoned-out hackers' theory could not agree on what would happen when a randomized decision-making process interfaced with a scrambled data bank. Boris believed that feedback loops might be set up that would short the whole mess out. Tanya opined that the process of dialectical materialism itself might speak through this tossing of the electronic coins of a cybernated I Ching. Grishka likened it to feeding the entire *Soviet Encyclopedia* through a tree-chipper and publishing what came out as the next edition of *Pravda*.

Ivan Igorovich Gornikov had no such theories, but now he was the one who was about to find out, as he booted up the decision-making program.

Pyotr Ivanovich stood there silently and motionlessly for a while, and then the lips of the corpse began to tremble, and the glass eyes began to flick back and forth in their sockets, and then the Chairman began to speak in a multi-tonal syntax cobbled together out of words and phrases from the recorded library of his old speeches.

"Fraternal Greetings, peasants and workers of the

Magnetogorsk refrigerator works, and welcome to the Five-Year Plan of Socialist Realism. . . ."

"What?"

"Gornikov! What's wrong with the Chairman?" demanded Marshall Borodin.

Ivan shrugged innocently. "Aside from the fact that he's been dead for ten years, nothing."

"The correct Marxist-Leninist solution to the present crisis in hooliganism is to express fraternal solidarity with the long-range class self-interest of the running dogs of agricultural production quotas. . . ."

"Then why is he babbling like that?" snapped Sergei Polikov.

"Babbling?" said Ivan. "Don't tell me an educated Marxist-Leninist intellectual like yourself has trouble following our Chairman's new Party Line when it seems so crystal clear to an ignorant but ideologically pure Soviet worker like me?"

"We must stamp out revanchist elements within the Kirov Ballet and send the New Soviet Man to conquer the stars on his way to Siberia. . . ."

"We can't put *that* on the hot line to the American President!" said the Foreign Secretary.

"What else can we do?"

Marshall Borodin scanned another communique. "Spy satellites indicate that the Americans have gone to Condition Black!" he moaned. "Everything they have is now directly controlled by this used-car salesman, this bumbling *civilian*, this Uncle Sam Carruthers!"

"They're preparing a first strike!" said Polikov. "We must launch everything we have at once!"

"But maybe the President has instead seized control from the militarist circles in order to *prevent* some crazy general from acting on his own. Have you never seen *Dr. Strangelove*?"

"He's right!" said the Minister of Production, arising from his stupor. "It's an implied invitation to a summit."

On and on they went, as the clocked ticked and the Bulgorny babbled, and finally Ivan Igorovich Gornikov could contain himself no longer. What did he have to lose by speaking anyway, since if the world were not blown to smithereens shortly, he would be shot for treason if the KGB still existed afterward to find out what had happened.

"You'll pardon my saying so, comrades," he ventured, "But why don't you ask *Pyotr Ivanovich* if he feels like talking to the American President before we all blow ourselves to bits? He may be dead, but at least he can always be counted upon to be decisive."

"Well what about it, Pyotr Ivanovich?" Marshall Borodin demanded directly of the stuffed and wired Party Chairman. "Do you wish to negotiate with the American President?"

". . . the Soviet Union is in favor of peaceful coexistence with the complete disarmament of all neo-colonialist tractor-operators. . . ."

"*That* should give the American President pause. . . ." mused Polikov.

"Let no one mistake our determination to fulfill our sorghum production quotas or take a capitalist road towards the dictatorship of the party hacks, for we will never submit to American demands that we make a profit-motive revolution without breaking eggs. . . ."

"A powerful dialectical line would seem to be emerging, wouldn't you say?" said the Minister of Production.

"I find it impossible to fault its logic. . . ." agreed Sergei Polikov.

"It would appear you are our only hope, Pyotr Ivanovich," said Marshall Borodin. "Will you now speak with the American President?"

Ivan caused the corpse of the Chairman to nod its

assent, and managed to smear a rictus grin across its face. "We have nothing to fear but bourgeois tendencies in American ruling class circles," said Pyotr Ivanovich confidently as the exoskeleton made his dead hand reach for the hotline phone.

"Jesus," said the Appointments Secretary, "that's the Russian Chairman himself on the hot line!"

"But he's *dead*!"

"He may be dead, but he's on the line demanding to talk with the President himself, and threatening to launch an all-out pre-emptive ideological dialectic against the class self-interest of malingerers and black-marketeers, whatever that means, if we refuse."

"What the hell can we do now?"

"Well, you assholes, I'm getting tired of waiting for your answer," the voice of Samuel T. Carruthers shrieked on the speakerphone. "I'm horny, and I'm bored, and I want to go out and get some nookie!"

The White House Staff exchanged terrified speculative glances.

"We can't!"

"Got any better ideas?"

"Isn't this what we hired him for?"

"I'm gonna count to three, and then I'm gonna tell Bo Bob to have them drop fifty megatons on Washington. One . . . two . . ."

"He may be crazy . . ."

"Two and a half . . ."

"But at least he won't take shit."

"I thought you were dead," President Carruthers said when they had patched Air Force One through on the hot line.

"The state will wither away only when all production quotas for sugar beets are exceeded by non-proliferation treaties between revanchist troglodytes and the vanguard of the working software," said the weird voice on the phone.

"My dong will wither away if I don't get me some nookie soon!" the President said crossly. "What do you want, you Rooshian stiff?"

"I want to take this opportunity to express my fraternal sympathies with decadent capitalist sensualism...." replied Chairman Bulgorny. "Owing to temporary bad weather in the Ukraine, the nookie crop in Central Asia has been shipped to the Gulag by mistake...."

"Oh," said the President much more sympathetically, "you're also having trouble getting laid."

"Socialist morality has advanced by leaps and bounds since Rasputin...." Pyotr Ivanovich Bulgorny admitted. It figured. All those Rooshian women looked like science fiction fans as far as Uncle Sam was concerned, and besides, it must not be so easy to make out in singles bars when you're a corpse.

"What you need, buddy, is some Red White and Blue One Hundred Percent American Used Nookie!" the President told him. "I hear tell that they got hookers in Las Vegas that'll make even a dead Russian Chairman whistle the Star Spangled Banner out his asshole!"

"Cultural exchange programs between our two great peoples should not be interrupted by linkage to ideological differences between trashy western popular literature and the Red Army Chorus ..."

"Tell you what, Mr. Chairman, why don't we have a meeting in the grand old American tradition?" the President suggested helpfully. "We'll go to Las Vegas and party with some hookers, and who knows, once we've gotten stewed, screwed, and tattooed, we might even get down to doing some business."

"Long live the solidarity between progressive elements of social parasitism and to each according to his need," agreed the stuffed Soviet leader. "Let us conduct joint docking maneuvers together in the spirit of Apollo-Soyuz while continuing peaceful competition for the available natural resources."

"See you in Vegas," the President said happily. "For a Rooshian and a corpse, you sure sound like a real party animal!"

Blinking against the cruel glare, Ivan Igorovich Gornikov maneuvered the Party Chairman down the ramp onto the broiling tarmac of McCarran Airport, following as inconspicuously as he could while of necessity lugging the portable control console.

"Two hours of this heat, and poor Pyotr Ivanovich will start to stink," Boris Vladimirov whispered unhappily in Ivan's ear as the full force of the noonday Las Vegas sun hit them in the face like a hot rocket exhaust.

Ivan groaned. No one had had time to think of that.

No one had really had time to think of anything. The hardware arrangements were as hastily improvised as the summit meeting that the Chairman had somehow managed to arrange with the American President. Access to the main memory banks and mainframe software of Pyotr Ivanovich back in Moscow was a shaky affair involving a satellite link to the airplane and a modem-mobile phone link to the control console that Ivan carried, cleverly disguised as what the decadent capitalists called a "ghetto blaster." It even had AM-FM cassette capability for the sake of realism.

But the KGB technicians, who admittedly had done heroic feats of socialist labor putting the electronic linkages together on such short notice, had entirely overlooked the limitations of even advanced socialist embalming technology. True, the corpse of the Chairman had survived ten years of service without beginning to rot, but a few short appearances atop Lenin's Tomb in brisk Moscow springs and falls were one thing, and the 100-degree heat of the Great American Desert quite another!

Ivan, Boris, and the Chairman were met at the foot of the ramp by the Vice President, the First Lady, and a big blond Air Force Captain.

"Welcome to the monkey house, mon!" said the Vice President.

"You look pale as as a pissant parson, boy," said the Air Force Captain, regarding the Chairman with an idiot grin. "Guess it's pretty hard to keep a tan back in Moscow!"

"I am pleased to convey the fraternal dialectic of the workers and peasants of the Lubianka collective gulag to the militaristic elements of progressive world youth," said Pyotr Ivanovich, grinning mechanically of its own accord, as it had been taking to doing lately.

"Say what?"

"The Chairman's English is somewhat less than perfect," Ivan said hastily. "Would you prefer we switch to Russian?"

"So you can do the talking?"

"Who *me*?" exclaimed Ivan. "I'm just the Chairman's . . . how do you say it, *roadie*. And Boris here my assistant."

"Where's the Foreign Minister and the Defense Minister and your KGB chief?" demanded the American Vice President.

Cowering with the rest of the Central Committee in the Dacha where they hope to save at least their own cowardly asses when the bombs start to fall! Ivan almost answered. Not one of them dared accompany the dead but gallant Party Chairman on his eleventh-hour mission to save the world from nuclear destruction. The randomized decision-making software was not only in control, it was entirely on its own. Even Marshall Borodin, after a fatuous charade of reluctance, had readily enough in the end ceded direct computer-link control of the Soviet strategic forces to the decision-making software of Pyotr Ivanovich. Collective Leadership had been entirely surrendered to a new Cult of Personality.

"Our Glorious Chairman, Pyotr Ivanovich Bulgorny, Hero of Socialist Labor, inheritor of the mantle of Marx and Lenin, has the full unquestioned support of the KGB, the Red Army, and the Party Machinery which he embodies," Ivan was therefore able to declare quite truthfully. "But if there has been no militarist coup in American ruling circles, why is your President not here to greet him?"

The Vice President and the First Lady exchanged peculiar glances.

"Sam has . . . got his hands full at the Court of Caligula. . . ." the First Lady finally muttered, grinding her teeth.

"The Court of Caligula?"

"The hotel where the summit will be held," said the Vice President.

"Don't worry boys," boomed the Air Force Captain, "it's got the wildest casino floor on the Strip, you're gonna love it!"

"Time to go down to meet the Rooshians, girls!" the President said, pulling up the pants of his Uncle Sam suit but forgetting to zip up the fly. If he had not yet gotten stewed or tatooed, he had certainly at last gotten quite properly screwed while Margot was occupied at the airport. He wondered if boffing four hookers in two hours might be one for the *Guinness Book of Records*.

"I hope your Rooshian friends don't think they can pay for pussy in rubles!" said the blonde bimbo.

"Yeah, Mr. Prez," said the brunette, "I mean the world may be about to blow itself up, but business is business!"

"Don't worry girls, you just show old Pyotr Ivanovich a good time, and send the bill to the State Department," said the President. "Those Foggy Bottom fruits have been pimping for foreigners ever since FDR sent Eleanor to spread her legs for Joe Stalin!"

The Air Force helicopter set down in the outdoor parking lot of the Caligula's Court Hotel and Casino, a huge gleaming glass phallus looming behind a half-scale replica of the Roman Coliseum domed like an all-weather stadium.

Igor, Boris, Chairman Bulgorny, and the Americans were met at the colonnaded entrance by a phalanx of body-builders done up as Praetorian Guards, replete with spears, shields, and skin-tight rubber body-armor.

They were ushered down a short wide corridor embellished with audioanimated Romans and animals cycling through entirely un-Disneylike couplings and through a great vaulted archway overlooking the casino floor.

A long spiral ramp wound down around the circumference of the huge room where the grandstands in the real thing would have been, a continuous arcade of slot-machines, where fat blue-haired women squeezed into pastel tights, small children, gum-chewing off-duty hookers, and bleary-eyed drunks stood pulling levers mechanically and staring into space.

Below, the roulette wheels, blackjack and poker games, and craps tables were interspersed with both live sex acts and audioanimatronic figures performing hideous tortures and perversions too beastly to contemplate. The cocktail waitresses wore black leather panty-hose, chrome chains, and slave-collars. The dealers and croupiers were done up in rags as captive Christians, and the lurking bouncers were gladiators.

A big stage jutting out from the curving wall was presently dressed as the Emperor's Box, replete with two cushioned thrones, couches, fan-waving Nubians naked to the waist, groaning tables heaped with fruit and meats, and a plethora of nude serving girls.

The cocktail tables in front of the stage had been entirely taken over by reporters, cameramen, and TV technicians in the process of getting stony drunk, and the stage itself was garishly lit by bright shooting lights.

On one of the oversized thrones lolled Samuel T. Carruthers, the President of the United States. He was dressed in an Uncle Sam suit. Four hookers in red white and blue garter-belts and pasties managed to drape themselves over various portions of his anatomy. He sat there stroking the red phone to the button room with his fly open and his staff at half-mast.

"Somehow, Ivan," Boris said as they made their way across the casino floor towards the Presidential spectacle, "I don't think we're in Kansas."

"Sam Carruthers, how dare you!" the First Lady shouted before any more official greetings could be exchanged. "Get rid of these bimbos at once!"

"This is my new White House Staff!" the President said. "Candy is the Press Secretary, Lurleen is National Security Adviser, Marla is Chief of Staff, and Sue Ellen is my new expert in domestic affairs."

"You can't appoint a bunch of whores to be the White House Staff!" exclaimed the Vice President.

"Why not?" said the President. "Why should I be any different than my illustrious predecessors?"

Fast Eddie shrugged. For once he had to admit that the old goat had a point.

"Well if that's the White House Staff, then Bo Bob here is going to be my appointments secretary for the duration," the First Lady declared. "Come on, Bo Bob, you sit down here with me and peel me a grape."

"Well come on and get your ass up here, Pete!" the President told Pyotr Ivanovich after the American delegation had sorted out its seating protocol, patting the cushion of the adjoining throne. "These lovely ladies are ready for some stiff negotiation."

Ivan hesitated, holding the Bulgorny motionless, for he wouldn't give Pyotr Ivanovich more than an hour or two under those hot lights.

But Pyotr Ivanovich, it would seem, had developed some more ideas of his own, or perhaps the linkage with Moscow was not quite as static-free as promised with all these slot machines going off around the control console, for without any say-so on Ivan's part, the Bulgorny ascended to the stage and seated itself. Two of the prostitutes detached themselves from the President of the United States and turned their ministrations to the corpus of the Chairman of the Soviet Communist Party.

"Greetings to the Plenary Session of the Supreme Soviet of the decadent West," said the Chairman. "I wish to take this opportunity to propose a new five-year plan for drill press production."

Ivan and Boris collapsed behind a cocktail table and ordered a bottle of vodka, determined under these conditions to catch up to the American TV people, which, by the looks of them, would take some doing.

"Haw, haw! That's a good one!" the President exclaimed, slapping the Chairman on the back. "Well you've come to the right town to do it!"

"Mr. Chairman!"

"Mr. President!"

The cameras started rolling and the reporters were up and shouting, and all at once a press conference had begun.

"Mr. Chairman! Is it true that you're dead?"

"The Cult of Personality has been tossed in the dustbin of history and the Party machinery now functions as the Collective Leadership of the Brezhnev Doctrine."

"Mr. President, if the Israelis ignore the Korami ultimatum, and Koram defies the Israeli counter-ultimatum, how will you respond to the Soviet threat to launch a nuclear attack on the United States after the Israelis reply to the Korami response to their rejection of the original demands?"

"Huh?" said Samuel T. Carruthers. What was the flannel-mouthed sucker talking about? He turned to his National Security Adviser. "Lurleen," he whispered, "what you got to say about that?"

"Tell 'em you'll think about it, hon."

"I'll just have to think about it. . . ."

"But Mr. President, within 24 hours, Hassan al Korami will launch his nuclear missiles at Israel if they don't capitulate, and if the Israelis retaliate, the Russians will nuke the United States! Isn't that what this summit meeting is all about?"

"They will? It is?" the President said perplexedly. He turned to face the Chairman of the Central Committee, who sat beside him maintaining a perfect poker-face despite this awful revelation. "I thought you just came here to get some nookie, Pete!" he complained.

"Mr. Chairman, do you deny that the Soviet Union has threatened to launch an all-out nuclear attack on the United States if the Israelis attack the Sheikdom of Koram?"

"The peace-loving Soviet People will never be the first to use nuclear weapons nor will we be the last. Long live the threat of long-range economic planning and mutual short-arm inspection between our two great nations!"

"Does that mean that Hassan al Korami was lying then? Are you now willing to promise the American people that Koram is *not* under the Soviet nuclear umbrella?"

"Owing to technical difficulties with the Proton supply rocket, the entire production of the Kiev umbrella factory was mislabled as fertilizer and shipped to Poland in place of the missing consignment of Marxist-Leninist dialectic. The Ministry of Production assumes no responsibility for the ideological reliability of misuse of the product."

"Just a minute now, let's get one thing straight, I'm the President here, this is *my* party!" said the President. This was getting out of hand. This smartass Rooshian was doin' all the talking.

"You tell 'em, Mr. Prez," said the Presidential Press Secretary, nibbling at his ear.

"That's right!" said Uncle Sam. "Why don't you guys start asking *me* some questions?"

"Well then what will *you* do? Will you force the Israelis to capitulate to Koram? Will you pre-empt the Russians? Will you attack Koram before the deadline?"

Uncle Sam's patience was wearing quite thin. Koram, Israel, the frigging Rooshians, they were all a bunch of foreign troublemakers, weren't they? "I'll nuke 'em till they glow blue!" he shouted, waving the red command phone.

"Russia?"

"Koram?"

"Israel?"

"Nuke who?"

"Nuke *you*, Charlie!" the President said crossly. "That's the part I haven't figured out yet!"

Slowly, the tumult began to subside, as the three major network anchormen rose to their feet in unison, and with the cameras rolling, went after the President before the world like a tag-team of wrestlers.

"Mr. President, within 24 hours, World War III is likely to break out between the Soviet Union and the United States unless you and the Chairman can agree on steps to prevent it. . . ."

"The clock is ticking towards midnight. . . ."

"And there you sit before the American people with your fly open and the button in your hand telling us you'll think about it?"

"The American People have a right to know what you're going to do right now!"

"What am I going to do right now?" the President asked his Chief of Staff. She grabbed his crotch as she whispered in his ear.

The President grinned happily. "Right now," he said, "we're going to party!"

"Boy Mr. Prez, your friend is really weird," said the Presidential Press Secretary, emerging from the adjourning bedroom on wobbly knees, and plunking herself down on the bed between the National Security Adviser and the Chief of Staff, who lay there torpidly dragging on cigarettes. "He's already worn three of us out, and we *still* can't make him come or quit!"

"And he talks so funny all the time while he's doing it, like some kind of speed freak phonograph record whose needle keeps slipping. . . ."

"He's a Rooshian, isn't he?" said Uncle Sam who,

now quite thoroughly sated, was making an effort to pull up his pants and be Presidential.

The Domestic Affairs Adviser emerged from the other bedroom suddenly, ghostly pale and green around the gills. "Give me a' luud quick!" she moaned. "You're not going to believe this! It fell off!"

"You don't mean—"

"I am proud to award you all the order of Hero of Socialist Labor for your stakhanovite efforts in overfulfilling your production quotas by 23%!" declared Pyotr Ivanovich Bulgorny, clad only in his baggy blue boxer shorts and suit jacket.

As he regarded the Soviet Chairman standing there, grinning hideously, babbling communist propaganda, and with his pecker quite literally in his pocket, Sam Carruthers remembered what in his severe horniness he had forgotten, namely that Pyotr Ivanovich Bulgorny was in fact dead.

Now he finally noticed the green cast to the Soviet leader's skin, and once having observed that, he began to smell the faint putrid odor of deer that had been hung just a wee bit too high.

Well dead or not, thought Uncle Sam Carruthers, *he can't complain I didn't show him a good time*. And dead or not, he realized, Bulgorny was a man to be reckoned with, because dead or not, he had run the show over there in Russia for twenty years.

"Fair's fair, Pete," he said. "We've had our partying, and now, in the grand old American tradition, it's time to sit down and talk turkey. We can't let this little A-rab pissant pull this stuff on us! We gotta figure something out. Lurleen, give me my National Security Briefing."

"Say what, Mr. Prez?"

"Tell me what the hell is going on!"

"Well hon," said the National Security Adviser, as they all repaired to the couches in the suite's sitting room, "it's the same dumb game we girls get you johns to play with each other when we're feelin' mean. You know, some girl will get two big bruisers pissed off at each other, and then stand back and laugh while they punch each other out. Well you and old Pete are the two nuclear heavyweight champs of the world, right, and this Hassan al Korami is the mean little bitch."

"That's right," said the Domestic Affairs Adviser, "you jerks are letting him make monkeys out of you."

"Oh yeah?" said the President. "If you girls are so smart and Pete and I are so dumb, what would *you* do?"

The Presidential Press Secretary eased herself down in between the President and the Chairman and threw an arm around each of their shoulders.

"You guys don't *really* want to punch each other out, now do you?" she purred placatingly. "You're not really mad at *each other* now that you've partied together, now are you?"

"Right," said the National Security Adviser. "It's the creep that's been trying to get you to blow each other up so he can sit back and laugh who deserves to get his ticket punched, now isn't it?"

"What do you got to say to that, Pete?" the President asked the Chairman. "Makes sense to me. Why don't we just get together and stomp the little pissant flat?"

"Marxist-Leninist doctrine clearly states that a fool and his missiles are soon parted," agreed Pyotr Ivanovich. "But on the other hand, the long-range interests of the Soviet consumer class cannot be decoupled from the national paranoia trip of Soviet prestige. *Pravda* by definition must always speak the truth."

"He means he'll look like a wimp if he backs down," explained the Domestic Affairs Adviser.

"I guess I can see your point, Pete," the President was constrained to admit, seeing as how the poor bastard looked like a corpse with his pecker in his pocket already.

"Why don't you guys just go on *America Tonite* and yell at each other?" suggested the Presidential Press Secretary. "Pete here, instead of threatening to punch you out if your pal Israel punches out Hassan, threatens to punch you out if *you* punch out Hassan."

"Right hon," said the Chief of Staff, "and you can jump up and down and threaten to punch out Pete if he punches out your pal Israel."

"You both get to look like big tough guys, and your troublemaking pals can't complain you let them down. . . ."

"But instead of blowing up the world, we all just get to sit back and laugh while the smart-ass that tried to start the whole thing gets the shit beat out of him."

"You girls sure beat all hell out of my previous appointments," the President said with satisfaction. "What do you say, Pete? It's almost show time. . . ."

"Long live dialectic solidarity between the collective leadership of working class software and the social parasites of decadent western oligarchs!" the Chairman of the Central Committee of the Soviet Communist party declared, shaking hands with the President of the United States, and with that, the Summit Meeting was concluded, and the participants repaired to the casino floor.

America Tonite had been on the air for ten minutes, and Terry Tummler had already gone on and died with his opening monologue when the President of the United States, the Chairman of the Soviet Communist party, and four disheveled hookers finally shambled arm in arm onto the Emperor's box stage set and flopped themselves down under the hot shooting lights.

The primo front-row tables had been permanently commandeered by the by-now thoroughly sodden world press corps, and lousy tippers these freeloaders were too, to the dismay of the waitresses. Ivan and Boris managed to keep their front-row seats by offering hash joints and vodka to all and sundry, and the Vice President, the First Lady, and Captain Bo Bob Beauregard found themselves squeezed together at a small table next to the Russians.

The rest of the night club seats were jammed with a demographic cross-section of ordinary Americans who had come to get drunk, lose their money, and tell the folks back home that they had seen *America Tonite* Live in Vegas, and instead found themselves sitting through dumb jokes waiting for the heads of state to emerge from their seclusion with the agreement that would save the world from nuclear holocaust.

And now, at last, with the deadline for doomsday only hours away, what they, and the vast television audience beyond, got was a former used car salesman in an unzipped Uncle Sam suit and a blotchy green corpse with its pecker in its pocket being interviewed by Terry Tummler bulging out of a comic Roman toga surrounded by fagged-out hookers.

"Well it's a pleasure to welcome two such extinguished world leaders to *America Tonite*," said the genial Terry Tummler, "and I'm sure we'd all like to know whether your writers have come up with any better material than mine have tonight. I mean, when *I* lay a bomb, only my agent dies, but if you bomb out the whole show gets cancelled!"

"Don't get your balls in an uproar, Terry," the President said, waving the red phone. "Uncle Sam Carruthers takes no shit from Ivan the Terrible here!" He stuck his tongue out at Chairman Bulgorny and let fly a juicy Bronx cheer. "If you bomb Israel, Bluto," he told Pyotr Ivanovich with a wink, "old Popeye here will nuke Rooshia back into the stone age."

At this, even the unflappable Terry Tummler blanched, covering it as best he could with a sickly grin. "Well ... heh ... heh ... I guess these are the jokes, folks," he stammered.

"What have we *done*, Boris?" Ivan Igorovich Gornikov moaned drunkenly.

They had been unable to control the Bulgorny for hours, yet somehow Pyotr Ivanovich had managed to function autonomously. The randomized software had taken over entirely. There was nothing in any hacker's theory to account for it. If he were not a good atheist, Ivan would have crossed himself.

Come to think of it, he thought, making the motions, *better safe than sorry*.

"What about you, Chairman Bulgorny?" Terry Tummler burbled. "Got any hot new projects?"

Some sapient spirit seemed to peer out from behind the glass eyes of the corpse of Pyotr Ivanovich Bulgorny, which certainly was beginning to look a little worse for wear. When it spoke, Ivan wondered whether some chance conjunction between programming fragments and bits and pieces of randomized old speeches had not conjured the true spirit of the bureaucratic socialist state, the voice of pure dialectical determinism itself, the ghost in the Party machinery.

"The peace-loving malingerers and hooligans of the Red Army will not stand idly by while neo-colonialist war criminals in high Pentagon circles vaporize reactionary Third World criminal elements," Pyotr Ivanovich Bulgorny declared forcefully.

"Oh yeah?" roared the President, mugging at the audience. "So's yer mother!"

"Now guys, come on, we've still got an hour of air time to fill, I mean, if we have World War III now, all that's left backstage to go on afterward is a chimp act and a gypsy violinist!"

"Well I'm ready to just sit back, open a six-pack, and watch the big fight on television if he is," said the President, leaning back, throwing one arm around a hooker, and elbowing the dead Soviet Chairman in the ribs with the other.

"If our illustrious allies wish to beat the shit out of each other," agreed Pyotr Ivanovich, "then both the long-range interest of the international working class and the spirit of non-interference in the internal sporting events of friendly buffer states require that our two great peoples do nothing to interfere with their right to express their national identities outside in the alley."

"You tell 'em, Pyotr Ivanovich!" exclaimed Ivan. "Ah Boris, does not such sterling cybernetic leadership make you proud to be a member of the Russian Computer Underground?"

"Cowards! Camel-suckers! Perfidious Infidels!" roared Hassan al Korami when he heard the news bulletin on K-RAB. How dare the scorpions he had sealed together in a bottle refuse to fight each other to the death for his delectation?

"No more Sheik Nice Guy!" he screamed, storming into the control van where his missile controllers sat before their screens and joysticks ready to play *Cruise Missile Commander*.

"Launch all our missiles the moment an Israeli plane crosses our borders," said the Lion of the Desert. "But you will fire only *three* missiles at Israel. The ones we reserved for Beersheba and Eilat will

instead be diverted to attack the American and Soviet fleets in the Mediterranean."

He rubbed his hands together, sucking on the nearest hookah. "Let's see the two arms of Satanic modernism talk their way out of *that* one!" he cackled
maniacally, drooling smoke and spittle.

"Pyotr Ivanovich's nose has fallen off!" moaned
Boris.

It was true. The Chairman was visibly beginning
to decompose under the shooting lights for all the
world to see. His face had turned a sickly brownish
green and gas bubbles pocked the surface of its var-
nish. Now the nose had melted like a piece of overripe cheese and fallen into his lap, exposing wet
white bone.

Armand Deutcher sweated nervously before his news
monitors in the control room of the Rockin' Voice of
the A-rabs. An ABC camera satellite was trying to
focus a clear picture of a flight of objects proceeding
due south across Saudi territory from Israel, on their
way to Koram. At the same time, Israeli TV was
broadcasting *its* satellite coverage of the Korami cruise
missiles waiting on the desert sands. Meanwhile, one
of the other two American networks was running an
old movie, while the third dominated the ratings
with *America Tonite* as never before. Radio Moscow
was playing patriotic music.

Now the NBC camera zoomed in tight on the for-
mation of Israeli aircraft. Alors, they were neither
Slings of David missiles nor fighter-bombers of the
Israeli Air Force, but a few dozen cheap obsolescent
light-weight drones powered by lawnmower engines!

"Bedouin spotters report a vast armada of Israeli
aircraft crossing our sacred borders, O Lion of the

Desert," declared Hassan al Korami's radio operator. "From horizon to horizon, the sky is black with F-21s, SuperKfirs, and supersonic cruise missiles!"

"Launch all missiles!" shrieked Hassan the Assassin, biting through the stem of his hookah in his ecstasy and spewing splinters of bloody ivory.

Hurriedly, Armand Deutcher readied his own control console, and ordered K-RAB off the air so he could patch it into the Rockin' Voice of the A-rab's monster transmitter.

For the Israelis could have only one thing in mind by sending in this handful of old junk instead of a sophisticated all-out non-nuclear attack force.

Thanks to the crazy American President and the rapidly decomposing corpse of the Soviet Chairman, his own plan was now back on course.

The Israelis obviously intended to provoke Hassan into firing his missiles first. Even now their own satellite cameras were showing the world five rusty F-111s wobbling shakily into the air then roaring off at supersonic speed right down on the deck in the general direction of Israel.

And, even as Armand had expected, the NBC satellite camera now showed the Israeli drones self-destructing just inside Korami territory.

Wonderful! Soon the Israeli controllers would take command of the Korami cruise missiles. They'd drop four of them harmlessly into the ocean off camera, and then use their satellite cameras to show the fifth one veering crazily off course and taking out Mecca.

Then they could nuke Koram out of existence while even their Arab enemies applauded, and when the dust cleared, they would sit astride the entire Middle East after having shot their way into the club as a nuclear superpower.

Or so they thought.

But Armand Deutcher had much better uses to put that cruise missile to than starting a nuclear potlatch, which, if it didn't escalate into World War III, would result in a Middle Eastern Pax Judaeaica which would severely suppress arms sales for decades to come. His multi-billion-franc smart-money bet was on a far more profitable nuclear option. . . .

A battery of monitors had been dragged out onto the stage set of *America Tonite*, and Terry Tummler, the President, the Chairman, and the hookers of the White House Staff sat there watching TV on camera, including, bizarrely enough, the live coverage of themselves watching it.

"Hey . . . heh. . . ." burbled Terry Tummler. "Looks as if the boys in the bedsheets have launched their missiles. . . . Got anything funny to say about that, Mr. Prez?"

"I'll lay 6 to 5 against any of them hitting Israel," said Sam Carruthers.

"You're faded, Mr. Prez," said the National Security adviser.

"I'll lay even money them Israelis clean old Hassan's clock in the next twenty minutes," declared the Chief of Staff. "Any takers?"

"The peace-loving revanchist vanguard of the Soviet People accepts your challenge to make a fast ruble," declared Pyotr Ivanovich Bulgorny, whose stainless steel teeth and bony jaw were now clearly showing where more rotting flesh had fallen away from his face.

Israeli TV now made a great show of having its satellite cameras lose track of the wobbly F-111s as the five Korami cruise missiles peeled away from each other. On came the Israeli Prime Minister with a terse announcement.

"The Skeikdom of Koram has launched an unprovoked nuclear attack on the State of Israel. The Israeli Defense Forces will confine themselves to a non-nuclear counterstrike in the interests of world peace. Unless, of course, this maniac Hassan al Korami should actually manage to hit anything with his nuclear missiles, in which case, we shall naturally be forced to nuke Koram out of existence in the interests of Biblical justice."

Armand Deutcher had the Korami missiles on his radar screen now. Three of them were zigging and zagging more or less in the direction of Israel, but the other two were making a bee-line across the Mediterranean towards the Russian and American fleets! Good Lord, if the Israelis didn't dump those two missiles *tout suite,* all bets were off!

"What is happening?" demanded Hassan al Korami, chewing the soggy end of his spliff to bits, as his controllers twiddled furiously with their joysticks. On their monitor screens, fuzzy purple airplanes were bobbing and weaving over cartoon landscapes dotted with medieval castles, fire-breathing reptiles, and giant apes.

"We have racked up three million points already!" one of the controllers reassured him. "According to the control computers, we are approaching the arcade record!"

One by one, the blips dropped off Armand Deutcher's radar screen, as the Israeli controllers seized control of the Korami cruise missiles and ditched them into the sea. Now there was only one F-111 still on the screen, headed in the general direction of Tel Aviv. Suddenly it veered off, did a ragged one-eighty, and set off on a new tack to the south.

"Well that's four out of five into the drink, isn't

it?" said Terry Tummler. "Maybe there won't be a fireworks act before the last commercial after all. . . ."

"It ain't over till the Fat Lady sings," said the President. "What do you say, Pete, will you give me three to one on at least one Big One going off before the show is over?"

But Pyotr Ivanovich Bulgorny sat there silently, his expression rendered all the more unreadable by the fact that most of his face had now fallen away, revealing a gleaming wet skull with two glass eyes set in its sockets, a hideous stainless steel grin, and shards and tatters of shriveled skin and decomposing flesh clinging to the bone.

The Israeli satellite cameras had now managed to "find" the errant F-111.

"The last Korami cruise missile has now been spotted over Saudi Arabia and headed in the general direction of Mecca!" declared the Israeli TV announcer with a great show of outraged horror as the rusty old plane jerked into focus buzzing low over the head of a camel caravan.

"Whatever this maniac Hassan al Korami is up to, and whatever misunderstandings may have existed between our two great peoples in the past, the Government of Israel wishes to assure our Arab friends that we will regard any Korami nuclear attack on their Holy City as an attack on our own, and will retaliate accordingly with the full resources of our nuclear arsenal in the Spirit of Camp David."

Armand Deutcher keyed in the override command, which went out over the mighty Rockin' Voice of the Arabs to the lamprey circuit he had planted on the control chips that the Israelis had secreted in the phony remote control machinery.

Reaching for his joystick, he bent the F-111's course slowly towards the west, fighting to turn the jury-rigged cruise missile around against the unexpectedly stiff resistance of the Israeli controllers.

On all the control screens, the same little purple airplane was weaving among giant black pterodactyls and laser-firing flying saucers towards a huge dim black castle at the top of the screen. Robots and centipedes poured out of it and began firing frisbees and lightning-bolts.

"A million bonus points for getting the Black Castle!" exclaimed one of the controllers.

Hassan al Korami squinted at the lettering on the screen.

Where in Israel was "Mordor"?

"Merde!" grunted Armand Deutcher, stirring sweatily at his joystick.

All three American networks now showed the F-111 stunting crazily over Mecca as Deutcher fought the Israelis for control.

It buzzed low over the bazaar, sending goods and awnings flying with its supersonic shockwave, zigged and zagged among the sunbleached buildings, suddenly shot straight up, then dropped down again and came within ten feet of taking out the Kaaba, before pulling out into another steep climb, and then—

—And then all at once Deutcher had it. He managed to bring the jury-rigged cruise missile back down on the deck and bend its course more or less to the north as its wings beginning to develop an all-too-familiar flutter. . . .

"Son of a bitch, look at that boy *fly!*" Bo Bob Beauregard exclaimed admiringly.

More monitors had been set out in Caligula's Court for the benefit of *America Tonite's* live audience in order to hype the action, for by now even the tables and slot machines had been entirely abandoned as everyone in the casino watched the network satellite cameras track the Korami cruise missile upon whose eventual destination thousands of bets now hung.

"Wow," said the President, excitedly stroking both his red phone and his dong, "this is just like the fourth quarter of the Superbowl!"

The F-111 was putting on quite a show.

Jerking and bobbing about twenty feet above the Mediterranean like a drunken dragonfly, its wings shaking and juddering, the rusty old jet missed a supertanker by inches, buzzed a cruiseliner, decapitated a seagull, and then came in low over the crowded harbor of St. Tropez, France.

It weaved crazily among the pleasurecraft, scattering waterskiers, starlets, beach bums, and Greek shipping tycoons, headed straight for the line of yachts lining the primo beachfront property, and then suddenly managed to veer off at the last moment, east along the Cote d'Azure in the general direction of Monaco.

It wobbled along the coastline until the prime beachfront real estate was replaced by rocky cliffs falling directly to the sea and then—

—the right wing of the F-111 sheered off and went sailing away like a kite as the plane went into a steep left turn—

—it skittered crazily across the sky and smashed directly into the seacliff with a blinding flash—

And the satellite cameras pulled back to a medium shot of a mushroom pillar cloud blossoming evilly on the southern coast of France.

A great groan of dismay rose up from the casino floor. No one had any money riding on *France*!

"All bets are off!"

"The hell they are! They didn't hit Israeli, did they?"

"But they didn't hit Mecca either!"

"Fork over!"

"Pay up!"

"Screw you!"

"Tu madre tambien!"

Only Pyotr Ivanovich displayed admirable slavic stoicism during this unseemly tumult. There he sat, silent and imperturbable, as fistfights broke out among the gamblers, and the American President masturbated nervously with his red phone.

Indeed the Chairman had not moved or spoken since the flesh had melted from his bones revealing the death's head grin within, as if he had become embarrassed by his poor appearance on television, or more likely, Ivan Igorovich Gornikov thought, as if his melting gush of body fluids had finally shorted the whole mess out.

But now a tremor went through the Bulgorny and the jaws of the skull clacked open and stuck, revealing the speaker grid within stuck like an overlarge morsel in its skeletal throat.

A horrible ear-killing shriek of static and feedback stopped everyone in their tracks and thin tendrils of smoke began steaming out of the rotting corpse's ears.

"... Brak! ... Scree! ... Wonk! ..." the Chairman of the Soviet Communist Party observed forcefully in a crackling metallic robot voice. "The dialectical requirements of socialist realist esthetics require a beginning, a middle, and an end to all cautionary Russian folk-wisdom in keeping with the Marxist-Leninist principle of from each according to his assholery, to each according to his greed."

"Are you saying what I think you're saying, Pete?" said the American President.

"You can't make a revolutionary omelet without breaking heads," Pyotr Ivanovich pointed out. "When confronted with homicidal reactionary maniacs and tinpot nuclear pipsqueaks, all progressive peace-loving peoples must reach for their revolvers."

"Like the man says," agreed the National Security Adviser, as she soothed the President's throbbing dork, "nuke 'em till they glow blue!"

"Oh boy!" said Bo Bob Beauregard. "Do we get to take out the Rooshians now?"

"*The Rooshians?*" the President exclaimed. "Shit no, us and the Rooshians are going to bomb the bejesus out of that wormy little bugger Hassan al Korami! Why the hell should we be nuking each other with maniacs like that running around loose! Isn't that right, Pete?"

"As Chairman of the Central Committee software of the Party machinery, I hereby declare the extension of the Brezhnev Doctrine to encompass peaceful co-preemption with the United States of all reactionary Third World autocrats who try to join the club."

Armand Deutcher, sipping cognac, puffing away at his huge Havana cigar, leaned back in his chair, and watched the grotesque spectacle that all world news networks were now carrying with the wry amusement of a connoisseuer of political buffoonery who no longer had any investments hanging on the outcome.

There for all the world to see was the President of the United States with a prostitute sitting on his lap and the red telephone cradled against his cheek, and there was the Chairman of the Soviet Communist Party, a rapidly-decomposing corpse out of some cheap Hollywood horror movie, with the last tatters of rotten flesh sliding off his skull and into his lap, and the smoke of burning electrical insulation pouring out of his ears.

Vraiment, thought Armand, *as the anglophones have it, one picture is indeed worth a thousand words!*

"This is the President of the United States. . ."

"And the Personality Cult of the Party Machinery of the Union of Soviet Socialist Republics. . ."

"My friend the Chairman here may be a moldy corpse. . ."

"And Uncle Sam may embody the final pussy-obsessed imperialism of the stewed, screwed, and tattooed West on its way to the fertilizer production quota of history. . ."

"But even a corpse and a sex maniac know better than to let any little pissant who's even moldier and crazier than we are try to get his dirty little mitts on one of these red telephones again!"

"We will now bury an object lesson in the historical dialectic of socialist surrealism and peace-loving ass-kicking so that any revanchist reactionary oligarch with delusions of nuclear destiny will think twice before pissing us off again!"

"Go get 'em, Bo Bob!" the President ordered, and collapsed in sweet ecstasy.

"Overfulfill your nuclear production quotas where it will do the most historical good," said the Chairman of the Central Committee as sparks shot out of his rictus grin, and he collapsed into a pile of old bones and burned-out circuitry.

The Black Castle was spewing forth bats and rockets and flying saucers and yellow munching circles in desperation now, for the little purple airplane had almost reached its target!

"Die, Zionist Dogs, die American Imperialists, die Russian Infidels, die Corrupt Modernism, die O Great Satan!" shrieked Hassan al Korami as a huge dark shadow shape with a fiery grin arose out of the Black Castle. "Fire! Fire!"

The controllers pressed their joystick buttons.

The Great Satan laughed.

"YOU LOSE, SUCKER, DON'T TRY TO PLAY AGAIN," said the words that appeared on the screen just before a brilliant white light exploded.

Fast Eddie Braithwaite, President of the United States, gazed expansively out at Washington from the helicopter carrying him to his first weekend at Camp David.

When twenty ten-megaton American warheads and twenty ten-megaton Soviet warheads had slammed into the Sheikdom of Koram as an object lesson to nuclear upstarts in the name of newfound Soviet-American solidarity, Uncle Sam Carruthers had been a hero for a brief moment.

But 400 megatons on an area the size of Los Angeles had been more than enough to shatter the collapsing rock-dome above the depleted oil table, and the entire skeikdom had plunged with a fiery splash into the oil pool beneath, setting it ablaze.

When the mushrooms clouds cleared, there was nothing left but a huge cauldron of burning oil where the Sheikdom of Koram had been.

While this made for some spectacular footage on the evening news, when it became apparent that the fire was spreading like termites in balsa wood throughout the Middle Eastern oil fields, that was finally enough to convince the powers that be to give Samuel T. Carruthers the hook, and send him off to get his ashes hauled on an endless Second Honeymoon in Atlantic City.

Anyone who was *that* bad for business was, ipso facto, insane.

It was a good life being a member of the new Soviet elite in the dawn of the Moscow Spring, a life of luxury apartments, dachas in the country, and

Mercedes-Benzes, in a Russia freed from the dead hand of the moribund Party Machinery.

In the revision of Marxist-Leninist doctrine which had been forced upon the Central Committee with the passage of the unifying figure of Pyotr Ivanovich Bulgorny from the scene, the Russian Computer Underground had emerged from the electronic catacombs as the only force capable of saving Mother Russia from total economic chaos.

The Communist Party and its functionaries had been retired honorably to the status of a collective royal family to preside at state funerals and make speeches atop Lenin's tomb on May Day and the Anniversary of the Revolution, and the practical matters of necessity had been put into the hands of the Computer Underground, who were the only people capable of keeping the newly decentralized and computerized Soviet economy going.

There were even those who called this the perfection of Communism, since the State was indeed in the process of withering away.

But sometimes, late at night, Ivan Igorovich Gornikov experienced a perverse nostalgic twinge for The Bad Old Days of Pyotr Ivanovich Bulgorny, even as his parents had come to consider the memory of Stalin something of a sainted monster once he was safely dead and buried.

Say what you like, dead or not, the noble Pyotr Ivanovich was responsible for Ivan's present good fortune, and for the present Soviet-American detente! There was a man who, whatever his shortcomings, would live in history!

Besides, now that the KGB no longer had a customer like Hassan al Korami to soak, the filthy capitalist roaders had jacked the price of hash in Moscow three hundred percent!

* * *

"Ca va, Zvi?"

"Business, believe me, could be a lot better," Zvi Bar David complained. "You were shrewd to get out and into real estate when you did, Armand. Ever since the Russians and Americans so forcefully discouraged Third World customers from seeking state of the art, all we can move are small arms and cheap old junk."

"Don't worry, Zvi," Armand Deutcher said expansively. "Someone will start a nice little war somewhere, they always do."

"Easy for you to say, Armand, look how you've made out!"

"I'm certainly not complaining!" Deutcher admitted.

There he sat on the terrace of his palatial mansion atop the highest point of the rimwall, looking down and out across the artificial bay carved out of the seacliff when he had brought the F-111 down on this formerly empty piece of formerly worthless coast.

Land he had previously acquired for a relative song.

Ah, but now a gleaming beach of pulverized and certified non-radioactive glass ran around the noble curve of the bomb crater, crowded with sunbathers, and lined with brand-new luxury hotels, casinos, and marinas choked with yachts. Quaint age-old streets lined with souvenir shops, boutiques and fancy restaurants had been laid out to climb the crater wall to the heights, and what wasn't a deluxe emporium was a condo building or townhouse as the multibillion-franc development glittered and glitzed up the cliff like a Gucci amoeba.

And Armand Deutcher owned every square centimeter of the land it was built on, renting it out to his glitterati serfs for a third of the take.

"To tell the truth, Armand," said Zvi Bar David,

"how well do you sleep at night? Almost we had World War III, and all for a petty real estate deal!"

"Come come, Zvi," Deutcher said goodnaturedly. "*This* you call this a *petty* real estate deal?"

"But what about your social conscience, Armand?"

"Pure as the driven snow!" Armand Deutcher declared. "Am I not the secret hero of the present era of easing international tensions? Thanks to me, no tin-pot little maniac will ever dare to acquire nuclear weapons agan, the United States has accepted a black man as President, Israel and the Arabs have made peace, and the Russians have been forced to take care of business."

"True," admitted Bar David. "But on the other hand, an entire nation has been been expunged from history, and the Middle Eastern oilfields are on fire."

"As for the first," said Armand Deutcher, "would you have preferred World War III to World War Last?"

"And as for the second?"

Deutcher shrugged philosophically. "As for the second," he said, "I'm already diversified into coal and horse-breeding, Zvi, and I strongly advise you to do the same."

The survival of any homogenous group depends ultimately on its females—their ability to survive and rear young. Today in England, the Netherlands, West Germany, women sit in the tiny village that is Europe and discuss strategy for battling the Bomb. Their pickets and demonstrations are instinctive reactions that transcend politics: it is self-protection on a very basic level. Flanders Field would not survive a new world war.

Nor, perhaps, would anywhere else on Earth.

The "nuclear winter" theory has been hotly resisted ever since it was born. That was in 1975, when the National Academy of Sciences published "Long-Term Worldwide Effects of Multiple Nuclear Weapons Detonations"—a study nobody wanted to hear but everybody quoted. More evidence—and more controversy—sprang from a study commissioned several years later by the Swedish environmental journal Ambio.

There are many unknowns in the nuclear equation, but computer models show that the Earth's climate will suffer some effects at almost any level of nuclear combat. A worst-case scenario shows ground bursts generating enough dust and debris to shroud the Earth for months, even years.

In all likelihood, the parameters of a nuclear winter will remain a mystery until the war that begins one is fought. Least knowable of all is how—even if—the men and women who survive will assemble a new order. For that will be a challenge not for computers and theoreticians, but for the human spirit.

with a hundred swords here says most of the

WHEN WINTER ENDS

Michael P. Kube-McDowell

I.

It was just 10 A.M. when Daniel Yates drove his four-year-old Honda into the Larchmont Executive Pavilion's parking lot, but he was already tired.

His day had begun five hours earlier, with a "from our affiliate in Baltimore" appearance on the *Today* show to debate a utility spokesman on the question of restarting Three Mile Island Unit 2. When that three-minute free-for-all was over, he drove 70 miles to the Choptank River under a sky dawning grey and gloomy. There he climbed into a Boston Whaler to inspect the heavy-metal sampling buoys in the channel downstream from the new Noble Electroplating plant at Cambridge.

By the time he returned to the office plaza in Glen Burnie, the dark sheet of clouds had begun to deliver on their threat, and the only open parking spaces were at the farthest corner from the six-story structure's entrance. As he dashed across the lot through the drizzle, dodging between cars and dancing around puddles, Yates wondered why he had rejected the perquisite of a reserved space.

I could have parked there, he thought as he left the blacktop for the sidewalk.

There was occupied by a blue sedan with U.S. Government plates and "Department of the Air Force" stenciled on the driver's door. The sight brought a reflexive scowl to Yates' face. But since three other organizations shared the building with Yates' Life Studies Foundation, he spent no time wondering why the sedan was there.

Then he entered the LSF suite and saw a uniformed man standing in the waiting area—and the presence of the car in what was always the first spot to fill each morning set warning bells ringing. Yates was no student of military insignia, but he knew at a glance that the visitor was high-ranking.

Jeanne, the LSF receptionist, waved Yates toward her desk.

"Who the hell is that?"

"Major General Rutledge. He's been here since eight, waiting to see you and Bernadette."

"What does an Air Force general want here?"

"He hasn't said."

"Bernie's not here?"

"She's waiting in your office. The general refused to talk to her without you there," she explained.

"I'll bet that sat well with her."

"She asked to see you for a minute before I show General Rutledge in."

Yates glanced over his shoulder at the visitor and frowned. "Give us five."

"You picked a great day to waltz in late," Bernadette Stowe complained, coming to her feet as Yates entered the office.

"I went out to Choptank to check on the water

monitors. One of them went off-line during the night, and I wanted to check for tampering," Yates said defensively, dropping his six-foot frame into a chair.

Stowe swept her flowing black hair back off her shoulders with a flick of her hands, an idiosyncratic gesture that told Yates of her anxiety. "I know, I know. I just don't like keeping generals cooling their heels."

"He can stay out there a week as far as I'm concerned. What's this about? Did we tread on any hobnailed feet? Who is he?"

Stowe clucked. "Didn't Jeanne tell you? That's Jack Rutledge—Major General Jacob Rutledge, number one in the Air Force's Logistics Command."

Yates lifted his hands. "Means nothing to me. Know anything else about him?"

"As it happens, I had some time to dig a little. Graduated the Academy in '67 and served two years with a C-130 wing in 'Nam. Came back and taught at Sheppard AFB in Wichita Falls for six years. He applied to NASA as a Shuttle pilot candidate in '78 but was turned down—not enough hours in high-performance jets. Wing commander in the Central American campaign."

A cold look passed over Yates' face. "That's enough for me."

"He's been at Logistics five years next month. Rep is that he's smart and tough, not flashy, not overly ambitious, a good administrator."

"I didn't hear anything in that that would bring him to our doorstep."

Stowe shook her head. "Me neither. But I bet he'll tell us if we give him the chance."

Maj. Gen. Jacob "Jack" Rutledge walked into the conference room with the feline grace and carefully measured movements Yates associated with military automata. There was no wasted motion, no nuance that spelled personality. *Here's your dehuman syndrome, Montagu—the military bureaucrat, the ultimate example.*

"I must apologize again for the delay, General," Stowe said when all were seated.

You don't have to do any such damn thing, Yates thought. *Not to him.*

"Your office gave us no notice you were coming, and it's not uncommon for one or the both of us to be out at a field site," she went on.

Rutledge acknowledged and dismissed the apology with a bare nod. "I have a project for you," he said.

Yates whipped forward in his seat and rested his folded hands on the table. "Not interested."

Stowe placed a restraining hand on Yates' arm and dug her fingernails in for emphasis. "What Dr. Yates means is that, in the past, we've found that the military's needs and our expertise had a very low correlation. We'll be happy to hear you out."

You'll be happy—not me. What the hell are you thinking? Yates demanded with a sidewise glance. When Stowe ignored him, he shook his arm free but said nothing.

"The project is very simple to define but may be rather complex to execute," Rutledge said. "I want you to devise a way to assist the survivors of a nuclear war. I'll provide you with the attack model— how many weapons, what yields, what targets, what coefficient of success. You figure out what conditions the survivors will be living under. You figure out what they'll need most to guarantee their survival and how to get it to them."

Yates twisted in his chair and dug in his pocket. "If you want to do something to guarantee survival, try this," he said in a hard-edged voice, and slid a green plastic card across the table.

Politely, Rutledge picked up the card and glanced at it. Yates followed his eyes as he read:

Daniel R. Yates, Ph. D.
Atlantic States District Supervisor
People's Disarmament Alliance

Rutledge slid the card back. "I'm aware of your leanings. I trust you are realist enough to treat seriously the possibility that disarmament will never take place."

"And that nuclear war will?" Yates said challengingly.

"Yes," Rutledge said quietly, meeting Yates' eyes. "That's what this project is about."

"What do you mean, you know my leanings?"

"Just that. I wouldn't have told you even as much as I have already without knowing a great deal about both of you, both the important and the insignificant." A hint of what might have been amusement appeared played briefly on Rutledge's lips. "For instance, though I have never been in either of your offices, I can tell you that Dr. Stowe has all four of her diplomas and most of her awards displayed on the walls, while Dr. Yates' equally impressive credentials are packed away somewhere—I wouldn't be surprised if even he didn't know where they were."

"Is that sort of trivia supposed to impress us?" Yates asked.

"It's not trivia," Rutledge corrected. "As for impressing you, I don't care what you think of me. In point of fact, I have a fair idea of what Dr. Yates thinks of me. When I said I knew his leanings, I meant all of them."

Yates scowled.

"That doesn't matter," Rutledge continued. "What matters is that you're one of the very few organizations capable of pulling off this project under its very tight time constraints."

"Meaning you need to spend your budget surplus before the end of the fiscal year?" Yates sniped.

Rutledge studied the younger man for a long moment before answering. "When you work for us, you adopt our calendar and our timetable," he said finally, with a note of irritation in his voice.

"These survivors—" Stowe interjected. "We'll have to know where they'll be at the time of attack."

Rutledge's gaze flicked from Yates' unfriendly face to Stowe's hopeful one. "You misunderstand me, Dr. Stowe. I'm not trying to assure that any particular person or group of people survives."

"Not even your own family?" Yates asked cuttingly.

Rutledge answered without emotion. "Since we live midway between Bolling and Andrews, it's unlikely my wife and I will survive a general nuclear war."

"Then you're talking about assisting the random survivors?" Stowe asked.

"Yes."

"That is a more interesting challenge."

"Dammit, Bernie, don't encourage him." Yates turned to Rutledge. "General, let me put this to you in words of one syllable. If you're serious about this, then I don't want to help you. If you're not, then I don't want to waste my time."

Rutledge raised an eyebrow questioningly.

"Let's say you are serious," Yates went on, "that for some unnatural reason you're really concerned about the fact that this nuclear war you've been building for and planning for thirty years would fry and poison a billion or so people and leave any survivors wishing they weren't. Let's say we're unspeakably clever and devise some way to do what you describe. I figure all we've done is make your kind a little more confident that nuclear war would be winnable and a little more willing to choose that option."

He leaned forward in his chair and slapped the table for emphasis. "On the other hand, if you're not serious, then all we're doing is wasting tax money and fattening a file somewhere in the Pentagon when we could be working on something that matters."

"I see," Rutledge said, and began to rise.

Stowe stood up abruptly. "General, you've heard Dr. Yates' opinion, but you haven't heard the firm's decision. If you could excuse us for a few minutes—"

"Done. But I need your answer today. This whole project has to be finished within six months." He glanced from Stowe to Yates and back again. "If you can pull it off on time, we won't have any problems between us in any other area."

Stowe sat on the edge of Yates' desk and gestured at the bare wall. "So—do you know where your diplomas are?"

"No," Yates said gruffly.

"Think it means anything?"

"Hell, I don't know. That's not what you whisked me out of there for."

"No." She hesitated. "Look, Daniel, I had a couple of hours this morning to think over the idea of working for the Pentagon, and I think we should take this project."

Yates shook his head vigorously. "I don't trust him. I don't really believe he's here for what he says."

"What would he want?"

"I don't know," Yates said angrily. "To compromise us somehow."

"We've done nothing to cross them." She looked down, rubbing the back of one hand with her fingertips. "If the money's real, he's real."

"I don't want their money."

Stowe sighed expressively. "That's all well and good as an ideal—if that's what it is."

"What do you mean?"

"Deanna—"

"She has nothing to do with this."

"I'll take you at your word. Even so—I know we set out to dedicate ourselves to the nuclear freeze, environmental issues, hazardous waste. But you know, there's a lot more money on the other side. I don't think what he's talking about would compromise us. In a way, it meshes with what we do."

"How so?"

"Oh, Dan—I know you've got no love for the military. But can't you see? War is the premise, not the point."

"I know that," Yates said, throwing up his hands in surrender. "But there's still something wrong about his being here. Why come to us? They've got their own thinktanks, their own internal study teams. We're definitely off the beaten track."

"Maybe he is, too."

"What do you mean?"

"Well—I wonder how many generals go out to interview contractors and let contracts."

"You think he's freelancing? Wants to keep this quiet?"

"Could be."

Yates pursed his lips. "It's not like the Air Force to start thinking about consequences. Or to have a conscience," he agreed with venomous sarcasm.

"But one officer could. Even a major general."

"I doubt it," Yates said stiffly. "And taking Pentagon money is still wrong for us."

"I don't think so. Not when I have trouble meeting the payroll practically every month."

"I'll bet his prying told him that, too." There was a long silence in which he avoided her eyes. "We've always found a way to pay the bills, or to deal with not paying them. That's the wrong reason for us to take this."

She pounced on that. "What's the right reason?"

Yates blew an exasperated sigh into one cupped hand.

"Listen, Dan—I think he wants exactly what he says he wants. And it's something we should want, too. You know the state of Civil Defense in this country. We like to build the weapons but we don't like to think about the consequences of using them, at least not in human terms. This is a departure from form, and we ought to encourage it. Otherwise we're in the position of refusing to allow the leopard to change its spots."

"I don't want any part of it."

"You won't have, except to sit in on a few meetings for appearances. I'll handle the gruntwork."

Yates studied the earnestness in her expression. "You really want this?"

"Yes. Like you wanted the Consumers Power audit. Because I'd feel badly about turning him away and it not being done, or being done by someone for whom the money is the right reason."

Yates rested his chin on steepled fingers. "All right," he said finally. "You can have your project."

The contract arrived the next day by Air Force courier, who first obtained their signatures on a security warrant, then turned over a magshielded box and a check for $250,000.

"This isn't like them, to move this quickly," Yates said suspiciously when the courier left. "What happened to competitive bidding, supplier certification—the bureaucratic manna?"

"Hiring a consultant isn't like buying B-2 bombers," Stowe rejoined.

"Apparently not."

The box contained a DOD Standard Data Format diskette and a brief note from Rutledge:

Disk password = Damocles. Do it right.

Yates shrugged. "Let's take a look."

"Let me get a notepad."

They sat side by side at a single VDT and watched as Rutledge's war model unrolled:

ACCESS RESTRICTED TO CLEARANCE
LEVEL II AND ABOVE
DO NOT COPY

DOD 345.33.45-6
-SUMMARY OF SCENARIO-
INITIAL ATTACK: U.S.S.R, counterdefense. Targets: Vandenberg, KSC, Unified Space Command. Space Operations Center, High Frontier Command, High Frontier tiers 1 + 2. Mode: Ground targets 1 ea. SS-N-6 Sawfly submarine launched ballistic missles, total yield approximately 3 megatons (MT), orbital targets non-nuclear ASMs. Warning time: <6 minutes. Coefficient of success: 1.0 ground, 1.0 orbital.

"The man has a nasty imagination," Yates said with a shake of the head. "With the subs that close to the coast, that's practically a sneak attack."

"Which means we'll have to launch on warning," Stowe said. "They can't get Presidential authorization in 6 minutes."

Yates tapped a pencil rhythmically against the desk. "I'd bet we stand pat. Three SLBMs can't threaten the ICBM force. We won't know whether the Russians are just taking out the High Frontier defense or setting the stage for a real attack."

RESPONSE 1: U.S., counterforce. Targets: space launch centers at Baikonur, Volgograd, Northern Cosmodrome; submarines on station off East (4) and West Coast (2); Salyut 12. Mode: Ground targets 1 ea Minuteman III ICBM 3 × 170 kiloton MIRV, submarines P-3C Orion/ASW, orbital target F-15 Eagle/ASM. Time frame: within 45 minutes of confirmation of attack by IR satellite or equivalent intelligence. Coefficient of success: 0.85 land, 0.62 sea.

"Not on warning," Yates said with a touch of childish pride.

"No," Stowe said quietly through her folded hands. "They're allowing just enough time to get the antisubmarine forces in place."

"Still—the retaliation is less than I would have thought. We're still under 20 megatons. And there's no escalation. Each takes out the other's spaceflight capacity. What's the nuclear winter threshold?"

"A hundred megatons. I'll bet it doesn't stop there," Stowe said gloomily.

"Don't take it so damn seriously. "It's just a study model."

RESPONSE 2: U.S.S.R, counterforce. Targets: all SAC, ICBM, GLCM squadrons, airburst. Mode: 200 SS-N-6 Sawfly SLBM (1 MT), 200 SS-18 ICBM (20 MT), 200 SS-19 (66 × 570 KT). Time frame: launch on confirmation of Minutemen III launch, impact 6-20 minutes. Coefficient of success: 0.8.

"Looks like they were ready to go the wall and we weren't," Yates observed.

"It's too late to get the cruise launchers. They'll be deployed at the first alert," Stowe murmured. "And they've got no chance for the Tridents. Not that it matters. We might as well leave ours in the silos. They've aready screwed up the planetary heat balance. No point to poisoning everybody as well."

"Dreamer."

RESPONSE 3: U.S., counterpopulation. Targets: all cities >50,000 population. Mode: 240 ± 40 Trident C4 (8 × 100 KT), 190 ± 60 Poseidon C3 (10 × 50 KT), 440 ± 100 Cruise Missiles (GLCM, ALCM), all groundburst (target list follows). Time frame: >90 minutes <6 hours. Coefficient of success: 0.95

—TARGET LIST FOLLOWS—
—CASUALTY ESTIMATES AND DISTRIBUTION
FOLLOW—
—DAMAGE ESTIMATES AND DISTRIBUTION
FOLLOW—

"A revenge attack, that's all that is. Good one, too—look at that coefficient. Empty the fuckin' silos, boys, it's the bottom of the ninth and we're down a run," Yates said with cold humor. "Isn't that just like them?

"Why the delay, I wonder?"

Yates shrugged. "The 90 minute minimum could be retargeting time. The six hours—maybe that's how long he figures it'll take us to work up to a useless gesture. Or be forced into it by our allies and our generals' definition of manhood."

"Or how long it'll take the Cabinet to get out of Washington," Stowe said, and they laughed hollowly together.

Yates pushed his chair back and stood up. "That's enough to satisfy my curiosity. I'm not interested in looking at all the details."

"I think maybe Keith and Barb would be the best

ones to take this and draw out the survival parameters," she offered.

"If you want. Let's watch the hours, though. We've got other commitments to meet."

"I know. But he wants to see something next week, and he's already advanced us expenses."

"You can use a database search for the problem definition report."

"Already underway."

Five copies of the two-inch thick, 500-plus page report *NUCLEAR WAR SURVIVAL: Parameters and Options* were stacked up by Rutledge's seat at the conference table. The general settled in the chair, picked up the top copy, and regarded it dubiously.

"We're prepared to summarize the key points of the study for you, and then of course you'll need some time to digest it," Stowe said helpfully.

Rutledge folded back the cover and thumbed past the first few pages. "Just sit there while I look it over. I don't need someone to tell me what I can read myself," he said curtly. For the next twenty minutes Rutledge paged through the report, skipping large sections, stopping occasionally to read a passage in its entirety.

While he did so, Yates sat watching him with hands folded in his lap, swiveling back and forth in his padded executive's chair. *You getting the message yet? You reading between the lines? You can't save them. The only useful thing you can do is not fight the war.*

At last Rutledge snapped the binder closed and dropped it back on top of the others. "What the hell is going on here?"

True to form, Yates thought smugly. *I knew angry would be the first emotion we'd see from you.*

"Pardon me?" Stowe asked, looking up in surprise from her notepad.

"I thought you people were supposed to be good. There's nothing new here. This is a rehash of the same crap I could have gotten from FEMA or Army Civil Preparedness. Highway tunnels in Pennsylvania. Railway tunnels in the Rockies. Abandoned salt mines. Bomb shelters under the patio, for Chrissake."

Stowe laid down his pen. "It's necessary that we get a sense of direction from you as to where you want us to take this—"

"Goddammit, I told you last week what I wanted. And I told you that we were short on time. So you wasted a week on this idiocy."

"General—" Stowe said tentatively. "I thought you understood that this would be an interim report, so you can steer us in the direction you want to go. These studies proceed cooperatively—"

"I don't have time to handhold. You're supposed to be able to make judgements and decisions. That's what you're being paid for."

Yates took over. "Not without knowing what kind of financial and administrative commitment you're prepared to make. We want to keep this study in the real world, after all."

Rutledge looked unconvinced, but the tone of his words moderated. "I told you about that, too. I want more than a paper study. That's why I picked you people. You follow through. You get your hands dirty."

"And we'll follow through for you. But you've got to put some parameters on it," Yates said. "What's the ceiling? Who's going to implement this thing?"

"Dammit, why don't you listen? You're going to implement it. If something needs to be built or bought or someone needs to be hired, you'll see to it. So keep that in mind. This has to be do-able," he said, and paused to gnaw at his lower lip. "As for the ceiling, there is none. Not if what you decide on makes sense to me."

"A million? Two million?" Yates asked carefully.

"Or five hundred million, or a billion—if that's what it takes."

"And the only one we have to sell is you?" Yates asked.

"That's right. And so far I'm not buying. So tell me where you're going with this now, and when I can expect some real results."

Stowe looked at Yates for a cue but got none. "I've got one hangup about the model," she said slowly. "I thought High Frontier was supposed to protect us from an ICBM attack. Why can't it protect itself? You've got the coefficient of success at 1.00 for the first attack."

"High Frontier has to be operational to have any impact," Rutledge said.

"You mean you're modeling on the present—" Stowe stopped in mid-sentence and stared. "You're serious about this. Not five or ten years down the road. This model is for today."

"Yes."

"And the time constraint—you're talking about between now and next March, when High Frontier is finished." Stowe's face was pale.

Rutledge shook his head. "Not exactly. The announced operational date is next March, true. The actual operational date is this November, when the Command and Control center is ready. If the Russians are going to do anything about not letting us complete it, they're going to do it in the next six months."

"How likely do you think that is?"

"If I thought it *un*likely, I wouldn't be here. Let's just say if I were the editor of the Bulletin of Atomic Scientists, I'd move the hands up about thirty seconds to midnight." Rutledge stood up and shoved the stack of reports across the table toward Yates.

The one Rutledge had been reading toppled into Yates' lap.

"You see, I don't want it soon because I'm impatient. I want it soon because we're running out of time."

When the door closed behind Rutledge, Yates chuckled under his breath, then gathered himself together and rose to leave the room.

"Do you have to go?" Stowe asked, catching him by the arm. "I'd like to have you for a few minutes to bounce around some ideas."

Yates cocked his head questioningly at her pensive expression. "He hasn't infected you with his paranoia, has he?"

"I thought the six-month deadline was because he wanted to spend the money before the end of the fiscal year," she said, walking around the table and gathering up the reports. "I didn't think it was anything like this."

"Anything like what? That scenario is ludicrous. The Russians will have first strike capability with or without the High Frontier. It's only going to be able to knock down fifty percent of the missiles at best. They don't have to start a war over it."

There was a series of hollow thuds as she unceremoniously dropped the binders into the waste container by the door. "How do they know it's only going to be fifty percent effective? Because critics in Congress said so? Because a few pretty-boy science popularizers said so? Because the build-down alliance said so? If I were the Russians, I wouldn't take that at face value."

"They're not dummies. They've got their own technical experts, and the basic technologies of the system are no secret. They can add up the numbers just like we can."

"Then why does Rutledge obviously think otherwise?"

Yates frowned. "Hell, because that's the way people like him are trained to think. What, you think he knows something?"

"There's only ten major commands, and they trust him enough to give him one of them. He travels in the right circles to know."

"And what he knows makes him think we need some survivor's insurance?" Yates' tone was skeptical.

"Maybe. Look, that's not what I wanted to talk about, anyway," Stowe said with a wave of her hand. "This thing breaks up nicely into two problems: how and what. How do we get a CARE package to the survivors, and what do we put in it. Since the what is entirely dependent on the how, I think I'd better go ahead and start working on that aspect."

Yates shrugged. "Your decision. For the taxpayers' sake alone, we'll have to give him *some* value for his money. I just don't want to see it interfere with the Lilly study."

"I'll meet my other deadlines," Stowe promised. "But can I ask you to do some thinking about what should go in the caches? Not that I'm trying to draw you into this, but I would like to get your input."

"Sure," Yates said offhandly as he headed for the door. "But not today, huh? I've got work to do."

The halls of the LSF suite were darkened and quiet by the time hunger drove Yates to clear off his desk and go home. He locked his desk and disk file, then, keys jangling in his hand, headed down the main corridor to the entrance. En route, he saw a line of light at the bottom of the door to Stowe's office, and pushed it open. The associate director was seated sideways on the couch, shoes off and legs up, a notepad on her lap and an open can of Pepsi on the floor beside her.

"Ready to pack it in? I could stand a beer."

Stowe looked up. "What time is it?"

Peeling back a cuff, Yates looked at his watch. "Almost seven."

"Think I'll stay on a bit," Stowe said, stifling a yawn.

Yates glanced at the top sheet in the portfolio open in front of her. He read the her neat block-printed column headings upside down:

SURVIVABILITY   ACCESSIBILITY

A long list of notes in Stowe's symmetric handwriting filled the rest of the sheet.

Shrugging, Yates backed out of the room. "Suit yourself."

When he reached the parking lot, he looked back up at the second floor. The window of Stowe's office was the only one in the entire west face of the building bright with light.

"Bernadette, my sweet, you still haven't learned not to always volunteer for the front lines," he said softly. "You've got to pick your fights, and that one's not ours."

Then, shaking his head as though faced with the incomprehensible, Yates climbed into his car and drove away.

Two mornings later, Yates arrived before eight a.m. to find a blue Air Force sedan was again parked in the walkway spot. On seeing it, Yates hurried inside and upstairs.

He found Stowe and Rutledge just settling into chairs in the conference room.

"Daniel," Stowe said with a nod. "Glad you could make it."

"I thought you didn't need to see us until Friday," Yates said to Rutledge, taking a nearby seat.

"I asked the General to come in," Stowe said quietly. "I may have a recommendation for packaging a survival cache."

"May have?" Rutledge asked, a warning tone in his voice. "I didn't come here for more doubletalk and indecision."

Stowe tossed her head. "You won't get any. I think I have an excellent solution to the problem you posed. But there're certain requirements I'm not sure you'd be able to meet. I wanted to find out from you immediately, so that I didn't spend any more time on it if it wasn't."

Rutledge nodded to himself and waved a hand. "Go ahead."

"Whatever medium we use, the cache has to be both able to survive the war itself and able to be found easily afterwards. The problem is that those two factors cut against each other. There's a lot of places you could put something and know it was going to get through all right: buried in the middle of Indiana cornfields, hidden in salt mines. But it'd be just the wildest luck if they were ever found."

"Hell, you just need some way to tell everyone where they are. You could even put some sort of transmitter on them, "Yates suggested.

"Yes—but then you'd have to assume that the survivors have working radios, and we're better off making as few optimistic assumptions as necessary. And if you think it through, I don't think you'll want to publicize the existance or location of the caches until they're needed."

Fine. See if I open my mouth again.

"So what, then?" Rutledge asked.

"I'm thinking along the lines of putting the caches in water. Some sort of neutral-buoyancy canister which you anchor below the surface like a mine. You could put them all along the continental shelf and in the major lakes and rivers. As soon as the first one's found word'd spread pretty fast."

Stowe's rebuff had made Yates contentious. "Aren't you writing off the Great Plains?"

"To some degree. Most of the population lives on the coasts or near a major river. With municipal water systems destroyed, the survivors will come to natural water supplies eventually."

"Yes," Rutledge said, interested.

"The problem is that the places you'd want to put the caches are also heavily used for recreation—swimming, fishing, boating. They'd raise a lot of questions you might not want to answer, not to mention the possibility of vandalism."

Rutledge wagged a finger in the air. "I still like it. You could avoid some complications if you just deployed them at the last possible moment."

"But that leads to all sorts of logistic problems in storage, production, the manpower and organization needed to deploy them," she said.

Rutledge tapped his service insignia. "You forget who you're working for. How big would these be?"

"They could be any size, but I'd recommend restricting them to a size one person could recover. Say a metre in diameter, fifty or sixty kilograms."

"Then we could just drop them out of the back of C-119s. Make them float. Don't anchor them at all," Rutledge said, sitting back. "I presume you'd fill them with penicillin, high protein foods—"

"Medical supplies would probably be a low priority. If the nuclear winter hypothesis is correct, the greatest needs would be food for the present and seed stocks for the future. I do have one serious concern, though. I'd estimate a 40 percent wastage rate if the caches are floating free—"

"But they'd be simpler to make and more reliable," Yates interjected. "So we'll just deploy more of them."

She glared at him for interrupting. "I was going to say that if they're all the same, that's acceptable. But if you've got something of special importance, that method won't do at all."

Rutledge sat forward. "What do you mean, something of special importance?"

"Well—why shouldn't some art objects survive? What's the most valuable thing the nation owns? The original Constitution? Maybe we want to send a medical database instead of a few syringes of broad-spectrum antibiotics. Dan's looking at stocking the caches. He might have other ideas."

Rutledge looked to Yates. "Well, Doctor? What about it? What would you send?"

Yeah, she asked me, but I haven't given it a thought since. Thanks for putting me on the spot, Bernie. "How are you going to package the 'special' caches, Dr. Stowe," he asked, ducking Rutledge's question.

"In satellites," she said. "Big dumb satellites launched into unstable polar ellipical orbits—orbiting the earth the way a comet might orbit the sun. Very bright reflective coating, so that every time one reaches perigee it draws attention in the night sky. A nice low perigee so the atmosphere eventually drags it down. An ablative coating contaminated with nodules of copper and strontium chloride so the fireball is green and scarlet, and it's not mistaken for a meteor when it comes down. And just enough of a guidance system to see that it comes down on land."

I guess that overtime paid off, Yates thought with honest appreciation. *Very nice.*

Rutledge waggled a finger at Stowe. "This is why

you called me. You need to know if I could arrange for such a thing to be launched."

She nodded. "We'd be extremely limited in our payload if we had to depend on Space Systems International or even Arianespace, so much so that I'm not sure it'd be worth doing. But one Shuttle can get us 40,000 pounds into polar orbit from Vandenberg. I think I could get two specials in for that."

"You'd program them to come back here, I presume. If we can't help everyone then we need to make certain we help our survivors, not theirs."

Stowe nodded agreeably. "We should be able to target the North American continent as easily as any. The east coast, I would think, though we'll want to look at targeting and the distribution of our floaters."

Steepling his fingers, Rutledge stared into the tabletop for a long moment. "Time," he said finally. "Do you have enough time to do both, the floaters and the specials? We're looking at thirty, maybe forty-five days."

Rutledge's comment furrowed Yates' brow. *What happened to the six months?* Yates wondered, suddenly attentive.

"The floaters will be ready. I've felt out two suppliers, and if I get them plans tomorrow they'll start turning them out by the first of next week. The floaters are really pretty simple—a counterweight, a marker flag, a compartmented interior and a pictograph that shows you how to open it. If you're ready to authorize an overtime contract—"

"Done." Rutledge squinted at Yates. "Where are you, Doctor? You haven't said much. In fact, I get the impression you aren't really involved in this project."

Yates rocked back and folded his hands in his lap. "I suppose that's because I have trouble taking it seriously," he answered honestly.

"Any particular reason?"

"Lots of them. For one, I can't buy into your scenario. Everyone knows the High Frontier won't work. I don't believe for a minute the USSR would attack us because of it. That unravels the whole model, including what you want us to do."

Rutledge traced small circles on the tabletop with a fingertip. "I had a teammate like you once, Yates. All week he'd have terrible practices—dropping balls, missing his routes, cutting up. Game time came, and he played like a champion. He just couldn't take practice seriously. But when the pressure was on—"

His gaze flicked up from the tabletop to Yates' eyes. "You've been jerkin' me around. We're running out of time, and you're jerkin' me around. Dr. Stowe there knows this is the game, not the practice, but you're looking the other way."

"Do you want me to believe that scenario's anything more than a paper exercise?"

"Yes." Flint-gray eyes burned into sky-blue ones. "You don't know anything about Air Force security, or you'd realize that I have access to Class II materials but I can't show them around or grant anyone else Class II clearance. And I told you last time that the USSR is afraid of High Frontier. Maybe I'd better tell you why."

"Because they're paranoid, just like you," Yates said with a smirk and a shrug.

"No. Because some of the High Frontier satellites are carrying orbit-to-ground nuclear weapons. And the Russians know it."

The smirk slowly faded as Yates' eyes widened in shock. Then his lips curled in an expression of virulent hatred and he came up out of his seat. "You fuckin' idiots!" he screeched, shaking both clenched fists in front of him. "You goddamn snakebrain sons of bitches put *nukes* in orbit? Sweet Jesus—" His voice trailing off to a whimper, he squeezed his eyes closed as if in pain and melted back down into his chair.

Though equally shaken, Stowe allowed herself no such display. She folded trembling hands together and brought them slowly to her mouth, and then her body went rigid.

"I won't defend the decision," Rutledge continued in a soft voice. "It wasn't mine to make, and I think it was the wrong one. But it was made at the very top."

"The Chiefs of Staff?" Stowe asked in an unsteady voice.

"No. At the *very* top."

"Why?" It was question, plaint and protest all in one.

"They believed they had to do something to counter the USSR's advantage—2-1 in launchers and 3-1 advantage in throwweight, 5-1 in most conventional weapons. That plays on you after a while. And Congress kept knocking down almost every new system and giving away all the secrets on the few they approved. So we hid the funds for Damocles in the High Frontier project."

"Damocles," she echoed.

"You shouldn't have told us," Yates croaked at last. "I can't keep quiet about this. I've got to get it out."

"No, you don't," Rutledge said, standing. "Unless you want to be the cause of the war. Negotiations are underway at the highest level. You and I have to pray they succeed. But this can't be fought out in public. Neither side would be able to be flexible. Once everyone knows the warheads are there, the President would lose the option of ordering them removed. He can't back down to the Russians publicly. So hold your tongue, Dr. Yates—and get to work."

When the door clicked shut, Yates and Stowe sat beside each other for an interminable minute, isolated by their inexpressible thoughts, frozen by an overwhelming helplessness. Then without warning Yates leaped to his feet, toppling his chair backwards onto the floor, and fled the room without a word.

"Daniel!" she called out after him.

But it was not enough to slow his flight, though she followed and repeated the call down the stairwell. He took the steps three and four at a time as though pursued by a demon, and when he drove away tires and engine cried out protests that might have been his own.

Yates sat on his heels before the white marble cross and fingered the carved grooves of the lettering on the crosspiece. Around him, seventy thousand similar crosses stood in coldly precise lines and rows on the gently rolling land, acre after acre of mouldering bodies lying as regimented in death as in life.

Deanna R. Yates
Specialist 7th Airborne
May 13, 1990 Estanzueles, El Salvador

"Do you know how much I hate it here, Dee?" he said softly, withdrawing his hand. "Do you know what this place says to me? All the puffy-cheeked mothers and dutiful sons, the wet-eyed wives and fathers, all the lies they tell themselves and each other. Honorable death. Noble cause. I wouldn't have let them leave you here, little sister. If it had been up to me—"

I always talk to you as though you were still alive. Why is that, Dee? There's nothing here but the cloak your spirit wore. Why don't I go to the last place I saw

*you alive and try to catch a memory there? But I come
here, where all I can see is them folding the flag and
handing it to Mom.*

"If there was to be any point in what happened to
you, it would be if they learned enough from the
small wars not to fight the big one." His voice broke
and he bit at his lower lip, the corners of his eyes wet
with incipient tears. "But it's beginning to look like
there wasn't any point to any of it. Not to your
dying, or my living, or any of what we've done."

With a forlorn wail, Yates pitched forward and
pounded his clenched fists against the unyielding
ground. He fought the tears but they came nonetheless, his tortured sobs marking the struggle and leaving him weak and aching. It was a long several
minutes before he sat upright again.

"Oh, God. Don't they know?" he demanded of the
dead in a voice thick with anguish and anger, spreading his arms wide to include the skeletal crosses
from horizon to horizon. "Don't they realize what
they stand to lose? Don't they understand how im-
probable we are?"

He held his own hands out before him and studied
them as though seeing them for the first time, moving his thumb and each finger in turn. "A cosmic
alchemer's triumph, gifted with eyes that see beauty
and minds that create it," he said reverently. "Oh,
Dee. It's more than the body dying. You could tell
them how little that means. But they're going to kill
the spirit of what we were—Of what we wanted to
be. God, we're never going to go to the stars—"

With a keening cry, he flung his arms around the
cross, clutching it as he would have hugged Deanna,
flattening his tear-slick cheek against its smooth cold
surface. Great sobs tore through him, escaping as
explosive gasps and whimpers.

A hand on his shoulder that was not his own, a soothing voice repeating his name, and at length Yates lifted his head.

"Bernie," he said, with an unhappy laugh.

She crounched beside him. "Here," she said, opening her arms, and he gave up the grave marker's embrace for hers. They cried quietly together for a while, neither saying anything. Presently Yates pulled away.

"You followed me?"

"I knew where you'd go." She held his hands in hers. "It hasn't happened yet. It might not."

He flashed a maudlin smile. "You were always the realist in this partnership. Don't try to change your spots now."

Brushing his cheek with the back of one hand, she answered, "Even realists are allowed hope, Dan."

He cast his eyes downward, and in the moment of silence that followed both heard the sound of birds in a nearby tree and traffic on a distant road. "You know, I figured out why you hang your diplomas and I don't," he said, grinning crookedly. "Maybe it's some of the extra baggage that goes with being a damned good-looking woman—it was always important to you that people knew you came in the front door, that you were there on merit."

"I'm just a gold-star girl at heart," she said with a tender smile. "And you hide yours away because you don't want to belong to any club that'd have you as a member. Come on, Dan. Let's go. This isn't helping you any."

He used the cross as a crutch to pull himself to his feet, then helped her up as well. "Or anyone else, h'm? Can you meet me back at the office?"

"Of course—"

"Thanks. I'm going to need some help getting caught up before I'll be any use to you."

                          *   *   *

For two months they heard nothing from Gen. Rutledge except acknowledgements through his staff: 100 water caches received at Andrews for the Chesapeake, 300 received at Grissom for the lower Great Lakes. Stowe located two Hughes 570 modular satellite chassis about to be shipped to AT&T and flew to California to buy them away from their owner. She stayed to supervise their conversion into her special caches.

Yates remained in Maryland, but called her daily, both to keep track of each her progress and for reinforcement they both needed. Of his own progress, there was little to report. Deciding what was to go in the specials was a burden rather than a privilege, and the enormity of the responsibility led him to procrastinate. It was values and ethics class all over again: what do you take to a desert island, what do you rescue from a burning house? And do your choices describe a person you're comfortable being—

Choosing not for himself but for Bernie and his parents and the women he was dating and even Gen. Rutledge (he would not allow himself to think in terms of choosing for Earth's five billion strangers), Yates assembled an imposing list of possibilities and proceeded to raise ambivalence to a high art. He comforted himself with the thought that Stowe's hardware was the pacing item; unless and until the satellites were ready, the question of their cargo remained academic.

Steady progress on the satellites did not make him any more decisive; the pacing item became the availability of a launcher. His calls on that subject found Rutledge "not available" and the general failed to return them. After a week of waiting, Yates pressed the issue in person.

Deep worry lines and dark circles under the eyes

made Rutledge look older than when Yates had last seen him. "What are you here for?"

Taking a chair without being invited, Yates answered, "I could do with some good news."

Rutledge shook his head solemnly. "There is none."

"You said they were negotiating—"

"Talks are stalled. No, they're worse than stalled, they're frosty. And construction goes on."

"Why? The least we could do is hold the status quo."

"The official wisdom is that the Russians won't act," Rutledge said wearily. "The truth is that now that we've finally got the advantage, we're not willing to give it up."

"What are you telling me?"

He toyed with a pencil before answering. "That we've got two weeks, maybe three, before it all goes up. It's out of control. And there isn't anything that you or I or even the people'll that'll give the orders can do about it. The Joint Chiefs would rather use those warheads than give them up, and they've got the President convinced the Soviets are bluffing. Everyone will make what they think is the only right decision and it'll all add up to one very wrong decision. And if there's justice in this Universe they'll have at least a few hours to regret their part in it."

"We can get the specials launched. We can do that much."

"There's not enough time."

"Damn you, don't you quit on us! Do you think we took your six months as a promise? Bernie's been working 20-hour days—"

"And she's done a good job. We've got almost fifteen hundred water caches ready to deploy."

"The water caches are band-aids. The specials are what really matter. What have you done about manifesting them on a DOD Shuttle?"

"Nothing—"

Yates came to his feet and slammed his hands palm-down on the desk in front of Rutledge. "Why the hell not? You sang us a song about following through and now you don't."

Rutledge cocked his head and looked up at Yates. The intensity of the younger man's expression seemed to pain him. "You're still angry. I envy you that. I've gone past angry to something much less fulfilling," he said with uncharacteristic gentleness. "I did nothing because I had no reason to believe you could be ready. Now that I know differently, I'll make some calls. Go ask Mary to get us both some coffee, yes?"

Yates returned in five minutes to find Rutledge standing behind his newly cleared desk, pulling on an overcoat.

"You've got *Explorer* for a flight on the 16th. That's eight days. Can you be ready?"

"We'll be ready. Tell them to mount two 570-series cradles—"

Rutledge pressed a card torn from a Rolodex into Yates' hand as he moved past toward the door. "Tell them yourself. I've told them to expect you. I have other responsibilities to deal with. This is in your hands now."

"I've been wondering if I was ever going to see you," Stowe said, clutching Yates' arm as she joined him in the otherwise empty observation stands three miles from the Vandenberg Shuttle pad.

"Did you get the payloads integrated?"

"I wouldn't be here if I hadn't. But I had no chance to get inside them. What are we sending up?"

"Not enough," Yates said in a faraway voice. "Not enough." He glanced at the electronic clock. "Coming out of the hold."

"Oh, hell. You can tell me later. I don't want to

think about anything now except that we're going to make it. We're going to get them off," she said with a happy sigh. "I've worked harder on those birds than I've ever worked on anything ever in my life. And I've never wanted more for something I did to be totally unnecessary. Did you talk to Rutledge before you left? Where do we stand?"

"Rutledge dropped out of sight—went somewhere with his family."

"That's not good."

"I don't know. He seemed—I don't know." Yates squinted in the direction of the pad. "There goes the oxygen vent arm."

"Just a couple of minutes, then. I remember watching the first launches on TV as a kid," she said wistfully. "I knew the countdown sequence by heart."

They clung to each other in a fierce but asexual embrace as the last seconds ticked away.

"I've had a standing offer from Philip Cortieri for ten years to watch the grey whale migration off the Baja, but never took him up on it," Yates said as the clock reached 0:10. "When we're done here, how about going down there with me?"

She smiled wistfully. "Sure."

"If you can handle scuba gear, we can watch them from underwater. I'd like to get close."

"Maybe even hitch a ride?"

"Maybe."

Steam like white cotton billowed from the south side of the pad as a flicker of yellow marked the ignition of the main engines. At 0:00, the Shuttle rose off the pad and hurtled southward atop a dense pillar-like cloud lit from within by a furious white fire.

"Fantastic. Go go go go go," Yates murmured, and then the tsunami of sound washed over them and drowned out his urgings.

The echoes of the Shuttle's departure were still

rumbling when Stowe tugged at Yates' sleeve and pointed at an arcing contrail high in the western sky. "What's that?" she asked.

Yates shielded his eyes with a hand and studied the phenomenon with a sinking heart.

"There's another one," she said suddenly. "Daniel—"

They watched the incoming missles impassively, conscious of the futility of flight or protest. A halo of light more intense than a million Shuttle engines blinded them, and the radiation that accompanied it burned them where they stood, consciousness fleeing an endless instant after agony enveloped them.

But it was the death they would have chosen. For before long, the silo-studded plains were burning, and the cities which were home to pilots and sailors and soldiers were burning, and the furnace-like columns of air the wildfires created thrust their burdens of smoke and ash into the highest regions of the atmosphere, where they merged into a spreading cloud that turned day to twilight and then to night.

And then winter came to the world.

II.

Though the body of Garivan was beginning to smell strongly—having been dead a day even before being packed, cradled on Tola's shoulders like a felled deer, crosscountry to the Lonega family's homehill— the ceremony was held until twilight, the customary time.

In the intervening hours, Tola went to the stream to bathe, and Ledell, the keeper of stories, went with him to hear and commit to memory the deathtale. But there would be little glory in the retelling, for there was no glory in death by *dark*—the fickle scythe with a hundred different faces. This time, it had hardly marked Garivan's skin, instead making black blood run endlessly from his bowels until he was a hollow shell of agony.

Garivan's two surviving brothers meanwhile made a bier. As befit a provider and the first son of a Twelvenames, its frame was stout needlewood, laced and then crisscrossed with climbing vine.

The Twelvenames herself retired to her cupa alone, descending the notched log ladder into the domelike circular chamber without a word. Kenman, her husband prime, sat dutifully on the spider weed surrounding the cupa's smoke hole in case she should call for him. He did not expect a call to come. Belinda Twelvenames had outlived five of her children, and always she had found what she needed inside herself.

When twilight came on, the clacking of hollow rotwood sticks called the Lonega to the ring of sitting rocks which comprised the sky circle. The bier bearing the body of Garivan was hoisted high on the shoulders of his brothers and carried into the center of the circle, where four fist-thick waist-high stumps, each notched at the top, jutted up from the bare earth. Atop them the bearers placed their burden, then stepped away to where the rest of the family stood waiting.

There was silence in the circle as Belinda Twelvenames came forward and gripped her son's cold, stiff hand. In a voice younger than the forty years she wore with quiet dignity, she began to sing Garivan's song.

Garivan's song had no words, only the clear, unburdened notes that were the person who was gone—the soothing melodies that as an infant he had found pleasing, the happy sounds to which he had first given voice, the brief themes which evoked his gentle personality, and the never-before-heard cadence of his painful darkdeath.

When the song was ended, Belinda raised her head to the family. "A Lonega lies dead. I call on his family to remember him."

Since Belinda herself was beyond the age of breeding, she passed the right of first claim to Alice-Tonda-Ken, gravid with her third child. Alice-Tonda-Ken sang the first phrases of the family's song of remembrance, then placed one hand on Garivan's lifeless torso and the other on her swollen belly.

"What was good in you lives on. I take your love of the chase for my child," she said, and there was a murmur of approval.

Behind her came Kenman, who with his gravelly voice took up the remembrance song where Alice-Tonda-Ken had stopped.

"What was good in you lives on," he said clearly and loudly. "I take the laughter that lightened long travels in your company."

Nine others came forward in turn to make their claims for that which was well thought of in Garivan. The claims were made solemnly, in full recognition of the responsibility of the claimant to make that which was Garivan part of themselves. It was one of the rituals that set the Lonega apart fom the other Georgia families—the living remembrance, the preservation of the essence of the dead.

"He is well honored and will be well remembered, Belinda," Kenman said at her side.

"Will you find his body a good resting place, husband, where it will be devoured undisturbed by men?" she asked, touching his cheek.

He lowered his eyes. "Gratefully."

She raised her arms palm up. "I give his substance to the land that sustains us," she cried out, her voice touched by the first tremulous hint of emotion. "He is and will be with us, always. Open the larder, uncork warm spirits. Tonight we celebrate life."

*   *   *

Everyone in the Georgias knew that Belinda Twelve-names had the magic. She was the only Twelvenames within a month's walking, in large part because of the gift of twinning. Eight times she had been roundbellied, bringing forth eleven healthy children and but a single cull.

The cull had been her first, and the beginning of her legend. In defiance of Eloai, the senior mother at the time, she had given the child a name. Though the frail, armless creature died within a month, Belinda placed the dried, blackened stub of its umbilicus in a pouch on her belt as though she had bred a healthy child, ignoring Eloai's warnings that to do so was to invite barrenness.

Now there were a dozen proofs in the pouch, and Belinda Twelvenames was senior mother of the Lonega. Despite her age, she still kept four husbands, and could have had many more. Suitors young and old from other families still came calling on the Twelvenames offering gifts and making chivalrous entreaties.

The gifts took as many forms as the suitors, from a fresh hindquarter to a well-made blouse—though it had become known over the years that Belinda favored the works of the small muscles of a maker's head and hands over those of the large muscles of a provider.

When a gift pleased her she would lie with he who had brought it, as was her perogative. But she asked none to stay. They went away grateful nonetheless, for all knew that the Twelvenames's magic was contagious and they would reap the benefit when they returned to their own homehill.

In the same vein, Belinda's husbands were nearly as much in demand as Belinda herself, being asked to bring nothing more to the mating than a tiny bit of her gift. Custom gave Belinda a veto, and when the breeder was an Lonega the answer was always no. But from time to time, Belinda would unmarry Kern or Av or Denis, freeing them to go away a day or five and visit another family. Kenman alone she kept for herself.

But if the breeding magic was contagious, it was sympathetic as well. Alice-Tonda-Ken was with child again, and Kirsta, Belinda's first daughter, was suckling the child which had made her a Sixnames. Of the family's six breeders, only Tania had yet to bear a normal child, and she was still ten summers from blood-end.

In every wise the Lonega were rich in children, and the credit accrued to Belinda Twelvenames. But for Belinda itself it was a mixed blessing. The deathfeast only evoked memories of other children who had died too soon, and before long she withdrew from the festivities and went walking, away from the sky circle and the family's three cupas, down the west slope of the homehill toward the stream. Denis, assuming the duties of first husband in Kenman's absence, followed at a respectful distance.

Though there was but a sliver of moon to light her steps, she moved sure-footedly across the shallow stream atop the slender log Av had placed there for her. On the other side of the stream was the meadow, her favorite watching place, and there she slowed and gestured to Denis.

"Let me make a pillow of you," she said, and he came to her. They lay down in a bare patch together, and she rested her head on his belly as she looked up at the sky.

"The sun sets late, the Twins set early. Hot days are coming."

"Andor counts six phases to north-sun day," Denis said in an agreeing tone.

"How foolish the sun is, to give the summer all life and warmth and then punish us with the short-day cold," she said with real anger. "How much harder to enjoy the gift of light when we know it will be taken from us."

Denis understood the source of the anger. "Just as the breeder of many will see many deaths."

"I would take a lesser gift that I could keep forever."

Saying nothing, Denis stroked Belinda's smooth, dry forehead. She reached up and caught his hand, then brought it to her mouth to kiss the palm.

"Does our family eat well?"

"Yes, Belinda."

"Are our family's songs strong ones?"

"Yes, Belinda."

"Are our breeders fertile and fecund?"

"Yes, Belinda."

"And is there nothing more to life than that?"

"Those are the highest blessings."

"It seems to me that to have all the highest blessings should bring more happiness."

"Are you unhappy, Belinda?"

"I am triply blessed," she said wearily. "Am I allowed to be unhappy?"

"A Twelvenames is allowed anything."

"So it is said," she agreed.

It was then that the nightfire appeared. Both saw it nearly at once, brighter by far than the brightest star in the sky, brighter than the five planets together, as bright even as the crescent of moon: a brilliant flame arcing up from the hilly north horizon, piercing the bowl of the Great Cup, searing the back of the Serpent, and then vanishing beyond the plains to the south. The entire apparition took but a hundred breaths.

Belinda had seen the nightfire two dozen times throughout her life, but each time she felt the wonder. "Why does it come?" she asked in hoarse whisper when it was gone.

She felt his shrug. "Because it has always come."

"That answer means nothing." She sighed. "Perhaps it comes to light the fires in young hearts, and I am too old to feel the warmth and know."

"Or perhaps it comes to honor the dead son of a Twelvenames," he said gently.

"Do you think me so special that the sky now bows to me?" she demanded with some indignation.

"You have always been deserving."

"You're a foolish man, Denis, foolish and vain." She sat up and began to loosen her blouse. "Love me," she said, and straddled his groin. Riding his hardness, surrounded by the living Earth and before the watchful eyes of heaven, she replaced her pain with pleasure for a time.

When Belinda awoke the next morning in the cupa, Kenman was sleeping soundly beside her, smelling strongly of sweat and the trail. Sitting up, she saw by the empty bedplaces around the cupa's perimeter that Kern and Denis had already risen, as had Alix-Ellet and her breed-family. Only Alice-Tonda-Ken still slept, a phenomenon becoming more common as she moved into the seventh month.

As Belinda stretched and yawned, Kenman stirred.

"Sleep, my husband," she whispered, bending over to kiss his forehead. Then, gathering a cloak around her against the lingering night chill, she climbed the log ladder to another morning.

A breakfast fire was crackling in the sky circle, tended by Tola and two of the younger providers. Several of the children were playing on the treeless east slope of the homehill, their high voices carrying to Belinda's ears. Mejein, Kirsta's oldest girl, walked shyly up to Belinda and offered to brush her hair, and Belinda settled crosslegged on the grass to allow it.

Shortly after, Kirsta herself came to them, touchad cheeks with her mother and daughter, then gently chased the latter away.

"I would help—" she said uncertainly.

"I am not in need," was the gentle reply.

"Does the wound heal so quickly?"

"You ask because you have not yet known the loss," Belinda observed, touching hands. "But because you have not known it, I cannot answer you."

"My eldest is ready to take a craft. Another summer, and Mejein will be ready to choose a husband—"

"From such events you will learn the art of letting go."

"I do not want to learn it. I sometimes think, what if tomorrow Mejein did not awake—"

"It would not be beyond your coping. But you will do yourself a kindness to forgo such thoughts and live it only once, when it happens. Now—since you sent Mejein away, you may help by finishing her task."

With a small grateful smile, Kirsta took up the brush.

Across the homehill, Denis sat with his back against a tree, pushing green-stained threads through the back of a roughweave shirt as he began a provider's string painting. The sight reminded Belinda that she would have to choose a replacement for Garivan, either by accepting a petition from another family or by promoting one of the craftless children. The latter was more likely, and Kip the probable choice, but she would ask Tola for his thoughts before acting.

By the time breakfast was ready, Kenman had roused himself and joined Belinda.

"What you asked is done," he said as he settled beside her.

She squeezed his hand in acknowledgement, but gave no sign of wanting to hear more. "Did you see the nightfire?" she asked.

"I did."

"Is it just that I grow old, or does the nightfire come more often these last years?"

"I cannot say. I am no watcher."

"I am no watcher either, yet my memory tells me that when I was a child with the Unicoi the nightfire came but once or twice a year. When I was eleven it came three times, once in autumn and twice in spring. Our senior mother worried greatly over it. The next year it did not appear at all."

"The nightfire owns its own spirit, and moves as it chooses."

"So it is said," she said resignedly.

Five days later, the family had just scattered from the high-sun meal when a shout went up from the north slope of the camp, drawing the attention of all within earshot.

"It's Av!" someone called over the hooting and happy laughter.

Belinda stood and took a few tentative steps toward the commotion. It was indeed Av, her youngest husband and one of the family's runners, in a group bearhug with Modris and several others. When he saw Belinda he disengaged himself and pushed through to where she stood. His right hand went up with her left; their fingers entwined, and he stepped close to lightly press his cheek against hers.

"Welcome home, husband," she said softly into his ear.

"They tell me Garivan died the darkdeath," he said. "I am sorry I was not here."

"He is well remembered," she said reassuringly, and stepped back, breaking the formal embrace. They went to the sky-circle hand in hand, and Bria, Belinda's youngest, brought Av a bowl of the hot fruit mash. Those who were not needed elsewhere settled on the sitting stones nearby to hear Av's news.

"No stories till all can hear, tonight," Belinda said warningly at the group of eager young ones beginning to gather.

"I have something better than stories," Av said, unhooking a small pouch from his belt. It was his seedbag, in which he carried and scattered along his route the germ of their homehill's plants—a tradition Av had brought with him from the Chats. Usually the seedbag was empty at the end of a run. But from his Av drew a dozen small, rounded streamstones. Hands cupped, he held them out to Belinda and then, when she had chosen one, to the children.

"Water skippers," one exclaimed.

"Look again," Av instructed, and they obediently scrutinized the stones.

"Mine has a needletree!"

"I have a deer!"

"Look, a killkenny!"

Belinda peered at hers and found a picture scratched in its surface. The scratches were fine and deep, the execution—in her case, of a clawed beetle—skillful.

"This is fine making," she said in a neutral tone.

"I got them from the Cantona, from the hand of a maker named Brian. He takes stones from the Allatoona and makes fertility amulets for his homefamily. A good stone is highly prized there—a breeder will give her stone to her favorite when she reaches bloodend, and men will fight to own a stone that has shown the magic. We have no need of such, nor would he have allowed me them if we had. But he consented to turn his skills to other subjects."

"Did you see the making? How is it done?" Belinda asked.

Av squirmed uncomfortably. "A maker has his secrets—"

Belinda thrust the stone before Av's face. "These are made with cutters of shinestone."

"Yes, Belinda."

"Shinestone comes from the time of dark and carries the darkdeath. How can you bring these here as gifts and toys for children?" she demanded.

"These are streamstone, not shinestone," Av protested. "They carry nothing but their maker's mark."

She looked to Kenman, then to Denis. Both wore looks that said *You can forbid it, but you lose more than you gain.* The look on Av's face said something else, something cautionary, something conspiratory.

"Yes. This is fine making," she repeated, slipping the stone into a pocket. "You were thoughtful to bring them for us. Thank Av, children. Then leave us."

The adults retired to the fire circle of Belinda's cupa for privacy. It was a full council—besides Av, there were Belinda, Kenman, Kirsta Sixnames and her senior husband, and all the firsts of the crafts: Andor, Tola, Ledell, Elul the maker, Modris the guardian. Because she was just rising, Alice-Tonda-Ken was there as well.

"I was surprised to hear that you had gone far enough south to visit the Cantona. The news is bad?" Belinda asked.

"The news is bad," said Av.

"Begin at the beginning. You visited the Gaddis," Belinda said. The Gaddis's homehill lay just less than a day's run to the north, in the wooded hills. "How did you find them?"

"It is as Adrian said," Av replied, naming the family's youngest runner. "Their songs are fading, Belinda. Their first maker is dead and his tools lie unused.

The children are thin and rarely laugh. They have only three breeders, who cannot keep the family in milk."

"Who is senior mother now?"

"Sylva-Mark-Juniper."

"A breeder of two is senior mother?" Kenman shook his head. "What became of Dione Sevennames?"

"Bitten by a clawed beetle last summer and died of the froths. Sylva was her eldest."

"But not the keeper of her remembrance, it would seem," Belinda mused.

"No. She is flush with a senior's privilege and does not see what has happened."

"Bad news indeed, Av. The Gaddis have a fine homehill and a good heart," Kenman said.

"They are in danger of losing both."

"Perhaps there is some way to help them," Kenman said, with a brief sideways glance at Alice-Tonda-Ken, who was seated on the second tier. "We are strong enough to share some of our substance."

"We will talk of it at another time," Belinda said firmly. "Continue, Av."

"You have heard the best of it already. I had hoped to continue on to the Blue Ridge. But the Gaddis warned me that there has been fighting among the lake families, and the black flag hangs along the runs."

Belinda shook her head. "The lake land is as rich as any in the Georgias, yet they fight like killkennies over a dinner scrap."

"They must have a poor excuse for a keeper, if he allows them to forget the lessons of the time of dark," said Ledell, defending his craft. "There is more lost in fighting for food than gained in winning."

"It's not food they fight over," Modris said. "If they were more hungry, perhaps they would not have the time to think of such foolishness."

"There's truth in that," Av agreed. "Sylva says that the senior mothers have allowed their husbands too great a voice in the family's life."

"An eternal danger," Belinda said, directing a smile and a sideways glance toward Kenman. "Where did you go, then, with the runs to the North closed to you?"

"To Ellijay," he said, to their surprise.

A runner away from his homehill has much time for thinking, and as he covered the leg-numbing miles in the long shadow from the western hills, he thought about his destination: Ellijay.

Nearly all of what he knew came from Ledell's stories. Ellijay was, literally, a daughter family of the Lonega, founded on the east shore of Carter Lake by Belinda's breed-sister Maryn. The division had been amicable, and many of the Lonega had breed-relations there: Kenman had a brother, Kirsta Six-names a son and daughter, Belinda two sons, Elul a sister.

For all that, contact between the families was infrequent. Maryn was several summers older than Belinda, and with three good pregnancies before she was twenty had had reason to think about being senior mother to the Lonega some day. But the three healthy boys were followed by an equal number of culls, just as Belinda was beginning her string of twins. At the time of Eloai's death, Maryn had but four children to Belinda's eight, earning the younger the right of succession.

With the title came problems Eloai had left unsolved. The family's two cupas were crowded and a third was needed. But the spring had come cold and dry, and those who might have built the new earth lodge were busy with the task of providing. The addition of Maryn's resentment in that situation could well have been incendiary.

Belinda resolved all three problems with one wise decision that cemented her claim to be senior mother. The split relieved the crowding and the pressure on the Lonega's foraging range, and took the proud Maryn out of her younger sister's shadow.

Maryn had seen to it that the new family's homehill was more than three days away on a difficult run, and made the distance seem greater by sending out her own runners but rarely. Belinda reciprocated, allowing Maryn the independence she craved. Av's visit would be the first in four summers and only the third he could recall.

If he could find them, that was. Av was dependent on the reliability of Ledell's directions and the sightings he took of the dayrise and dayset, since he had never made that run before. He had followed the valley southwest from Gaddis, detouring through hilly country and picking up the blackrock run the second day. He had only to find the great lake and then work his way along the shore to its northeastern end.

—Or so the senior runner from the Gaddis had said, though by the look of him it had been several summers and many meals since he had done any running.

"Stay to the blackrock runs," he had said. "You'll see the lake and the fires of the Ellijay clearly from it."

Despite his misgivings, Av complied as well as he could. Twice he lost the blackrock, once for more than an hour, and twice he found branches he was not expecting, and had to guess at which to follow. Finally the run ended on the bank of a briskly moving stream which seemed large enough to feed a good-sized lake.

The light was fading as the sun's disk neared the

peaks of the next range of hills. But his view west into the valley was unobstructed, and he saw neither sun-sparkled water nor curling smoke plume. Certain he was lost, Av followed the stream west in the hope it would lead him to the lake.

He was still walking and hoping an hour later when he came upon an abandoned cupa.

Dug into the ground and then roofed over with needlewood planks and earth, a cupa gives litte sign of its presence apart from the smoke hole. That is especially true of an older one, where the shallow dome of the roof is covered with a natural scattering of needles or growth of spidergrass. Summer cool and winter warmth are the goals, but deception is often the effect. It is the presence of people and the activity aboveground that mark a homehill for what it is.

There was none of that as Av came upon his discovery. There was only a creak of warning and the shifting of the ground beneath his feet. Av tried to scramble clear, but there was nothing solid under him, and he dropped heavily into darkness along with a cascade of dry soil and splintered wood.

Immediately he bounced to his feet and drew his jasper knife from a belt pouch. He peered into the dimly lit recesses of the cupa, looking on the powdery dust kicked up by the fall. Humans were not the only form of life to find the cupa a congenial home. Among the frequent secondary tenants was the razor-toothed killkenny, which could negotiate a smoke hole ladder as agilely on its four clawed pads as a human could on two skin-wrapped feet.

Nothing moved, and no eyes glinted back at him.

Still wary, he clambered out of the hole. When he was standing in the light again, he called the runner's recognition call. No answer came.

He spotted a second cupa a few dozen strides further on, and crawled to the edge of its smokehole. There was no ladderlog, and the darkness inside was complete.

Av was confused. If this was Ellijay, where were the people? But it could not be Ellijay, for where was the lake? He would have to go into the cupa for answers, and for that he needed light.

Rather than wait for tomorrow's mid-morning sun, he ran to the nearest west-facing slope and climbed a hundred steps, until he could see the disc of the sun between two peaks and fell its fading warmth. With his fireglass, he focused that warmth on a bed of needles, until they smoked and burst into flame. A stout stick with a long strip of bark wrapped around one end made a passable torch.

Returning, he thrust the torch through the smokehole of the intact cupa. Immediately, the rattle of chiton broke the silence of the chamber, and Av saw the furtive shapes of a hand of clawed beetles as they skittered away from the light. He also saw what had drawn them there: a formless scattering of skeletons on the dirt floor of the cupa. There were large bones and small bones and the palm-sized empty backshells of a hundred or more dead beetles. But except for the ladder, lying across the fire pit where it had fallen, the chamber was bare of all human sign.

Abruptly, Av broke off his narrative. Belinda was not looking well. Bent forward, face flushed, she stared blankly at the floor, her palms pressed against the sides of her neck.

"Go on," she said hoarsely. "It is no less the truth if I do not hear it. Go on."

Hesitant at first, Av complied. "I counted six skulls, five adult and one child. There were two killkenny skulls as well."

"The bodies would have drawn both the killkennies and the beetles," Tola said authoritatively.

"Yes. The 'kennies probably knocked down the ladder, the way they fight over a carcass. The ones that were trapped inside were eaten by the beetles. And then the beetles ate each other."

Kenman broke in. "The Ellijay were twenty, at least. What about the others? Were they in the cupa that collapsed?"

"No," Av said, still watching Belinda with concern. "It was a living place—bowls, roughweave, a woodpipe—"

All knew that the objects would carry the mark of their making. "Ellijay?"

"Yes."

"Perhaps a daughter family," Belinda said hopefully. "Did you keep looking for the lake?"

"Yes—in vain. I was where the lake was. The lake is gone. The downstream wall is broken."

Belinda's demeanor brightened. "That must be why. The others must have left, moved to some better homehill."

"I do not think so, Belinda. I think it is that no one troubled to find a resting place for the last few to die, that they were too weak to do more than drag them to the other cupa and push them in. I don't know what killed them, they were so scattered by the 'kennies and picked so clean by the beetles. But I wanted to know before I returned here if it had touched me as well."

"So you went on, as far as the Cantona."

He nodded. "If I were dying I thought I should at least see new faces and new places before surrendering."

"This is a new death, then, that saps a family's traditions first," Elul said, his tone a criticism.

"For every star there is a way to die," Ledell said.

"This is not a new death but an old one. Do you not remember the silence? Even the Lonega have lost family to it. They crawl inside themselves, insensate to pain, oblivious to hunger, until their song ends. It is said they have asked the question 'Why not die?' and found no answer."

Belinda stood, hugging herself, and faced Av. "No!" she said fiercely. "That is *not* what happened." With the light, quick steps of a hunter's quarry forewarned, she ascended the ladder and was gone.

"In the time of dark, the water spirit fed us," Ledell said, and all turned to look at him. "I will say that it has taken the Ellijay in payment."

There was a stunned silence. "You think the end of time is coming, Ledell?" Kenman said at last.

"Our mothers' mothers' mothers lived in darkness on the gifts of the water-spheres. Then the sky-sphere brought a greater gift, sweeping away the darkness. We grew healthy in the light. But we forgot out debt to the water." Then he shrugged, as though discounting his own words. "I am the keeper of the past, nothing more. Tomorrow is always a surprise."

"Come to the meadow with me."

Kenman looked at Belinda with surprise. "They are gathering to hear Av's story—"

"They do not need us for that."

"There are too many clouds for watching."

She crossed her arms and cocked her head. "Why do you resist me?"

"Perhaps because I have no answers to your questions. For such things you are better served by Denis, or Av himself."

"And what questions are those?"

"The ones that steal the smile from you."

The smile appeared, tender. "And if I prefer you, despite your ignorance?"

Kenman bobbed his head submissively. "I will go and tell them not to wait on us."

They walked with hands clasped to the stream and crossed to the meadow beyond, then settled in a familiar spot.

"Does it not seem as though our family is the only strong family left in the hills?" she asked.

"Burdens fall unequally."

"Yet we all live better than our mothers did. There is more food, warmer days. Why should families fail in plenty when they thrived in scarcity?"

"Gifts also fall unequally."

"What do we have that the Ellijay did not?"

"A Twelvenames called Belinda," he said readily.

Annoyance crossed her face. "Is it not clear to you that I too will die? If not this winter, then the next, or the next. Where is the breeder who has seen forty summers?"

"You will. Surely life will grant that to a Twelvenames."

"You have made too much of me," she said, annoyance turning to anger.

"You have the magic."

She pushed his solicitous touch away angrily. "Oh, yes. Belinda Twelvenames has the magic. Everyone believes it. But how much of the magic is in the believing and how much of it is in me?"

"I don't understand why you doubt—"

She threw her hands up in a gesture of frustration. "What honor is there for a Twelvenames who has outlived half her brood? Perhaps I will be further honored, and see them all dead."

"It pains me to see you unhappy—"

"It pains me that you do not understand," she said curtly, grasping his hands tightly. "What is the purpose if death always follows life? Why sing the songs? Why keep the tales? If I am the meaning, then there is no meaning, for I know none. If I am the heart, then we are empty, for I am empty. If I am the reason we live, then why not die now, for I surely will."

"I said I would have no answers," he said helplessly.

"Which I forgive. But you fear the questions, which I do not," she said with contempt.

Fat raindrops began to pelt them, kicking up tiny puffs of dust and striking the leaves with a slapping sound. A seamless rumble of thunder echoed among the hills. Unexpectedly, Belinda laughed.

"The sky rebukes me for my angst," she said. "Go back home. I wish to bathe myself in the new water and absorb its spirit." She undid the side ties of her blouse and lifted it over her head, then removed her cloak. "Go, good husband," she said as she began the dance. "In the morning I will be well again."

"Damn the light!" Andor exclaimed, peering at the faint marks cut in the flat surface of the split stick he held in his hand.

Rain had been falling every night for a week. The deluge had left the Lonega sodden and surly, prolonging and deepening the distressing sense of custom violated which came with learning the Ellijay had died unremembered.

Cut off from his own watching by the sheets of grey clouds, Andor absorbed himself in the records Av had brought back from the Gaddis and the Cantona. The Gaddis records were easily understood, since Polton, the Gaddis's senior watcher, used the marking system common to all the hill families.

But Polton's observations filled few of the gaps in Andor's own, since it was rare for two families so close together not to suffer the same weather. Only those observations which Polton himself had gotten from families still further north were of any use.

Andor was much more interested in the Cantona records, since their homehill was more remote and he had no recent observations from that part of the world. But the marking system was unfamiliar and Av's explanations confusing: /\ was the observer's mark, / a wanderer. What, then, Andor demanded, did

/\ //*> //′/\ | | | |

or

/\ /> = =//

mean? Av did not know.

Patiently, with the help of his own records, Andor puzzled out the remainder. There were marks for the rising and setting of the moon, for night's arrows, and, it seemed, for the nightfire itself—though the disagreements between their sightings and his own raised doubts in his mind about the skills of their watchers.

Veracity aside, the Cantona records were elegantly concise, and despite their brevity contained most of what Andor wanted to know. But by the time he recognized that, Andor was too aggrieved with the Cantona to admire their invention.

On the eighth day after Av's return, the air changed and the low clouds broke apart to reveal a high, shimmering blue sky. Andor celebrated by setting off for the high observatory, which lay in a mountain gap a tiring two-hour climb to the west. In truth, it was a trip better left to the younger watchers.

But the high observatory was special. A great circle of stick markers preserved the positions of dayrise and dayset, nightrise and nightset as seen from the circle's center during earlier watchings. Some of the placements were made by Andor's predecessor Nirel as long as a hundred summers ago. Though his legs always regretted his mind's enthusiasm, it was by far his favorite place for watching. From there the whole bowl of heaven and the whole disk of earth seemed on display for his inspection.

As the reddened face of the sun touched the far horizon, Andor held the sighting rod vertically and noted how its shadow fell across the circle. It was three phases to the north-sun day, the end of the sun's summer march north along the horizon. Soon it would begin its retreat, foretelling the short-day cold to come.

Andor remained at the high observatory until distant clouds obscured the yellow wanderer, precluding his observing at what point it also slid down beyond the horizon. By that time the cool breezes that blew almost steadily across the observatory had brought the chill-ache to Andor's bones, and he gathered up his things to go. His last duty was to sing the song of the wanderers, which he did in a high, reedy voice. Then he headed back down the mountain to the homehill.

He was nearly there when his eye caught the glint of a brilliant light climbing the curve of the night from the north: the nightfire. His mind recorded the sighting automatically, registering mild surprise since it had been only fourteen days since the last apparition. Then he turned his face fully toward it, and what he saw caused his muscles to fail him, dropping him to his knees, the sighting stick falling from his numb hand. He knelt, his hands clapped over his mouth, and beheld a wonder.

For racing toward the zenith were *two* nightfires.

Andor was frozen for a moment, then leaped to his feet and began to run, his way lit by the lights above. Branches whipped his face and arms, and deadwood strained to trip him. *They must see or they will not believe*, he thought, heart pounding, *they must know*, and raced on recklessly. But as he neared the homehill, a foot slipped sideways and he went down heavily,

pain shooting through his ankle. He lay there help-
less, mortified by his failure, then forgave himself as
he heard the cry of a Lonega guardian:

"By the mother of the light! By the light herself!
Belinda! Kenman! Kirsta! Arise! Come quickly! The
nightfire! By the Twelvenames, the nightfire has
twinned!"

"Ask, ask, ask, so I can parade my ignorance,"
Andor moaned, the blanket slipping off his shoulders
as he threw his arms wide. The watcher was still
agitated, though enough time had passed to herd
back to bed the young ones awakened by the guardian's cries, and to wrap Andor's swelling ankle with
dur-soaked roughweave.

"Calm yourself, Andor," Belinda said. "I do not
expect perfect knowledge from you."

"But I am senior watcher. I should know the
meaning—"

"Enough! Andor, what brings the nightfire?"

The watcher averted his eyes. "The nightfire owns
its own spirit, and moves as it chooses."

"Spare me well-worn sayings that are empty of
meaning," Belinda reproached. "What do you hold
the nightfire to be? Is it kin to the sun, or to the
wanderers, or to the moon?"

Taking a clay bowl in hand, Andor dragged himself
across the dirt circle and crouched in front of an
anthill. "They are as we are," he said, pointing. "They
live in the earth, in a homehill, and take their life
from the earth." Then Andor inverted the bowl and
set it upside-down over the anthill. "This is as the
sky is, a great, smooth bowl of blue rock over us. The
spirits of the sky crawl across its face and give us
their light. They are all kin to each other."

"You do not remember, then, the story of the founding?" Ledell asked indignantly. "How the nightfire

carried the spark to the sun and ended the time of dark?"

Elul caught the note of alarm. "If this new nightfire should twin the sun, would we not burn?"

Ledell's expression was grave. "We would."

"I will not have this muddied by stories of times which no one here witnessed," Belinda said sharply.

"You question my keeping?" Ledell was too astonished to be insulted.

"Your keeping is splendid," she replied. "But you forget that I have heard the stories others tell of me, and know that what is kept is not always what is true." She turned back to Andor. "You have not answered my question. What is the nightfire? Is it flame, spirit, substance?"

Andor grunted his unhappiness. "How am I to know these things?"

"Have you never considered such a question?"

"No. It is the nightfire. Why should it be anything else? How could I attempt to take its measure? Av—were you not with the Adako when the nightfire came last summer?"

"I was."

"And how far is that?"

Av considered a moment. "A run of twelve days."

"And did not the nightfire still rise beyond the farthest tree or mountain? Was it any larger, any brighter?"

"No."

Andor turned an apologetic look on Belinda. "Do you see? It is so far away that twelve days' run brings it no closer. And yet if it is so far away it must own a terrible flame. The nightfire is not part of the land. It is over us, beyond us. It is not meant that we should know its substance, that it burns without being consumed. It is not meant that we should know what moves it, that it chooses a path unique in the sky. It is not meant that we should know its purpose, that it alone comes without pattern or plan. There is a great space set between us, and we may not cross."

"Is there truly no rhythm to its apparitions?"

Andor shook his head vigorously. "No watcher has found one, and many have searched. As recently as Nirel's time, the nightfire went two years without appearing, yet this spring there were two apparitions in three nights."

"How often has it come this year?"

"I do not know."

That drew a quizzical look from Belinda, and Andor hastened to explain. "Our family has recorded five sightings before tonight. But there were many clouded nights this winter, and our knowledge could well be incomplete."

"What about the records I brought you?" Av asked.

"The Gaddis saw as we did. The Cantona claim five more sightings, but I cannot believe it."

Belinda's eyes narrowed. "Why not?"

"There has never been such a number of apparitions."

"What was the count last year?"

"Eight—the most ever recorded."

"And the year before?"

"Five."

Belinda stood and walked to the far side of the sky circle, craning her head to look up. The clawed beetle was overhead, the tiny skylights that outlined its carapace sharp against the inky night. "How can you say there is no pattern? Where when I was young it came once each year, now it comes once each month. What will happen when it comes once each night?"

Ledell followed her halfway across the circle. "The Seneca say that in times to come, the nightfire will awaken the cold light of the moon and drive away the last of the dark. *That* is what is coming. There will be no more death, and no more need of remembrance. We will all live forever in the light." His voice changed from a warning hiss to a patronizing sneer. "But forgive me—you do not believe the stories of an old keeper," he said, and stalked off in high dudgeon toward his cupa before she could reply.

"Andor?" she called across the circle. "Is this your belief as well?"

Andor struggled to his feet with an assist from Kenman. "Mother Belinda, I would gladly give you the answer you desire," he said unhappily. "But I am still as I was an hour ago. I do not have an answer, for you or for myself."

Kirsta, who had stood hugging herself and listening at the periphery of the circle since Andor's return, spoke for the first time. "I do not see why we could not travel to where the sky meets the earth and climb it, as the ants climb the inside of the clay bowl. Then we would behold the sky spirits as we behold each other, and know them."

Andor shook his head, his expression wistful. "I asked the same question of Mirel when I was younger, who had asked it of his teacher in turn. The received wisdom is that no runner could go to where the sky meets the earth, because it lies a life's journey away beyond a great lake."

"To all points? The north, the south—"

"This is more than legend. I have not seen the lake-of-the-horizon, nor have any of our living runners. But Weneta did, and betimes we hear of it from other families. I am afraid we are forever in the lesser world and the skyfires forever in the greater."

Belinda sighed and gathered her nightcloak about her. "If true, it is a great pity." She glanced at each of her husbands in turn. "Come, Kern," she said, deciding. "I grow chill."

* * *

It was Belinda's habit to go walking in late morning. The long walks gave her the exercise she desperately needed to fight off the sedentary, pampered life the family tried to force on her. Her sojourns likewise took the edge off her hunger before the high-sun meal, saving her from the round-bodied fullness that was common to seniors beyond blood-end.

Sometimes Kenman, one of the children, or, when killkennies were known to be about, a guardian accompanied her. More often she walked alone, and relished the privacy and the temporary sense of privacy it allowed. On her purposeless sojourns she was just Belinda, not a Twelvenames, not senior of the Lonega; and beholden to no one.

But there were times when she could not free herself, could not shed her concerns as though they were clothes left behind in the dust of the skycircle. As the days before the north-sun day slipped away in the easy rhythms of a practiced life, Ledell was such a concern. Sleep had not improved the keeper's disposition, nor had he forgotten the perceived affront.

In fact, he made an ongoing issue of it, telling his version of the Seneca endtime tale in his persuasive way to audiences of any size, always mentioning in a manner calculated to stir indignation that the senior had scoffed at the wisdom of the Seneca (and, by implication, of Ledell himself.) All this came to Belinda secondhand, for Ledell avoided Belinda and her husbands when he could and was surly to them when he could not.

There was no mystery in any of this. Like most keepers of any skill, Ledell was suffused with male ego. It was what made them good keepers: they thirsted for the high seat, the center circle, and the attention their tales could command. It was also the reason so few keepers were taken as husbands, for rare was the breeder that would stand for such nonsense once the tale was over and the spell broken.

Belinda knew what Ledell wanted, what would end the backstabbing campaign. Ledell expected an apology, one at least as public as his humiliation. More than one earnest family member had taken it on themself to come to her, tell her of Ledell's unhappiness, and gently suggest how she might end it.

But she balked at giving him what he wanted, as much because of the campaign he was waging as because she in fact thought the Seneca tale to be foolishness. It was not in harmony with the watchers' knowledge of the sky, or with her own instinctive beliefs. Families knew beginnings and endtimes, but surely the world did not. She did not even quite believe there had been a time of dark, but if there had been, she was sure it had not been the beginning of anything but legends.

Her thoughts were interrupted when someone called her name. She stopped and turned, looking back through the trees the way she had come. It was Alice-Tonda-Ken, barefoot and breathless.

"Have you come all this way looking for me?"

Alice-Tonda-Ken nodded vigorously, not yet having caught her wind.

"You have walked enough, then, I think," Belinda said. She led the pregnant girl to a newly fallen log, one not yet taken over by armored scavengers.

When Alice-Tonda-Ken had arranged herself on the log, Belinda crouched on the ground facing her. "Why did you follow?"

"You promised there would be talk and there hasn't been. Or did I miss it, and the decision is made?"

"About what, child?"

"What are you going to do about the Gaddis?"

There is rebellion in that question, young breeder, Belinda thought. *But you at least come to me alone with it.* Shrugging, she said aloud: "What is there that can be done?"

"Kenman said it the day Av returned. We can send them some of our substance."

Belinda made a gesture of demurral. "We would only weaken ourselves without strengthening the Gaddis. Then both families might go the way of the Ellijay. I plan no family gift." She cocked her head and her eyes bored into the girl's. "What is your concern with it? You have no broodkin among the Gaddis."

Alice-Tonda-Ken looked suddenly uncomfortable, as if realizing her motives had been plumbed. She opted for directness. "There are those who would go if you gave them the chance."

"Oh?" Belinda said as though it were a surprise.

"Perhaps some of us love the Gaddis more than you do."

"I love none better than the Lonega. That is my flaw," Belinda said, gently asserting herself by rising to her feet. "You are one who would be willing to go?"

"I would."

"And your two husbands?"

"They would go with me."

It is Maryn all over again. "Any good husband would," Belinda said in a neutral tone. "Alice-Tonda-Ken, are you so unhappy with us?"

Alice-Tonda-Ken squirmed. "My song is not heard clearly here," she said finally. "The family hears your song, and the song of Kirsta Sixnames, and—" She stopped. "You will take me wrong."

"No, I understand quite well," Belinda said. "With the Lonega, you stand third among our breeders. But among the Gaddis you would stand higher, and your song might be heard very clearly indeed. If your new child is healthy you could displace Sylva-Mark-Juniper as senior of the Gaddis."

Alice-Tonda-Ken nodded eagerly, taking understanding for agreement. "Ledell said—" She stopped short, realizing her mistake, as Belinda's features twisted into a chilly grimace.

"And does Ledell wish to go, too? Perhaps to see that the Gaddis hear the stories of the time of dark and become strong in the hearing."

The young girl nodded sullenly.

I should let them go, Belinda realized. *They could weaken us more by staying than by leaving, if they cannot accept their lot.* But she could not bring herself to acquiesce to their demand.

"You are too unseasoned to be a senior," she said coldly. "If you understood what it means to be senior you would know that there is something wrong in wanting it too much."

"I will never become 'seasoned' here," she said angrily . "I might still be a child for all that breeding has brought me."

Belinda clucked disapprovingly. "Those are Ledell's thoughts, which he has put into you for his own purposes. A senior must know not to listen too much to men. That is in Ledell's tales, too, but he does not like to tell it," she said, answering anger with patience. "You will grow here, if you will let yourself. The strength of a family comes not from numbers alone but when each member knows and accepts her role. When you understand that, then you will be ready to help the Gaddis."

The fire of rebellion in Alice-Tonda-Ken's eyes, flickering feebly by that time, died. "Yes, Belinda."

Belinda held out her hands and helped the breeder to stand. "Let's walk back to the homehill together," she said, her tone deliberately light and friendly. But her heart was heavy, with a new concern to possess it. Ledell would no doubt try again, and Alice—self-centered, impatient Alice—would no doubt take courage from his blandishments and offer new challenge.

Fighting without and within, forgetting the songs and neglecting the crafts, even quietly giving up life— what is happening to the families of the Georgias?

By the time they reached the homehill, Belinda had decided to grant Ledell a concession after all. Not an apology, but a gesture that could be taken as one if Ledell was so inclined—and would be taken as one by the rest of the family. She called for a circlefire that night.

The response to her call was as always, though perhaps a degree more intense, a sign she had been neglecting the emotional life of the family. The children were openly excited, because a circlefire meant they would be allowed to be up and about after dayset. The adults went about their chores with a lighter step, remembering their favorite stories and songs and lobbying for them to be a part of that night's celebration.

Ledell himself grumbled that he could not be expected to be at his best on such short notice, and asked snidely if Belinda wanted to approve each story before he told it. But he did not refuse to take part. Just as Belinda had anticipated, the lure of the audience was strong enough to make him cast aside his disaffected posture.

When the dayset meal was finished, runners and providers pitched together to build the circlefire in the sky circle: a tinder bed and a great mound of dry treewood too small and fast-burning for cooking.

When the sky overhead had darkened to a velvet black, the call went up from Kenman, and the family came to the sky circle—all save Belinda. They filled all the sittingstones but one, the largest and northmost in the circle, and sat there in in the darkness in silence, hands linked one to the next, child to mother, husband to breeder, guardian to maker to runner to watcher.

Then from the north they heard music, a woman's clear voice giving life to the mournful song of dark. It was a song never heard except at a circlefire, and its melody evoked the loss of friends and children, a cold transcending that of winter's short-day nights, the terror of living a life in dark at the mercy of its unknowable powers.

They heard the singer but they did not see her, until Belinda pulled the shroud from the ceremonial torch she carried. She held it high, its feeble light marking her passage as she came to them, entered the circle by stepping across her own sittingstone, and touched the flame to the edge of the woodpile.

She stepped back as the needlewood spat and crackled, and began to sing the song of the sun. The family joined her, even the youngest, for it was the song mothers sang to children cradled in their arms. The circlefire blazed high and filled the clearing with dancing light. At a gesture from Belinda the family raised their joined hands high.

"We are the family Lonega, bound by blood and fire to each other and to life," she cried. "Out of dark we have come and into dark we will go. But today we live well in the light, sharing the gifts of the earth with each other." She moved to her place in the circle and grasped the upraised hands of those to either side of her, completing the circle. "The fire is with us. The magic is in us. May both remember the Lonega forever!"

She lowered her arms to her side with a sudden motion, and a happy cheer went up from the family. As she settled on her sittingstone, Ledell rose and came before her.

"Belinda Twelvenames, mother of Kirsta and Gar-

ivan, mother of Alix and Bria, mother of Erik and
Erin, mother of Dette and Madee, mother of David
and Ajit and Cherim, senior to the Lonega and beloved of the Georgias. The right of first request is
yours."

Belinda smiled inwardly. The formal address was
Ledell's apology, as the circlefire was hers. She met
his eyes and saw the gesture as honest. "Keeper's
choice," she said, with a little nod.

His eyebrows flicked upward in surprise. Then he
rose from his crouch and turned toward the fire.
"Belinda Twelvenames has granted me keeper's choice.
I thank her, and give the choice in turn to—" He took
a comical leaping step and came down in front of
Belinda's youngest daughter. "Bria."

The child tittered. "Tell us how the killkenny lost
its fur."

Ledell bounced to his feet. "Why, it wasn't just fur!
It was a golden cloak, as yellow and soft as Alix's
hair. And long—as long as your hand, so it blew in
the wind and the little killkennies could hide in it
when danger came—"

Ledell recounted that and two other short, amusing etiologies. His seductive voice could be heard
clearly over the crack of the exploding firegrass tinder and the crackle of the burning treewood fuel.

Then he stepped aside to let young Kip try his
hand at an adventure. The keeper coaxed a song
from sad-faced Tania and, with Cherim as the quarry,
played out an amusing ill-starred hunt by a maledict
provider. I was one of Ledell's best performances, even
before he turned serious and called for silence.

"I wish to tell of the founding of the Lonega," he
said solemnly, "of First Mother Christiana and her
flight across the ice at the time of the first dayrise."

Ah, you could not resist, Belinda thought. But at

least it is our darktime tale. The rest of the family settled in comfortably, for, unlike some of Ledell's keepings, Christiana's story called for rapt attention rather than participation.

"Before Eloai, before Chaldan, before Jennif, before Deborah, before grass grew on the homehill of the Lonega and game flourished in our forests, the world was without light," Ledell began in his most somber voice. "The dark lasted a time without measure, and the world was cold. There was no sun to warm the day, no dayrise, no dayset. There was no moon to protect the night, no nightrise, no nightset. There were no stars to mark the seasons."

As he continued, Ledell began to walk around the circlefire with slow, deliberate steps. "The mountains, the lakes, the southlands lay cloaked in shadow and gloom. Over all spread a blanket of snow and ice. No tree bore leaves, no bush bore fruit, no flower bore blooms. The darkdeath was everywhere—no family was untouched by it."

He paused for effect. "And into this world was born a breeder named Christiana.

"Though the land was without life, under the ice the deep lakes harbored many kinds of fish: wily fish, bitter fish, bony fish, and dinner fish," he recounted, taking a lighter tone. "The family of Christiana lived on the ice and took their meals from the lake through holes they cut in the ice. When they had eaten all the dinner fish one hole held, they would take down their homes and bundle their possessions and make another hole in another place. They were always cold, and they were always moving. But in a world full of death, they had found a way to live. And Christiana sucked strongly at her mother's breast and grew.

"But the world was changing," he said, his voice dropping to a whisper. "In the time Christiana reached first blood, warm winds would blow without warning, puddling the skin of the ice and making its body shift and rumble. The clouds overhead swirled about as though stirred from above.

"And in the time Christiana was to marry, the first spark of light entered the world: a tiny shimmering point of fire that appeared on the northern horizon and slowly rose into the sky. It gave no warmth, but the light was beautiful, and Christiana's family wept with joy for the sight of it.

"The spark climbed higher, higher, higher," he said with a slow, sweeping wave of one hand, "The black cloud that had hung over the land began to lift, growing smaller, smaller, smaller, until both met at the highest part of the sky.

"And when the nightfire touched the cloud, the cloud exploded into blinding light. The large part became the sun, and the smaller part became the moon.

"And the light from them both healed the world.

"When the light touched the land, the snows began to melt, and the bowed limbs of trees to straighten and green. The light drove the darkdeath into the shadows, where it still hides, waiting for when the sun and moon are absent and the sky grows dark once more.

"Since they were closer to the sun, the mountains to the north were the first land so transformed. From them the nightfire had come, and to them it gave life. Christiana saw the life there and knew that it was time to leave the lake, that the hills would be a better home for her children and herself. And so she took the hand of the young fisher she had chosen for her husband, and together they walked off the ice and climbed into the hills.

"They had barely reached the first ridge when the earth shook, and the air was filled with a roaring sound. When Christiana looked back, she saw the surface of the lake in turmoil, the ice shattering, and the lake taking back the food it had given up—"

There were loud squeals from several young ones on the far side of the circle, and Ledell glared at them crossly for the interruption. Belinda added her chiding look, and with a nudge dispatched Alix-Ellet to quiet the noisemakers.

But before she could move, Elul, who was seated across the circle near the children, jumped up and pointed a trembling finger at the northern sky.

"Andor!" he cried. "Andor, explain!" The harsh circlefire light showed each line of his fear-contorted face.

Heads began to turn, and alarmed adults came to their feet in a wave that spread in both directions from Elul. The noises of the youngest children changed from gleeful cries to frightened crying as they sensed their parents' alarm.

"Be silent!" Ledell raged, his back to the north, still taking the interruption personally.

But now even those on the north side of the circle could see what Elul still pointed at, could see that the upturned awestruck faces were lit not by the circlefire but from above. Now Belinda realized that not all the crackling came from the circlefire, not all the squealing from the children, but that both had been joined by a harrowing cry from above.

The apparition was larger than sun and moon combined, and burned with colors never seen in the sky: a ghostly blue, a harsh scarlet, a hot green. The colors streaked the flickering trail it left as it flashed through the sky.

Belinda found Andor at her elbow. "Could it be a night's arrow?" she whispered.

"No, Belinda," he answered in a strangled voice.

"Mark its speed. Look at it grow larger. Listen to its roar. This is a great spirit, not a lesser one."

"I feel its nearness," she said with a shiver.

The apparition crossed the zenith, moving ever more slowly, the thunder-like rumble of its passing increasing. None took their eye from it as its multi-colored trail grew thin and then vanished. The apparition itself underwent a metamorphosis, giving up its flaming halo for the cold glitter of broken fire-glass.

"The uncrossable void is crossed," breathed Belinda. "It is the nightfire. The nightfire falls to earth."

"No, Belinda. It is an illusion," Andor said, shaking his head vigorously.

Jewel-like, the apparition hung in the sky for long seconds before vanishing over the trees like the moon at nightset.

"Illusion or no, mark its fall well, Andor," Belinda said firmly. "For I will expect your help when I go to find it."

The resistance began the moment Belinda and her husbands descended into the privacy of their cupa.

"Belinda, will you hear an appeal?" asked Kenman.

"I will not."

"This journey cannot end well for the Lonega," he said, presuming on his seniority by ignoring her reply. "We will be divided and weakened."

"I need only Andor and whatever of my husbands choose to come with us."

"I will go," Av said quickly. "We know too little of the runs leading south."

"I will go as well," Kern quietly concurred.

"Spare me your echo, Denis," Kenman said harshly, holding his hand up in a plea for surcease. "How can any of us refuse and still call himself Belinda's husband?"

"I am a breeder and a Twelvenames. I go where I choose," she said curtly.

"That right is yours," Kenman said pleadingly. "But your wisdom has been to put the family first. That is what has made us strong."

"All the more reason that I should now put myself first, if that were all that figured. But it is not. As you have told me yourself, you are no watcher. You do not understand the importance."

"The family is of first importance, always."

Belinda sighed. "If you did not think so, you would not be the fine guardian you are. But that is also why guardians should never rule the family. It is not in them to suffer change or weigh uncertainty."

"If you won't consider the family, then think of yourself. You will be at risk every moment you are gone."

"A Twelvenames has friends everywhere," Av protested. "Who would dare harm her, or even wish to?"

"Stop," Belinda said sharply, preempting an angry response from Kenman. "I will not have my husbands arguing on this. Nor questioning me. Tomorrow I will leave with Andor in search of the resting place of the nightfire. Such of you as are willing to do so in good spirit may come with us. There is nothing more to be said."

Then she retreated to her bedding in a manner that made clear none were welcome to follow.

Preparations for the expedition consumed much of the morning. There were seed pouches to fill, snare ropes to coil, guardsticks to sharpen, dur and burnweed leaves to gather. Dward directed his providers to dig up the winter store of dried meat from the floor of the greater cupa and remove half for the use of the travelers.

In the midst of the bustle, Kirsta Sixnames suddenly appeared at Belinda's elbow. "Belinda—"

"Kirsta, I have been looking for you. In my absence, you must serve as senior—"

"Belinda, I wish to come with you."

Belinda masked her surprise. "Then come. You have the right."

"I prefer your approval and consent."

"Then I require your reasons."

Kirsta's eyes misted and she looked away. "I barely know them myself."

"You have never wished to head the family," Belinda stated in a softer tone.

"No."

"It has been enough for you to see your children grow to take husbands and crafts."

"Yes." Tears began to stream from her eyes and she threw herself into Belinda's embrace. "Belinda, I am drying up. I near the blood-end. Before Sonda I was six summers between children, and I know that when Sonda leaves my breast there will be no more to follow her."

Belinda stroked her daughter's hair comfortingly. "I know," she whispered. "I know. It is the breeder's curse. There are times I think that to live with the emptiness brings more pain than to die of the dark."

"What Av said—about the Ellijay," Kirsta sobbed into Belinda's shoulder. "I find myself also asking, why not die? Mother, I do not want to end up like the Ellijay. But I fear that if I do not do something, find some answer, the silence will take me as well."

"I understand," she said. "I understand all too well. You are welcome to join us. In fact, I will relish your presence, as it will relieve the endless empty babble of the men."

"It will leave Alice-Tonda-Ken as senior in trust," Kirsta said timidly, pulling away.

"I considered that before I spoke. It will be good for her. She will learn either to fly or to be happy on the ground. And the firsts of the crafts will be here to see that she does not fall too hard. Or will you bring Elul and Piter?"

"No. Not even Sonda. Alix-Ellet is in milk and will care for her. I would like to know what it is like to live without them."

Belinda nodded. "Perhaps you will find that you were not so empty as it seemed. Go, then, and make yourself ready."

By the highsun all preparations were complete, and the seven travelers gathered at the sky circle before departing. Only then did the family realize that Kirsta's preparations were not for her mother but herself.

"Belinda!" Alice-Tonda-Ken cried anxiously. "Does Kirsta go with you?"

"She does."

"I will have my child before you return. Who will attend me?"

"There is Alix-Ellet, and Kim-Averic, and Tania—"

"Tania's touch will make me barren," Alice protested with careless cruelty. "I have a right to have the senior present for the birthing."

"The senior will be present. You are to be senior-in-trust until we return—"

The news did not placate her. "You have always despised me because I am not your child," she said angrily, her voice rising to a screech. "You do this to keep me here, away from the Gaddis. You would be happy if I bore a cull, to insure that I stay here where you can—"

Ledell suddenly stepped between Alice and Belinda. His back was to the senior, so that she could not see his expression. Nor could she hear his words, though she caught the intensity with which they were delivered. When he stepped aside, Alice spoke again, this time with a chastened civility.

"You will remember that Kip's birth taxed me, and the memory of it has made me afraid," she said, ending the awkward moment. "I regret my words and ask that they be not-spoken."

"They are not-spoken," said Belinda, silently grateful she had mended relations with the keeper. "I leave the Lonega in your hands, Alice-Tonda-Ken. Do well by them."

Alice answered with the traditional traveler's blessing. "May you run forever downhill."

"Aye to that," Andor growled, to general laughter. "Has there been enough talk? My legs are getting no younger."

"Then take the first step, old one, and we'll be that much closer," Av said playfully, and led the way as the party turned its back to the homehill and headed south.

They kept a runner's day, dayrise to dayset, though in deference to Andor they did not try to keep a runner's pace. On the morning of the fourth day, they skirted the great Christiana Lake, thought to be the setting of the founding tale Ledell never got to finish. Even near the lake there were no runs to speak of, and they picked their way across fields of snarlgrass and needlewood copses guided only by the navigational instincts of Andor and Av.

By that night they were in unfamiliar and apparently uninhabited terrain, on the fringe of the scalded lands. Here the snarlgrass was thicker and more vigorous than they had ever seen it, and yet the land seemed brown and barren. With the new moon in the day sky, the party spent that dark night restless and uneasy. A short time before dayrise, Kern piked a killkenny which, out of uncharacteristic bravery or desperation, was drawn by the smell of food into the light of their fire. From that point on there was no sleep had at all.

The land became flatter with each day, until it was the nearby flora rather than distant hills that limited how far one could see. That was no advantage, since Andor had taken his sighting of the nightfire's fall on those hills. From that point, they would be dependent on dead reckoning and whatever could be learned from whoever they encountered.

About once a day, they encountered broad, white-rock runs unlike any in the northern hills—arrow-straight and elevated, with a central trough dividing them in two. The ridge runs, as Av dubbed them, were clear enough for good traveling, but none would take them south. On the afternoon of the fifth day, as they were crossing yet another of the ridge runs, they were halted by a ringing challenge from the trees ahead.

"Far enough, *porci*. You trespass against the Forsyth."

Kenman moved to the point, his guardstick in the low-ready position at his hip. At the same time Av pulled Belinda back across the run to a less exposed position.

"This is the party of Belinda Twelvenames, senior of the Lonega," Kenman called ahead. "If you have a watcher we ask to speak with him. If you do not, then we ask safe conduct to the south."

"What is a Twelvenames, porci, and why should we grant it passage?" The voice seemed to be coming from the right.

"What is a Forsyth, voice-that-cowers-in-trees, that it is so ignorant? The Twelvenames is our senior breeder, mother to eleven fine children, gifted with the magics of twinning and song."

There was a rustling in a tree off to the left, and two bare legs appeared dangling beneath a limb. A moment later the rest of the body appeared as the young Forsyth guardian dropped lightly to the ground.

"I have never heard of a breeder birthing eleven young," he said suspiciously.

"Then take us to your homehill and we will share the story," Av replied readily.

The guardian hesitated, seemingly torn by conflicting impulses. "Come," he said suddenly, and set off at a trot without looking back to see if they followed.

At the Forsyth's camp—it could not be called a homehill, with lean-to homes and without a sky circle or any other mark of permanence—they were better welcomed. The family leader was a grey-bearded man named Duane, a novelty which discomfited Belinda and her husbands alike. For his part, Duane was slow to adjust to Belinda's precedence over her husbands, and tended at first to address both his questions and answers to Kenman.

But beyond that Duane seemed earnest, wise-eyed, and curious, and he called in from his watch the guardian who had best seen the nightfire fall, so that Andor could talk with him. Then they shared food with the Forsyth in what was almost a meeting of equals, since there were only eleven of the family in camp.

The capacity of the lean-tos suggested that few if any providers were away, and Belinda wondered to herself if the family were in as much trouble as its small numbers suggested. *I myself have bred as many children as there are Forsyth here tonight*, she thought at one point.

That fact was not lost on Duane, who after the meal pressed Belinda to tell of her children, first in a way that betokened skepticism, then with growing credulity and respect. Av made up for all the bragging Belinda herself declined to do, with the result that as dayset approached, Duane excused himself to conference with another of his family, then returned with a proposition.

"We have a new breeder two moons past first blood. You would honor us if the husbands of the Twelve-names would lie with her. We much need the touch of your good magic. In the last five summers our family welcomed but one new child."

"And how many culls?"

"Two hands' and more."

Belinda nodded gravely, then smiled a laughing smile at the hopeful look on Kern's and Denis' faces. "With my blessing, my husbands."

The girl, Alinda by name, lay on her back in the spidergrass by the lean-tos and squirmed fetchingly. Before she rose again she had opened her thighs to all five of the Lonega men in turn, and the Forsyth had sung and clapped their way through their best songs of breeding.

Then Belinda herself brought the sweat-happy Alinda a cloak, and combed out the young breeder's hair while singing her own song of breeding. The Forsyth watched and listened in a respectful hush, their hearts full of gratitude for such an unexpected blessing. For the Lonega men, the song was an anthem of fond memories, for all but Andor had had it sung soft-voiced to them in the confines of the Twelvenames's bedding.

When she was done there was little talking, but it was a good silence, the silence of full hearts and reflective minds. And the mood and the memory of the song brought Lonega and Forsyth alike a peaceful night's sleep under a watchful full-eye moon.

Declining Duane's repeated invitations to stay and share another meal, another breeder, another night of communion, the Lonega left the Forsyth at dayrise, taking their first meal on the trail as was their pattern.

Av led them, followed by Denis and Kern, who were arguing the merits of the Forsyth breeder, as well as of their own performance with her. Trailing the party were Kenman and Kirsta. In between, Belinda walked with Andor, and asked what he had learned by questioning the youth who had seen the nightfire fall.

"He was eager for me to know he had not been frightened, so eager that I am sure his bowels were loosed by fear," Andor said amusedly. "Beyond that—he seemed to think that the nightfire was overhead when the colors vanished and it regained its former aspect. I do not trust that very much, so it is not so bad that I do not know what it would mean."

"Have you heard of others who saw it, or had any word from families still further south?"

"It seems they do not use runners, nor much welcome them, as we saw. The nightfire was not cause for exception."

"I am amazed that they made so little of it."

"I am afraid we are not yet very near to its resting place. We are sure to encounter those who know of it before we come on it ourselves—"

Without warning, Kirsta cried out, stumbled, and dropped to her knees. As she doubled over, the others could see the rough wooden shaft protruding from her back. Strangely, the shout of dismay that followed came not from the Lonega but from well back on the trail.

Belinda started to move to Kirsta's side, but Av grabbed her and pressed her flat to the ground instead, shielding her body with his own. From there she watched as Kenman whirled and ran back down the trail, gripping his guardstick in the two-handed attack position. She saw a second arrow whip past him and bury itself in the brush. Kenman did not flinch or hesitate, and a moment later Belinda saw his target: the grey-bearded Duane, standing in the trail less than 100 strides away and reaching to notch yet another arrow.

Perhaps the Forsyth leader, accustomed to fighting with coward's weapons, expected Kenman to halt his charge once the the next arrow was ready. Perhaps Duane realized the charge was simply too fast, too furious for a mere arrow to halt. For whatever reason, he never gave the arrow flight. At the last moment, he turned the bow sideways as if to use it to fend off a thrust to the body.

But the thrust never came. Keeping his wide-spaced two handed grip, Kenman swung the point of his guardstick to one side and swept it back in a short, slashing arc that intersected Duane's throat. Even a hundred strides away, Belinda saw the blood spurt, saw the ragged gash that meant a quick and quiet death.

Abruptly, crying "Andor!" Av leaped to his feet and left her. Only then did Belinda realize that the battle was all around her as well. Kern was standing over a fallen body. Denis was still wrestling with an ambusher, with Kenman hastening back to aid him. Andor was down, crawling and making pitiful sounds, his assailant stumbling after him with knife in hand—that was where Av was headed.

The Forsyth heard him coming and looked back over his shoulder, and Belinda saw that it was the young guardian who had stopped them the previous afternoon. He saw her as well, and for a moment their eyes met, her gaze accusatory, his unreadable. Then he fled, leaping over Andor's supine form and disappearing through the brush, with Av and Denis pursuing closely.

Coming to her feet, Belinda brushed the dirt and

detritus from her forearms and went to where Kirsta lay on her side. Her breaths were wet and raspy, and a bloody froth trailed from one corner of her mouth.

She held her daughter's hand until the light died in her eyes, then walked back down the trail. Standing over the still form of Duane Forsyth, she met his open-mouthed death stare unflinchingly. His head rested in the puddle of blood that had flowed from his own wounds.

You could have taken us while we slept, for we posted no guardian of our own. A decision made late and unwisely, she thought sadly. *Yet part of the blame is surely ours, for parading too proudly our riches before the poor—*

Av joined her, made a shapeless noise deep in his throat, and raised his guardstick as though to strike at the still form in vengeance. Belinda's hand shot out and grasped the stick, forfending the blow.

"No," she said simply.

"Why do you protect him? He struck down Kirsta," Av protested in hurt and anguish.

"The arrow was meant for Kenman."

Av gaped at her, taking a moment to digest her meaning. "He would have taken you and Kirsta, to breed for him?"

"His family was dying. He could do nothing else."

"You excuse him."

She shook her head slowly. "No. I understand him. Come, let us see to Andor."

The Forsyth's shinestone knife had pierced the muscle of Andor's right thigh twice, once deeply, once not. Kenman had stanched the bleeding, but there was nothing to be done for the watcher's pain.

"He lives, but I am afraid we will have to carry him back to the homehill as well," Kenman said as Belinda arrived.

"I could stay with him until the healing begins, while the rest return with Kirsta," Denis offered.

"Have you both volunteered to make my decisions for me?" Belinda snapped. "This changes nothing. We will continue on."

Kenman's eyes narrowed. "Kirsta must be remembered by her family. She must be taken back—"

"Do not presume to tell me what my daughter needs," Belinda snapped with sudden fury. She closed her eyes, caught her breath, and continued in a more controlled tone. "She came with us looking for something and she has not yet found it. She had a yearning to find place and purpose and found neither. I have right of first claim, and I take her search for my own." She glowered at them as if daring them to argue. "Kirsta would not have turned back, and I will not."

Kenman would not be headed. "You think no more of her than of those who killed her, and would leave both to litter the trail?"

"We will find her a good resting place," Av said quietly.

"I do not understand you," Kenman said, shaking his head in disgust.

Andor answered, his voice weak but his tone commanding. "We have paid for something which we do not yet have. If the price seems high, how much higher must it seem if we never receive what it has bought?"

Kenman threw his hands up and stalked away, and Belinda looked to Av. "When we have sung the song of remembrance, will you find her body a good resting place, where it will be be devoured undisturbed by men such as these?"

Av nodded deeply.

"Then let us begin, so that we can leave this place and the memory of this morning may begin to fade."

*   *   *

In a hour they continued on, assured by Av that he would be able to follow their trail sign and catch them when his task with Kirsta's body was completed.

The main party, wounded in both body and spirit, made comparatively slow progress. Their speed was limited by Andor's crippling, their outlook darkened by Kirsta's absence. Kenman brooded, saying little when addressed and nothing of his own volition. Andor used Denis and Kern as human crutches, yet still winced at each jolting step.

Absenting herself from the group, Belinda walked alone, alternately outdistancing the others and then stopping until they drew near again. She needed the time to weave an emotional shroud into which to place the kernel of pain she held inside. It was almost a tangible process, as she saw herself methodically walling off the emotion and moving it beyond reach. But unlike in the past, this time when she was done something remained outside: guilt.

I gave you life, Kirsta, but could not give that life meaning, she thought. *I am responsible for your emptiness and for the hurt it brought you.*

Near dayset they spotted a tendril of smoke rising into the sky from among the trees ahead. Kenman peremptorily dispatched Av to head toward the smoke, which Kenman led them in a wide arc to the west to avoid the community it might represent. Av was not long in rejoining them, since he had but a single question to ask: "Where did the nightfire fall?"

The family called themselves the Doerun, and the answer was as vague as always: south, far south. A runner had gone five days in search of it and returned, having found nothing. The Doerun runner did bring back a report that the ice star, as it was called in that region, had fallen at the edge of the great lake-of-the-horizon.

"That's why he came back, it seems. They said we would find few people and fewer families the nearer we get to the lake, that it is a place of storms and sickness," Av reported.

"How far to the lake?" Kenman wanted to know.

"Twelve days."

Hearing that seemed to bring Kenman out of his funk. They would not be journeying on forever; the lake-of-the-horizon would stop them, and soon.

For a time, Andor's wounds grew better, and the fourth day after the attack he walked unaided for much of the morning. But the next day the deep slash was swollen and began to weep a cloudy fluid. Within a week the leg had begun to stink, and Andor to quietly admit a loss of feeling in his foot and ankle. By then all knew that Andor had been touched by the darkdeath, and that at some point the journey would inevitably claim a second victim from among the travelers.

If all knew it, none gave voice to it. All took their example from Andor. The watcher could not hide the tight-lipped grimace he wore throughout the early days, but as the nerves died and the leg went numb he began to show the good humor he had claimed from Kirsta.

"There, take the upwind side," he would invite Av or Denis as they helped him up. "Now if you could tell me how I could walk upwind of myself I'd be grateful.

"Now that I can't feel it, I walk more lightly, don't you think?" he asked. "If my whole body went numb I believe I would float like fluffseed."

In the dark when they had turned to bed, he would mumble aloud, "A blessing that the nose sleeps with the rest of me."

Though his jokes were frequently as lame as he was, they relieved the tension by telling the others he had accepted his state, and inviting them not to make his problems theirs. He underlined that along the trail, never flagging or complaining, never asking the others to stop for a rest and always being the first to call for them to continue.

Nevertheless, when one of Av's side trips brought him on a passable black-rock run which promised to take them due south, they gave up the open country for it out of consideration for Andor. On the run's hard surface, the watcher could do for himself (at the price of some speed) with the aid of a pair of walking sticks.

"Couldn't stand to take your turn with me again, eh?" Andor jibed, shaking a finger at Av. But that night he confided to Belinda that he was grateful for the change, saying, "If you lean on too many shoulders you can forget how to stand by yourself."

Near highsun the next day, they came on a small family living along the side of the run, a breeder with a single husband and two small children. But Belinda learned nothing from them, since they startled at Av's recognition call and then fled at the Lonega's approach.

At the end of the day, the dayset was spectacular, a broad band of bright red across the western horizon. Noting it, Andor warned the others, "We'll lose the good sky tomorrow."

True to Andor's prediction, that night during Denis's watch the air changed, becoming uncomfortably thick as the stars vanished behind a curtain of clouds. Shortly before Denis would have woken the others, there was a brief heavy rainshower that did the job for him. They stayed up to see the morning come without a dayrise, as a blanket of low, water-swollen clouds covered the sky from horizon to horizon.

Rain resumed falling before they had been on the run long enough to break sweat, and with the rain the wind from the east freshened. At first both rain and wind were constant but gentle. But with each step the Lonega took, the raindrops grew in size and the pitch of the wind rose, gusting, then ebbing, then gusting to a new peak. The caressing rain Belinda at first welcomed began to batter exposed skin, and the bursts of wind made them stagger and Andor fall. From heartbeat to heartbeat the sky grew darker, the changing canopy of clouds growing ever more turbulent, until it was hard to believe it was day at all.

Before long, the unrelenting assault drove them off the run and into the nearest copse. But there was little comfort and less shelter as the wind pelted them with leaves and small branches stripped from the trees. The six huddled together at the base of one stalwart needlewood, turning their backs to the sky, joining hands in a tight circle with Andor at the center. Almost unconsciously Belinda began to sing the song of the Lonega, and the others reflexively joined her, the familiar sound the only balm against the onslaught.

And still the fury of the winds rose, bending the treetops to astonshing angles, the percussion of snapping branches punctuating the gale. A great limb crashed to the ground near them, its central bole as thick as a man's thigh.

Then, in rapid succession, the clouds broke, the rain ceased, the winds died to the faintest breeze. The transformation was as complete as it was sudden. Above them was the high blue sky of a peaceful summer day; around them was the wreckage of a war. Though the direct rays of the sun could not reach them where they huddled, the air around them was dramatically warmer.

Belinda was the first to rise, brushing absently and ineffectually at the bits of wood and leaf in her sodden hair as she gazed up at the sky. "Has there ever been such a storm?" she breathed. "What a wonder!"

There was a fit of coughing behind her, and she turned back to see Andor doubled up, with Av and Kenman each supporting him by an arm.

"Yes, a fine storm, a fine storm to drown in," Andor croaked when the fit passed. "Especially breeders too foolish to keep their mouths closed when they look up." He tipped his head back in an open-mouthed mockery of Belinda, then grinned crookedly to encourage them to laugh.

None did.

"Belinda, it is time to go home," Kenman said, his voice half iron and half sugar. "This can only end in us dying unremembered in a strange land."

From the apprehensive expression on Denis' face, it seemed he agreed. Av scowled in disapproval, while Kern merely looked on with stoic curiosity.

"Nonsense," Belinda said lightly. "We are wet and perhaps a bit shaken, but we are far from dead."

Kenman took a step toward her. "By craft and marriage, I am obliged to protect you. How can I protect you from such as this?" He spread his arms to take in the destruction. "How can I protect you when you take such risks?"

"If the challenge is too much for you I will gladly free you from your craft and your marriage," she said with icy condescension. "But Kirsta and I are continuing on."

Kenman's jaw worked as he bit back the fury her response raised in him. The faces of the others, even Av's, showed varying degrees of shock, for, though both expulsion and unmarriage were perogatives of the senior, the threatened punishment far exceeded the crime.

But the threat ended the discussion, and when Belinda turned her back and started off, they hesitated only briefly before falling in behind her. They picked their way back to the run to find the ditch beside it transformed into a thigh-deep swiftly-moving stream. Wading through the muddy torrent, they found the run itself littered with broken branches and a plaster of wet leaves. The run shimmered with moisture returning to the sky.

Turning south, they found the way was nearly blocked by a shattered tree which had fallen across the blackrock at an angle. Denis was the first to look beyond the tree, and his face turned ashen. A vertical wall of black, boiling cloud filled the southern sky, and it took only a moment's observation to know it was bearing down on them.

The sight of the storm returning froze them for a hundred heartbeats. Then, with only by a whimpering sound deep in his throat as farewarning, Denis broke and ran, not into the woods but back up the road, toward home. Within a dozen steps, he slipped on the slick surface and went sprawling, but he scrambled to his feet and regained his stride. Kenman called after him, but Denis gave no sign he heard, never hesitated, and never looked back.

"Let him go," Belinda shouted, and waded into the rushing water, heading for the trees. The others hastened to follow.

They were barely ensconced in their imperfect hideaway when the storm struck again in full fury, this time with the downpour driven by howling winds from the west. But this time Belinda knew what to expect, and was not afraid; in truth, she was excited in a frankly sexual way. She knew Kenman would have thought her mad if he knew her thoughts, but that did not change them:

Beautiful! she reveled silently as the rain lashed her face and the trees around them danced at the whim of the wind. *Your power is your splendor. And in your fury you are beautiful.*

By the next dayrise, the rain had eased to a drizzle, and the clouds, higher and lighter, gave the promise of breaking to open sky before dayset.

By that time it was also clear that the ordeal of the storm had drained much of Andor's remaining strength. The cough that had been shallow and intermittent had become deep and incessant, and at turns Andor shivered and shook uncontrollably. Though he insisted on trying, he could no longer walk on his own, as even the uninjured leg buckled beneath him.

Watching him try, Kenman's face became a mask of determination. He pulled the roughweave wrap tight around the dwindling stock of dried meat, then set it aside. Quietly stripping off all but his genital pouch, he stood and announced, "I am going to find Denis."

"No," Belinda said, whirling to face him. "If he is alive, he is on his way home. If not, then he is already eaten."

"He came out of love and duty and did as well as could be expected of a maker," Kenman said. "You owe him."

"I owe him what I owe Kirsta—to see this through. If we are ready to travel, then we will all go, and we will go south."

Kenman pointed at Andor, again seated by the tree. "Is he ready to travel? He will have to be carried, like a corpse or a kill."

Tears of humiliation shone in Andor's eyes. "I will have to be carried whichever way we go," he said. "I would rather the view be of where we.are going than where we have been."

"You are on a fool's quest, the both of you," Kenman upbraided. "What if you reach the lake-of-the-horizon and the nightfire is nowhere to be found? Will you insist on traveling the shore a hundred days in each direction to find it?"

"The Doerun said that it had fallen at the edge."

"The Doerun heard a story already three times re-told. Did you not remind Ledell that what is kept is not always what is true?"

"But we saw it fall. And it has not been among the stars for sixteen days now," Andor protested.

"And is that so strange? Has it not been months, even tens of months, between apparitions? You are like the boy who climbs the highest tree to try to touch the sun. You do not understand your place."

"You insult us unfairly. The nightfire fell to earth," Belinda insisted.

"It did not fall because it could not, no more than the sun or moon could. It is a fire of heaven and presently it will appear there again."

"That would prove nothing," Andor argued. "We saw the nightfire twin."

Kenman held his hand out before him with one finger upraised. "I have been thinking of that as well. I may twin my finger by looking at it *so*," he said, squinting crosseyed. "But all the same I have but one finger. What is seen and what is may differ."

"A guardian risks straining himself when he wrestles with reason," Andor said cuttingly.

"Reason has left you, Andor. If the nightfire fell to earth, would it not cause the ground to shake beyond imagining? Would it not set the sprawlgrass and needlewood burning such that no storm, not even such as we have come through, could quench it? But did the ground tremble? Is the world aflame? If not, then the nightfire did not fall. You search for nothing, for there is nothing to find."

"You are wrong," said a new voice.

Heads whipped up to see a slender runner wearing a brilliant red shawl and a glittering rope belt step from behind a tree and walk toward them. "I heard your voices and thought to see if you needed aid, so I listened. I did not understand everything that was said. But if you have come looking for that which left the trail of fire across the sky sixteen nights ago, it exists. I have seen it."

The runner's name was Jacobee, and he was not truly a runner, though he had the build of one. When a startled Kenman took his weapon up, Jacobee quickly shed his shawl to show he was unarmed. He was, he explained, a Floridian and a mystic. Neither term had meaning for the Lonega, and that was not the end of the strange language.

"We saw the *damikan* fall, and I was sent to measure its *palan*," Jacobee explained. "It rests on a shoal in the bay of shoals, west of the black marsh. From the ease with which I found it, I thought its *palan* strong, but I was wrong. I watched it from the shore for the prescribed period, and called the tenth-hour spells each morning, but it took all and gave nothing back."

"You could look on it without being blinded?" Andor demanded. "Did not the scorched ground sear your feet?"

Jacobee looked puzzled. "Did you not hear me? It is in the bay of shoals." He shuddered. "The dead ground is well west, and only a prime mystic would risk a *kelota* there. I have no wish to enter the spirit world early."

"But does the—damikan—not burn with a white-flame?" Belinda demanded. "Does it not boil the waters and consume trees like fallen needles?

Jacobee shook his head slowly. "I thought from the

fall that it would have such a palan, but its heart is cold."

"Then how does it appear?"

The mystic touched fingertips to fingertips, trying to make the shape, then gave up the effort. "It stands twice the height of a man, with a white face complexly marked. I have never seen the like of it—"

While the interrogation was taking place, Kern had picked up and examined the shawl Jacobee had shrugged off. "What splendid making!" he exclaimed. "Belinda, look on this. The weave is so fine, the color so deep—"

"And rain rolls off as though off the face of a rock," Jacobee said, reclaiming it possessively. "It kept me well through the storm."

"Who is the maker?"

"I do not know. I found it among the trees near the damikan. This is but part of the whole. There was more, much more than I could carry or use, plenty to cloak all of you." He seemed suddenly nervous, and glanced repeatedly at the well-muscled Kenman, standing two steps away with his guardstick in hand.

"You must take us there," Belinda said firmly.

"Do even strangers subscribe to the libel that a mystic can never be trusted? I have not lied. I have told you the place."

Av shouldered forward. "You know this land and we do not. We require your aid, as we would give you if you came to the mountains."

"I would not have come even this far inland except for the storm," Jacobee protested. "I am barely headed home and you would have me turn on my heel."

"Why, how far is the bay of shoals?" Andor asked.

He pointed southwest through the trees. "A hard run of less than half a day. You cannot fail to find it."

Kenman stepped forward and brought the guardstick up to the low ready position. "We have come a long way and paid with two lives for our senior's curiosity. You will take us to this place, and then we will ask nothing more from you."

Jacobee looked to the point of the guardstick and back to Kenman's determined face.

"Aye," he said. "I believe I will."

For the first time since leaving the homehill, the Lonega broke into a runner's pace.

Jacobee led, with Kenman at his heels. Swallowing the humiliation of his helplessness, Andor accepted a punishing ride on Kern's back. The watcher's slight frame proved little enough a burden for the broad-shouldered provider that it was Belinda herself who set the limit on their speed. But she pressed herself to stay with the others, the anticipation which placed a glow in her eyes making her steps light.

The land lay heavy with water, both the swollen swamps and marshes which dominated the open land and the puddled leavings of the storm which dotted the woods. They made many small detours around water shallow enough to cross, which Kenman questioned until Jacobee pointed out the sinuous form of a water snake in one of the small ponds.

"One-bite-death," he said, the reptile's name explanation enough.

As they neared the lake-of-the-horizon, the smell of the land changed, the breeze bringing them the scent of salt and putrefaction. Then suddenly, through a gap in the trees and across an expanse of marsh, they could see the greenish-blue hue and undulating surface of the bay. The last thousand strides were taken at a breakneck pace, and when the party reached the small shell-littered beach Belinda was in the lead.

"It truly is the lake of the horizon," she exclaimed. She ran to the waterline and squinting into the distance as small swells broke in front of her. The water melded into the sky at the horizon, a faraway haze masking any seam. "I can see nothing of the other side."

"Some say there is no other side," said Andor as he was lowered to the sand beside her.

"But where is the nightfire?" Kenman asked.

Shocked out of her awe by the question, Belinda's gaze swept both ways along the curving shoreline. The surface of the bay was unbroken by shoal, or daniken, or nightfire.

"It is gone. I feared this. The storm—" Jacobee said hoarsely as the first questioning gazes turned his way. "The stormwave comes taller than a man. Perhaps without palan, the danikan could not stand against it."

"You have no doubt this is the place?" Kenman asked.

"I slept on this beach for ten days."

"Could the stormwave change the beach so that you would not know it?" asked Kenman, indicating the downed trees and debris lying just inland.

Jacobee pointed east along the shoreline. "The beach *is* changed. But there is the inlet that feeds the black marsh," he said, and swung his arm to point west. "And there is Decision Point, which marks the edge of the dead land. *This* is where the danikan was."

Av took a menacing step toward the mystic. "Or perhaps you brought us to the wrong place. Perhaps your scare talk about the dead land is meant only to hide the danikan's true resting place."

"No!" Jacobee insisted, backing away and holding his hands up defensively. "I swear by my father, it was here!"

"Liar," snarled Av, and would have flung himself on the mystic if Kenman had not intervened.

"Stop!" he said forcefully, and with a gesture invited the runner to look behind himself.

There Belinda knelt, silently crying, fat tears falling from her cheeks to pit the sand. Beside her Andor sat stunned, his face slack, his eyes vacant. As Av watched, the tongue of a larger wave crawled up the beach and swirled around them, and they seemed not to notice.

Av turned back to Kenman and the mystic. "I do not want to think it ends this way."

"But it does," Kenman said firmly, and turned to Jacobee. "You have done what we asked—now you can go. We have no further need of you."

Jacobee nodded and began to retreat cautiously, backpedaling with his eyes fixed on Kenman's weapon. When he was beyond throwing range, he turned and ran, his shawl flying out behind him as he disappeared down the curving beach.

Kenman walked back to where Belinda still knelt and offered a hand. She grasped it mechanically, allowing him to help her to her feet.

"Now we go home, and make things as they were," he said, and this time there was no argument.

Andor died quietly that night, lying on a bed of soft grass on the edge of the run. Though his passing surprised no one, it nonetheless affected Belinda profoundly. From the first moment his death was discovered the next morning, she sat crosslegged beside his body and rocked back and forth, alternately crying and softly singing in a voice made husky by grief.

She heard them talking about her in worried tones:

"Something has happened—"

"She never cried over her own children—"

"I am afraid for her—"

"I am afraid for us—"

But the words were sounds without meaning in her

ears. She heard only an inner voice, a voice curiously calm, drained of feeling.

Even such as you, my teacher, becomes food for the 'kennies. And the sights you have seen and the things you have known will be washed away as dust in the rain.

I would take you inside me and give you life again but I am dry, barren. And you would be trapped there and die with me, having lived a second life without meaning.

When Av came and touched her shoulder consolingly, she angrily shook off the contact.

After that, they left her alone until their impatience to be moving on was too great. Kenman approached her, crouching where he could see her face, though she did not look up or seem to note his presence.

"Belinda Twelvenames—do you want to hold Andor's remembrance here or at the homehill?"

She ran her fingers slowly, tenderly, along Andor's cheek, then stood. "There is no point to either," she said, and headed off down the run.

"What of Andor's body?" he called after her.

"Leave it," she answered lightly. "It does not matter." She did not look back to see the horrified expression that heresy begat.

That day and those that followed, Belinda was tireless. As long as the sun or the moon lit the way, she kept on, stopping only as taboo demanded when both were absent from the sky.

Belinda stayed within herself throughout the journey. In the beginning when they spoke to her directly, she would not answer, but she at least acknowledged them with her eyes. Often, when they stopped for meals, she would sit and listen alertly to their conversations, though never taking part herself.

It's as if we were travelers unable to understand each other, but who have taken each others' company for a time, Av thought as he watched her.

But as they reached the rolling hills south of the known land, even those small concessions to their presence were fading. By the time they reached the first range of the Georgias, she was treating them as though they were not there at all.

Not even the reappearance of the nightfire overhead could stir her. When its passing brightened the sky as they rounded the end of Christiana Lake, she stopped and raised her head to watch it arc over them. But she said nothing, her face showed nothing; and when the nightfire was gone she continued on as before.

By the time they reached the homehill, there was no longer any doubt: Belinda was deep in the silence. Brushing off the embrace of her daughter Bria, dead to the welcoming cries and joyful faces, she headed directly for her cupa.

But as she neared it, Alice-Tonda-Ken appeared at the smokehole, ascending the ladder and stepping off to block Belinda's path.

"So you have come back," she said challengingly, crossing her arms over her chest.

Belinda stopped an arms-length away and met her eyes, but gave no answer.

"Where is Andor?" Alice continued, looking past Belinda. "Has he died yet?"

The question told the travelers that Denis had made it home. "He has, Alice," Kenman called.

It was Ledell who spoke next, appearing out of the darkness off to the right. "You will use the name of respect when you speak with the senior. She is Alice-Tonda-Ken-Marla-Zi, newly delivered of a fertile daughter and a strong son. Like the seat of leadership, the magic of twinning has passed to her."

"I celebrate the births with you," Kenman said. "But Belinda Twelvenames is senior of the Lonega."

"No," Alice said sharply. "Twelvenames or not, she is no longer senior. She gave that up when she placed herself above the family. She gave that up when she took from us a fine breeder and the first among our watchers. She gave that up when she held lightly the lives of her husbands and took them on a foolish journey into a place of death." An unpleasant smile tugging at the corner of her mouth, Alice looked expectantly at Belinda for her reaction.

The smile faded when she saw no reaction at all. "I have decided to allow you to stay with us," she continued with a degree less confidence. "You can keep your place in the cupa, and you will be called first breeder because of your songs and magic." She leaned closer. "But I will hear you acknowledge me, or I will send you away, and you will have no place here."

"No!" Av cried. His protest was echoed by some of the family who looked on, hinting that conflict had ruled the homehill since they had left. "This is Ledell's doing. He has had a month to fill her head with his ambitions. You are senior. Belinda! She has no claim to it."

Belinda raised her head slowly and met Alice's gaze with a chilling empty-eyed stare. "I am not a Twelvenames," she said with an effort. "I am just Belinda. And you are senior of the Lonega." Then she ducked her head again and stepped past Alice to enter the cupa.

Shaking a fist angrily in the direction of Ledell, Av quickly followed her down the ladder.

"Belinda, what is wrong? Why allow this? The right is yours, not hers. Why let her take advantage?"

She turned to him and for the first time in days there was emotion on her face: the emotion was relief. To his surprise, she reached for his hand. "It is all right, good husband."

Her response encouraged him. "Belinda, we will fight this. The Lonega will not prosper under her. Only ask, and you know we will stand with you."

"It is not a thing worth fighting over," she said softly, and would say no more. But inside, she was calling out to her daughter, joining hands with her. *Alice has freed me*, she exhulted. *Now we are ready. We will slip into silence together, the silence that none can disturb. You will not have to go alone, sweet Kirsta. We go together.*

With the next dayrise, the family began to learn that a breeder deep in silence is a disturbing presence. Talk stopped at Belinda's approach, and the sight of her deathly face turned heads away and banished smiles. As though paying her back for being cold to them, some of the youngest took cruel pleasure in pinching her arms and legs until purple bruises appeared.

But Belinda took no meals with them, spent long hours in the cupa, and only rarely emerged to sit in the sky circle or walk the homehill with leaden steps. That pattern minimized the disturbance, and for several days Alice tolerated Belinda's behavior.

But before long, driven by her own insecurities, Alice began to harden. Each sight of Belinda became a reminder, then an accusation. She followed Belinda on her walks so that she could taunt her at every step, reminding her of her barren loins and dry breasts, inviting her to drown herself in the deep pool downstream from the bridge. And to none of this did Belinda react, not even to an open-palm blow that left a livid handprint on her cheek for the rest of the day.

The next day Alice added Denis to her stable of

husbands in a sky-circle ceremony at which the joy was more forced than real. But even that drew no reaction from Belinda, though Kenman had to be restrained from taking after Denis for his disloyalty.

Av marked all this with sadness and wondered how long Alice would allow it to continue. *You make it impossible for her to enjoy her victory,* he thought as he sat beside Belinda's sleeping form in the cupa, *because your serenity denies it.*

Before that phase was over, Alice confronted Belinda publicly as she sat at the edge of the sky-circle. "You are almost dead, Belinda Twelvenames," said Alice with all the cruelty she could muster. "The dead do not sleep in cupas or walk the homehill. Go and find yourself a resting place."

When Belinda did not look up, Alice shoved her with her foot and sent her sprawling. "Do you hear me?" she screamed. "Leave us! Take your silence and your deathface away from here! I expel you! You are no longer Lonega."

Belinda gathered herself slowly and came to her feet. *Fight back!* Av pleaded silently as he looked on. *How can you let her humiliate you this way? Belinda Twelvenames! Known to all the Georgias! Oh, Belinda, find yourself!*

But neither Alice's excoriations nor Av's exhortations registered on Belinda, and she moved off toward the north with head bowed. As she did, a victorious smirk spread across Alice's face.

Av looked helplessly at Kenman. "It's better this way," the guardian said, shaking his head, then turned his back to avoid Av's eyes. Av looked to Kern, who only shrugged impotently and walked away.

He ran after Alice and caught her roughly by the arm. "You are sending away the good heart of the Lonega," he said fiercely. "This family will die with you as senior."

Alice jerked her arm free and glared at him. "Then you should be happy to leave now, too," she hissed. "I expel you as well. I have no need for those with your loyalties."

Only a lifetime of conditioning that breeders were to be valued beyond measure kept Av from striking her down at that moment. But she saw the hate in his eyes, and he the momentary fear in hers, before he turned away to follow Belinda away from what had been their home.

She led him wordlessly to the high observatory, where she curled up in the dust of the marking circle and closed her eyes. He settled near her, and drew shapes in the dust with a fingertip until it was too dark to see their outlines. He expected her to die that night, just as Andor had died when he lost whatever hope or purpose the fallen nightfire had given him. When the nightfire appeared over the north horizon just after nightset, Av regarded it with undisguised antipathy.

I know you now, better than Ledell, better than Andor, he thought. *You are the bringer of death. You are the maker of miseries.*

But Belinda surprised him. Though he failed in his effort to watch her throughout the night, when he awoke at dayrise she was still breathing. On rising, she brushed her hair when he offered her his bristle-stick, and washed herself when he brought her water. But she would not eat, and she would not talk.

That did not stop Av from talking to her. Much of the time she was awake, he would sit near her and quietly recount things he had seen while running, or recollections of Belinda's children. He asked her no questions, and never raised his voice or showed impatience. It was the vigil of one friend resigned to the death of another.

Each day she slept later, and was more listless when she arose. And yet she lingered, through a day of showers and a night of fog, through two passings of the nightfire just three days apart, through the remainder of the food Av had had in his pouch when he left the homehill.

"Even if you will not, I must eat," he said one morning, standing over her. "I will be away no longer than is necessary."

When he returned, he found her seated crosslegged on the edge of the circle, turning an egg-sized stone over and over in her hand.

"Look, Belinda—I found snapberries," he said as a mother might coax a contrary child. Loosing his pouch from his belt, he placed it before her.

At that moment, a rumbling sound like a long, rolling peal of thunder turned Av on his heel to stare into the cloudless northern sky. There, trailing a lacy white plume and sparkling like sun on the water, something was falling to earth.

"Belinda!" he shouted, afraid to take his eyes from it. "Do you see? The second nightfire is coming down!"

As he watched, the apparition underwent a puzzling transformation. Its smooth ballistic arc was interrupted, and the thing itself seemed to grow. When the transformation was complete, the nightfire was not falling but floating, descending gracefully under three inverted red and white bowls, and joined to them by fine strands that glittered like a bedewed web.

"Look at it, Belinda, look at it!" he cried, locking his gaze on the strange shape. When it at last disappeared over a ridge to the northeast, he fixed in his memory the place it was last visible.

Then he turned to Belinda, and his heart leaped. She had come to her feet, and was staring at the northeast hills. Slowly, as though it were an unpracticed movement, she looked to Av, and he saw eyes that once again harbored life.

"I know where it fell," he said tentatively, hopefully. "I know we could find it—if you wanted to."

With painful slowness, she brought her hands to her cheeks, which were flushed with new color. "Yes," she said, her voice a croak. She held out a hand to him. "Yes, good husband. Take me there."

Av wanted to rock the mountain with his shout of joy, and catch her up in his arms in a crushing embrace. But fear stayed him: that he would frighten her back to the place she had only just escaped. Instead his right hand went up, and she mirrored his action. Their fingers entwined, and he stepped close to press his cheek lightly against hers.

"I have missed you, Belinda."

She answered him with only a wistful smile and a nod. But he understood that that was all he could expect for the moment, and together they started off down the northeast slope of the high observatory toward their goal.

Belinda's stamina astonished Av as much as her convalesence delighted him. After not having eaten for nearly two phases, she downed a quantity of snapberries that would have knotted Av's stomach in the same circumstance. She held her head high and pressed close enough to Av's heels to step on them more than once.

But she was still not whole. It seemed to Av that she was fighting to escape the silence, casting about for the understandings that would tear down the walls she had been building. Her self-explanations were the tools of that struggle, tools she reached out to share with Av, as though by doing so she ensured she would not have to fight alone.

Yet the first effort had to be hers. It was time for

Belinda to talk, and Av to listen. And though her utterances spanned half a day, they were a single continuum of thought.

"I cannot see Kirsta any more. This was not enough for her, any more than the first time. She came with us on hope alone.

"If I were a maker, I might have understood sooner—but if I were a maker, I might never have thought on it. A maker's works outlive him. He leaves the family enriched by the exercise of his craft, and that purpose never leaves him.

"Breeding is the most special kind of making, and brings the fullest sense of purpose. But there is a price, a terrible price. Where is the keeper struck dumb by time, or the maker with life in his heart but not in his hands? But a breeder blessed with many summers is condemned to outlive her craft. And a breeder past blood-end is a breeder in name only. That which sustained her, absorbed her, is gone.

"If the works of a maker are lost, he still has the craft in his hands to replace them. If the quarry of a provider escapes, he still has his weapon. If a young breeder loses a child, as I lost Dette and Madee, she still has her husbands and the floor of the cupa. But when I lost Erik, and Ajlt, and Garivan, and Kirsta, I could do nothing.

"The loss of my craft and the death of my children emptied me.

"When I saw the first nightfire fall, I had purpose again. To see it—to know its nature—to take its measure—that filled the emptiness. But when I lost that purpose, I was more empty than before. I lost more than my purpose on the shore of the lake-of-the-horizon. I lost hope.

"That is when the silence takes you.

"I know why the families are struggling, why the Ellijay are gone. If tomorrow is just to be an echo of today, then there is no reason for tomorrow, and no purpose for today. Death is preferable to a life that leads nowhere.

"The purpose of today is to shape tomorrow, not to repeat yesterday."

Though heartened by the sound of her voice, what Av heard did not banish his one fear. He waited until they were nearing their destination with Belinda's reintegration largely complete, to voice it.

"Belinda—if what we find is not what you expect—or we find noting at all, like before—will I lose you again?"

"No, good husband," she said with a reassuring smile and a squeeze of his hand. "I already know that it will not be what I expect. This time it is not the finding but the searching that recalled me. I needed a focus to bring me back from self-chosen death. But when it is gone I will find another. I know how to fill the emptiness now."

From the top of the ridge beyond which the nightfire had disappeared, they spotted the splash of red and white that marked where it had fallen. With his keener sight, Av also thought he saw movement, movement that would mean they were not the first to arrive.

"Perhaps the Gaddis saw it as well," Av said as they began to pick their way down into the valley. "They were closer than we."

But by the time they reached the site, the others, whoever they had been, were gone, taking with them two of the three red and white smoothweave bowls. The third was entangled in the crown of a tree, its glittering ropes dangling and dancing in the gentle breeze.

The nightfire itself did not glitter, or glow, or burn. It rested at an angle at the edge of the glade, a teetering white monument streaked with black. A broad, shallow gouge across the ground and a litter of broken branches betrayed the path and force of its landing.

It was too tall for even the long-limbed runner to reach up to its top, where the ragged stubs of the glitter ropes were attached, and far too large for even the two of them to join hands around its girth. Av circled it cautiously, then came to where Belinda stood studying the lines, ridges, and shapes arrayed on its surface.

"How could this be the nightfire?" he demanded. "How could this light the sky so?"

Belinda reached out and touched its surface, and found it hot where the sun shone on it, cool in the shadow, everywhere smooth to the touch. She ran her fingers across one of the black streaks and wrinkled her nose at the smell it left on her fingers. She struck it with a rock, and saw it dent under the blow.

"It is a *made* thing," Av realized belatedly.

Belinda nodded excitedly. "Yes—a made thing that once kept company with the stars."

"How can that be?" Av demanded, almost angrily.

She breathed heavily, and took a long time answering. "Somewhere there are makers of such skill as we have never seen, makers who work in smoothweave and shinestone and place lights among the stars," she said finally, running her fingers lightly over a pattern of red markings on the side of the nightfire.

"Where?" Av demanded to know. "I have traveled more than any Lonega, and I have seen nor heard of such makers. And if it is a made thing, what is its use? What does it do?"

Her eyes found and fingertip traced a drawing of the nightfire and of a man—a guardian or provider, from the shape—standing beside it. There was an outline of a hand, and she placed her own against it.

The engraved hand grasped a recessed catch and squeezed it. Belinda's hand did the same.

There was a hissing sound, and the nightfire shuddered. A crack appeared across its face and up its side, widening to a handsbreadth as the hissing ceased.

"Help me," she said, and took hold of one edge of the door. Tugging together, they swung it back until light streamed into the opening.

The light lit a grid of a hundred small rectangles, each barely a handsbreath wide, each colored one of a hundred different pale hues and tints. From each of the rectangles dangled a small loop of shinestone. A single rectangle, at the center of the grid, was a brilliant scarlet red.

With barely a moment's hesitation, Belinda grasped the loop of the red rectangle and pulled. It moved—and more appeared behind it. She pulled again, and still more appeared. A third tug, and a piece of the nightfire came off in her hands, swung downward, fell open, and disgorged more than a hundred objects unlike anything either had ever seen.

Belinda cast the container aside and picked up one of the objects. It seemed to be some kind of smoothweave, though made stiff somehow. One side was a white square marred by black markings that reminded Belinda of Andor's watching records.

The other side was a revelation—a magic hole through which she saw the lake-of-the-horizon, and on it a long white shape the nature of which she could not divine. But the waves of the lake-of-the-horizon were frozen, without motion, and dry to her touch.

"They are too real to be drawings, but less real than the world," she exclaimed.

Av crouched with her and sifted through the pictures, noting that each bore a small colored disk in one corner of the back. There was one larger object in the pile, but it was nothing more than a number of the smaller ones fastened together.

Suddenly Av grabbed a picture from the pile and thrust it before Belinda's face. "This is the downstream wall of the lake at Hartwell," he said in amazement. "I know where I would stand to see this."

Belinda cocked her head to one sde. "They are something like memories, I think—as though you can hold one in your hand and see what you saw when you were there—"

"But where would you stand to see these?" he asked, taking in with a sweep of his hand a footprint in the dust of the Sea of Tranquility, a turtle-backed bridge arching across the Lower Bay of the Hudson, and a line of silver transmission towers bisecting a field of young corn.

"I cannot imagine," Belinda said.

Av picked out a memory of the Gossamer Condor in flight and marked the pale blue circle of color on the back. Taking it to the open door of the nightfire—the name seemed most inappropriate by then, but he had no other—he compared it to the color of each of the drawers in turn.

"Look—these are the same," he said, pulling the drawer open and dumping its contents, a hundred memories of the shapes of flight, onto the ground. "And inside there are more. Every one of these must be full of them. But can these be memories, or are they dreams?"

Belinda did not answer. She had picked up the book of memories and turned back its cover, where she found a loose white sheet with more markings. The markings said:

From the desk of . . . DANIEL YATES
  To the survivors—
    If you are ill and hoped for medicine, or hungry and hoped for food, there is nothing here

for you. Even in my time, millions needed both, and yet life went on. Because, for a time at least, we had something you may now need: hope.

Consciously or not, you already know the worst we were capable of. I offer you here reminders of the best. I have no way to teach you how to do what these photographs show. It will have to be enough that you know they can be done.

But to Belinda the markings were meaningless, and she cast the paper aside. A minor gust of wind lifted it and blew it into the brush, where it would remain until the next rainstorm would destroy both its form and its content.

Belinda turned her attention to the book's contents. The first memory showed a tall breeder standing between two skeletal shinestone shapes that reminded Belinda of the nightfire. Successive memories showed more skeletons, and in each they more closely resembled the object resting a few steps away from Belinda and Av. In every memory there were men, but their builds were covered by clothing and she could not otherwise decide their crafts.

Then she found a memory which showed the nightfire itself much as it stood before her, save for the dangling cut ends of the ropes and the fragrant streaks of black.

Still further into the book was a memory of a sad-faced young runner holding in his arms a container like the ones she and Av had pulled from the nightfire. In the next she saw vast numbers of memories being neatly stacked by oddly-dressed breeders—

Belinda quickly turned back to the beginning and stared at the face of the tall breeder. Then she flipped forward a few pages, studying the skeletal nightfire that appeared on each—then back to the beginning, and forward again even faster.

They are not different *skeletons—they are the* same! *One becomes the other—*

Closing the book, she clutched it to her chest. "Av—I understand now. Oh, Av! *We* were the makers!"

He only stared, uncomprehending.

"Don't you see, in a time *before* the darkness—oh, here is purpose enough for a hundred lifetimes, not only for one old breeder but for all the Georgias!"

Still he stared, nose wrinkled in puzzlement.

"Dear Av," she said, reaching out to touch his cheek. "Do not wonder, and do not be afraid, of me or for me, I understand but a piece of it myself, but we will understand everything in time. Now, gather as many memories as you can carry! We are going back to the Lonega—to my homehill, where I am senior.

"And when we have put things in order there we will share these memories with the Gaddis, and the Cantona, and the mystics on the shore of the lake-of-the-horizon," she exulted, radiant. "We will put thoughts in their heads that have never been there before."

And in the heat of that vision began the first thaw of spring.

In memory of Gary VanDerHeyden, 1968-1984, and all the other children of promise who die too soon.

A giant space station orbiting the Earth can be a scientific boon ... or a terrible sword of Damocles hanging over our heads. In Martin Caidin's *Killer Station*, one brief moment of sabotage transforms Station *Pleiades* into an instrument of death and destruction for millions of people. The massive space station is heading relentlessly toward Earth, and its point of impact is New York City, where it will strike with the impact of the Hiroshima Bomb. Station Commander Rush Cantrell must battle impossible odds to save his station and his crew, and put his life on the line that millions may live.

This high-tech tale of the near future is written in the tradition of Caidin's *Marooned* (which inspired the Soviet-American Apollo/Soyuz Project and became a film classic) and *Cyborg* (the basis for the hit TV series "The Six Million Dollar Man"). Barely fictional, *Killer Station* is an intensely *real* moment of the future, packed with excitement, human drama, and adventure.

Caidin's record for forecasting (and inspiring) developments in space is well-known. *Killer Station* provides another glimpse of what *may* happen with and to all of us in the next few years.

Available December 1985 from Baen Books
55996-6 • 384 pp. • $3.50

Here is an excerpt from Cobra Strike!, coming in February 1986 from Baen Books:

The Council of Syndics—its official title—had in the early days of colonization been just that: a somewhat low-key grouping of the planet's syndics and governor-general which met at irregular intervals to discuss any problems and map out the general direction in which they hoped the colony would grow. As the population increased and beachheads were established on two other worlds, the Council grew in both size and political weight, following the basic pattern of the distant Dominion of Man. But unlike the Dominion, this outpost of humanity numbered nearly three thousand Cobras among its half-million people.

The resulting inevitable diffusion of political power had had a definite impact on the Council's makeup. The rank of governor had been added between the syndic and governor-general levels, blunting the pinnacle of power just a bit; and at *all* levels of government the Cobras with their double vote were well represented.

Corwin Moreau didn't really question the political philosophy which had produced this modification of Dominion structure; but from a purely utilitarian point of view he often found the sheer size of the 75-member Council unwieldy.

Today, though, at least for the first hour, things went smoothly. Most of the discussion—including the points Corwin raised—focused on older issues which had already had the initial polemics thoroughly wrung out of them. A handful were officially given resolution, the rest returned to the members for more analysis, consideration, or simple foot-dragging; and as the agenda wound down it began to look as if the meeting might actually let out early.

And then Governor-General Brom Stiggur dropped a pocket planet-wrecker into the room.

It began with an old issue. "You'll all remember the report of two years ago," he said, looking around the room, "in which the Farsearch team concluded that, aside from our three present worlds, no planets exist within at least a 20-light-year radius of Aventine that we could expand to in the future. It was agreed at the time that our current state of population and development hardly required an immediate resolution of this long-term problem."

Corwin sat a bit straighter in his seat, sensing similar reactions around him. Stiggur's words were neutral enough, but something explosive seemed to be hiding beneath the carefully controlled inflections of his voice.

"However," the other continued, "in the past few days something new has come to light, something which I felt should be presented immediately to this body, before even any follow-up studies were initiated." Glancing at the Cobra guard standing by the door, Stiggur nodded. The man nodded in turn and opened the panel . . . and a single Troft walked in.

A faint murmur of surprise rippled its way around the room, and Corwin felt himself tense involuntarily as the alien made its way to Stiggur's side. The Trofts had been the Worlds' trading partner for nearly 14 years now, but Corwin still remembered vividly the undercurrent of fear that he'd grown up with. Most of the Council had even stronger memories than that: the Troft occupation of the Dominion worlds Silvern and Adirondack had occurred only 43 years ago, ultimately becoming the impetus for the original Cobra project. It was no accident that most of the people who now dealt physically with the Troft traders were in their early twenties. Only the younger Aventinians could face the aliens without wincing.

The Troft paused at the edge of the table, waiting as the Council members dug out translator-link earphones and inserted them. One or two of the younger syndics didn't bother, and Corwin felt a flicker of jealousy as he adjusted his own earphone to low volume. He'd taken the same number of courses in catertalk as they had, but it was obvious that foreign language comprehension wasn't even close to being his forté.

"Men and women of the Cobra Worlds Council," the earphone murmured to him. "I am Speaker One of the Tlos'khin'fahi demesne of the Trof'te Assemblage." The alien's high-pitched catertalk continued for a second beyond the translation; both races had early on decided that the first three parasyllables of Troft demesne titles were more than adequate for human use, and that a literal transcription of the aliens' proper names was a waste of effort. "The Tlos'khin'fahi demesne-lord has sent your own demesne-lord's request for data to the other parts of the Assemblage, and the result has been a triad offer from the Pua'lanek'zia and Baliu'ckha'spmi demesnes."

Corwin grimaced. He'd never liked deals involving two or more Troft demesnes, both because of the delicate political balance the Worlds often had to strike and because the humans never heard much about the Troft-Troft arm of such bargains. That arm *had* to exist—the individual demesnes seldom if ever gave anything away to each other.

The same line of thought appeared to have tracked its way elsewhere through the room. "You speak of a triad, instead of a quad offer," Governor Dylan Fairleigh spoke up. "What part does the Tlos'khin'fahi demesne expect to play?"

"My demesne-lord chooses the role of catalyst," was the prompt reply. "No fee will be forthcoming for our role." The Troft fingered something on his abdomen sash and Corwin's display lit up with a map showing the near half of the Troft Assemblage. Off on one edge three stars began blinking red. "The Cobra Worlds," the alien unnecessarily identified them. A quarter of the way around the bulge a single star, also outside Troft territory, flashed green. "The world named Qasama by its natives. They are described by the Baliu'ckha'spmi demesne-lord as an alien race of great potential danger to the Assemblage. Here—" a vague-edge sphere appeared at the near side of the flashing green star—"somewhere, is a tight cluster of five worlds capable of supporting human life. The Pua'lanek'zia demesne-lord will give you their location and an Assemblage pledge of human possession if your Cobras will undertake to eliminate the threat of Qasama. I will await your decision."

The Troft turned and left . . . and only slowly did Corwin realize he was holding his breath. Five brand-new worlds . . . for the price of becoming mercenaries.